THE PROMISE....

The memory of her eyes haunted him. That vexatious girl, whether she was aware of it or not, had managed to destroy his peace of mind.

As for the vexatious girl in question, she too couldn't fall asleep. She didn't love him at all, she told herself. She hated him more than she would have thought possible. He thought of her as a zany, histrionic disaster, and that was how she would remain in his eyes. Very well. If that was what he expected, that was what he would get. If he had found her behavior disturbing before, it would be *nothing* to what he would find in the week to come.

"There are some possibilities for mischief you wouldn't *dream* of, my lord," she whispered aloud.

A REGENCY MATCH
ELIZABETH MANSFIELD

Elizabeth Mansfield
A Regency Match

BERKLEY BOOKS, NEW YORK

A REGENCY MATCH

A Berkley Book / published by arrangement with
the author

PRINTING HISTORY
Berkley edition / May 1980

ISBN: 0-425-04514-5

A BERKLEY BOOK ® TM 757.375
PRINTED IN THE UNITED STATES OF AMERICA

Chapter One

EVEN HER ACERBIC, acid-tongued grandmother had to admit that Sophia Edgerton knew how to enter a room. Everyone said that there was not an actress on the London stage who could make an entrance to better effect. Sophia would pause in the doorway of a ballroom or drawing room just long enough to permit the onlookers to admire her graceful pose and her slightly eager smile, and to cause those who had not been looking to turn their heads. Then she would permit her smile to widen (thus allowing her entrancing dimples to make their appearance), and she would hurry in, her arms outstretched affectionately toward her hostess or whomever she'd chosen to greet. The sparkle of her eyes, the warmth of that dimpled smile, and the artful liquidity of her movements would hold every eye in the room on her until her entrance had been completed.

But her grandmother, the austere Lady Alicia Edgerton, was too familiar with Sophia's artifices to be impressed. She much preferred her granddaughter's manner when the girl was at home, the buoyant, sweetly-generous girl bubbling with good spirits and youthful enthusiasms, although even *that* aspect of Sophia's character could be trying to a world-weary old beldame in her sixties.

This very moment was a case in point. Lady Alicia was sitting peacefully before the mirror on her dressing table, submitting to the ministrations of her dresser, Miss Leale, who was attempting to coax Lady Alicia's wispy gray hair into some semblance of neatness, when Sophia, without so much as a by-your-leave, burst into the room waving a letter excitedly in the air. The entrance was a far cry from her grand entrances into the ballrooms of the great houses of London. "Grandmama, you won't *believe* my news!" the girl cried.

Lady Alicia favored Miss Leale with a look of hopelessness and turned to the intruder with one eyebrow reprovingly cocked. "Have you forgotten how to knock?" she asked coldly.

"Never mind that," Sophia responded, laughingly ignoring her grandmother's rebuke. "*Bertie*'s back! He's sent a note! Isn't that astounding?"

"Astounding indeed," Lady Alicia said drily. "I'm quite overwhelmed to hear it. Especially since his mother, your Aunt Isabel, has been writing to me for the past three months of their intention to return."

"Three months? You've known for three months?" Sophia demanded, shocked. "Then why haven't you told me?"

"Because, my dear Sophy," her grandmother explained, rubbing the bridge of her nose with weary fingers, "I wished to be spared your breathless fervor for as long as possible."

"Really, Grandmama," Sophy said with a pout, "that was most unkind. Bertie was the very dearest friend of my childhood, and you *know* that I haven't laid eyes on him since I was ten."

"It's just as well for you that your uncle took him off to India when he did. That child was making a hoyden of you, if memory serves. Really, Leale, must you pull my hair that way?"

"Sorry, m'lady," Miss Leale murmured, giving Sophia a wink. Those who knew the Lady Alicia well were quite aware that her acid bark had no real bite.

Sophia perched on her grandmother's chaise and tucked her legs under her. "I loved being a hoyden," she said, her eyes glowing with happy reminiscences. "We always had the greatest fun together during those lovely days when we all lived in Wiltshire."

"Aye," remarked Miss Leale fondly. "Prime for a lark you were, the two of ye."

Lady Alicia glowered at her maid in the mirror. "You needn't indulge yourself in sentimentality, Leale. I remember quite distinctly that those two were a constant source of irritation and worry. Always climbing trees and falling out of them. Or eating green apples in the orchard until they were sick. Or wading through the stream and ruining their boots. Dreadful stuff!"

"It wasn't dreadful at all. It was wonderful!" Sophia declared. "Besides, what *should* two children have been doing with their days if not larking about and making mischief?"

"One would think the answer is obvious. Have you never heard of good books and good works?"

"Oh, pooh!" Sophia said scornfully. "You should have sent me to a convent if that was what you wanted."

"I was often tempted to suggest to your mother that very course of action," Lady Alicia said mendaciously.

Sophia paid no heed to her grandmother's remarks, her mind full of her childhood memories. "Dear Bertie! The brother I never had . . . my only real chum! You know, Grandmama, I was horribly lonely after he'd gone—there wasn't anyone else to play with."

"I see no point in dwelling on the past," her grandmother said crisply. "What does it all mean now? You're certainly too old for a 'chum' at this point in your life."

"I suppose you're right," Sophia sighed. "I can scarcely expect a grown man of twenty-two to go chasing through the woods with me after grouse as we were used to do."

Lady Alicia turned from her mirror to frown at her granddaughter in irritation. "You cannot *want* to go chasing through the woods any more, you silly chit! You're almost twenty-one yourself. You should be married and raising a brood by this time."

Sophia tried to hide her grin, but her dimples appeared to give her away. "Is *that* what you want for me, Grandmama?" she asked with exaggerated innocence. "Marriage and babies? I thought you just said you preferred that I spend my life reading good books and doing good works.''

''Minx!'' Lady Alicia muttered in disgust. ''Much good it would do me if that *were* my preference. I've never seen you spend any time with either.''

Sophia giggled and jumped to her feet. ''Poor Grandmama. It must be terribly trying to be saddled with such a ninnyhammer for a granddaughter.'' She kissed her grandmother's cheek and went to the door. ''Wear something spectacular tonight to the Gilberts' ball, my love. Bertie writes that he's to attend, and we want him to be pleased with us when he sees us after so long.''

''Take care of *yourself*, Miss Prattlebox,'' Lady Alicia called after her disappearing granddaughter irritably. ''I know how to choose a gown for myself without your advice.'' But the remark was wasted on the closed door. ''That girl will be the death of me,'' she muttered to Miss Leale.

''She's the *life* of ye, and you know it,'' Miss Leale answered bluntly. She had been in her ladyship's service too long and had served her too intimately to be intimidated by her sharp tongue. ''I remember how it was in this house after his lordship passed on. Like a tomb it was, so quiet and dim-like. An' you keepin' to your room like you wanted to bury y'rself away with 'im. Never seein' a soul from one week to the next. This wasn't a house—it was a grave.''

She put down the brush and the hairpins and bustled about to find a suitable gown, hoping her activity would prevent the need for facing a sharp retort from her mistress. But Lady Alicia was staring into the mirror with unseeing eyes, her mind having taken her back to the day, five years before, in 1808, when Sophia had first come to live with her. Leale was quite right, the house *had* been like a mausoleum then. Her husband dead, her younger son in India and her elder one in Wiltshire, she had been quite terribly alone in the Edgerton townhouse in Russell Square. She had been unspeakably lonely yet had disdained the society of most of her circle. Finding them either too frivolous, too lackluster or too self-pitying to make good company, she'd withdrawn from the world. By the time her daughter-in-law, Sophia's mother, had died, she'd become an embittered, unhappy old woman who rarely left the house. Had her son not remarried, and had Sophia not fled from the tirades of her Evangelical stepmother, Alicia might be living still in that terrible isolation.

But Sophia *had* come to her. The child, sixteen years old and spoiled by an overindulgent mother, had been driven to desperation by the antagonism of her fanatical stepmother and had sought her grandmother's protection. With her son's permission and his new wife's relieved blessing, Alicia had taken little Sophy under her wing and as a result had found herself reborn. Sophia had been like a gust of wind, sweeping the cobwebs of mourning from the house and refreshing it with a breezy gaiety. Her youthful energy had infused the old woman with a new vitality. She had had to face life anew, if only to become strong enough to guide her granddaughter's future. She had to renew her friendships so that the child would have a social circle in which to move. She had to see to the girl's education, to take her to museums and libraries, the opera and the theater. She had to find her the proper clothing and accompany her to parties and outings. She had to oversee Sophia's come-out three years ago and to chaperone her when her dozens of admirers paid calls. In short, she had to mother the girl. And in return, Sophia had brought her to life again.

Lady Alicia loved her granddaughter dearly, but she would have been the first to admit that the girl was too volatile by half. But how could she have turned out otherwise? She'd lost an indulgent mother before she'd reached sixteen. Then she'd had to deal with a religious fanatic of a stepmother. And finally, she'd found herself in the care of a grandmother too old and embittered to deal patiently with the mercurial moods and obsessive enthusiasms of youth. Attractive in appearance and charming in manner, the girl had learned to win her way with everyone she met. Was it any wonder that she was spoiled, moody and self-absorbed?

Lady Alicia sighed as she rose to permit Leale to help her into her ball gown. Leale, like all the rest of London, was too easily beguiled by Sophy's charm. "You always eat out of her hand," Alicia grumbled accusingly to the startled abigail.

"Whose? Miss Sophy's?" the maid asked.

"Yes, Miss Sophy's. Don't you see how you spoil her with that sort of indulgence?"

"Me spoil 'er? Don't know what you mean, m'lady. She's as pretty-behaved a young lady as I've ever laid eyes on."

"That's bibble-babble! The girl's headstrong, willful and very likely fated for some sort of disaster before long," Lady Alicia prophesied gloomily.

Miss Leale, in the act of lifting the gown over her mistress's head, froze in the act and gasped. "Disaster! Bite y'r tongue, ma'am! I don't know how you can say such a dreadful thing."

"Never mind, woman. Don't just stand there. Are you going to help me into that dress or just gape at me?"

Miss Leale closed her mouth and proceeded with her chores. Her ladyship was in a taking, the maid told herself. Why, everyone knew that Miss Sophy was the sweetest, kindest, prettiest young lady ever. Why should anything disastrous occur to such a one? Lady Alicia didn't mean a word of it. With that comforting thought, the abigail put the conversation from her mind.

But Sophy's loving grandmother was not so easily comforted. A long life had taught her much, and one of the things she'd learned was that one paid a price for the flaws in one's character. Her granddaughter's willfulness and tendency to histrionics were characteristics for which the possessor would pay a price. And Lady Alicia had every expectation that her granddaughter's payment would soon become due. Unfortunately, she had not an inkling of the form which the disaster would take. And what was worse, she had no idea of how to prevent it.

If Sophia was facing imminent disaster, she showed no signs of having detected its looming presence. She hummed happily to herself as she studied the two ball gowns laid out on her bed. Picking up the cherry-colored Tiffany silk, she held it to her shoulders and twirled around her bedroom in the new waltz-step. This is the one, she decided happily. Bertie had liked bright colors as a boy. She hoped he hadn't changed too much.

The memory of her cousin Bertie had remained fresh in her mind all during the eleven intervening years. There had never been anyone like Bertie in her life. They had ridden together, played together, exchanged favorites stories and revealed to each other their most closely-guarded secrets. An only child, Sophy had treasured the company of someone close to her own age. When Bertie had been taken off to India with his parents, she'd been heartbroken.

Readying herself for the ball, she studied herself carefully in the mirror of her dressing table. Would he recognize her, she wondered? She had been a rather chubby little thing when he'd last seen her, her nose freckled and her bright red hair plaited down her back. Now she was stylishly slim, her skin was completely clear of the disfiguring freckles, her hair was more auburn than red, and it was cut in short ringlets that framed her face. He would not know her at all.

But she would know him. Of that she was certain. He had towered over her in their youth, so he would probably be quite tall. His skin would be swarthy from the Indian climate, but his blue eyes would be unchanged. She would know those blue eyes anywhere.

Lady Alicia had already taken a seat among the dowagers when Sophia (who had excused herself when they'd arrived at the Gilberts' to check her appearance in the mirror of the cloak room set aside for the ladies), decided it was time to make her entrance. Her smile was a bit wider than usual as she stood poised in the doorway of the Gilberts' ballroom. A number of eyes turned to watch the girl in the cherry-red silk dress as she hesitated on the threshold, her eyes roving over the faces in the enormous, crowded room. Although the many admiring eyes studied her appreciatively, they could not detect the rapid tremor of her pulse. Beneath the poised exterior, Sophy was quite tingling with anticipation.

She scanned the room carefully, paying particular attention to gentlemen who were above average height. Suddenly her eyes lit up and, lifting her skirts with a sweep of her arm, she flew across the room. "*Bertie!*" she cried as she neared a group of gentlemen who had been standing together near the dance floor chatting amiably. She made straight for a tall man who stood in their midst. His height, his dark skin and his remarkable blue eyes gave him away. "Bertie!" she exclaimed again as she approached. "Dearest boy, I'd have recognized you anywhere!" And she flung her arms around his neck with such ardor that he had to stagger to keep his balance.

Every dowager seated in the vicinity stared. Every stroller stopped and gaped. A number of dancers paused in their promenade to turn and watch the little drama being enacted nearby. The gentleman himself had looked startled and embarrassed in quick succession as she'd advanced on him, but before these emotions could be noted by the onlookers, his face became impassive. Taking her hands firmly from round his neck, he raised an eyebrow and said coldly. "I'm afraid, ma'am, that you've mistaken me."

"Mistaken you? Oh, Bertie, as if I could!" Sophia laughed.

The gentleman's face remained impassive, but his annoyance was clearly noticeable in the glint of his eyes. "I assure you, ma'am, that my name is not Bertie," he told her, smoothing the folds of his neckcloth, the pristine perfection of which Sophy had disturbed.

"Sophy, you goose," chortled a voice at her ear. She whirled around to face a rather rotund, ruddy-cheeked young man who stood grinning at her from a height not an inch taller than her own. "*I'm* Bertie."

Sophy stared at him for a moment, gasped, looked from him to the tall stranger and back again, and burst into giggles. "Oh, dear," she exclaimed sheepishly, "now that I see you, Bertie, I *do* recognize you."

"Still making a cake of yourself, I see," he grinned, holding out his arms to hug her.

"Bertie, *dear*," she responded warmly, hugging him in return, "it's been such an age!"

There was a loud laugh behind them. "Well, Marcus," snorted one of the men in the circle to the fellow Sophy had first embraced, "what do you think of the likeness? Can't say *I* see much of a resemblance."

The gentleman called Marcus merely flicked him an unamused glance and said nothing. Bertie, however, blushed furiously. "She's my cousin," he explained. "Ain't seen her since she was ten. Best of chums we were then, but it's been a long time . . ."

The gentleman made a polite bow in acknowledgement and turned to go. But Sophia caught his arm and caused him to turn back. "I am *so* sorry, sir," she said with her most disarming smile.

The gentleman stepped back out of her reach. "Think nothing more of the matter, ma'am," he said with scrupulous politeness.

Sophia's eyes brightened with sudden interest. The gentleman's swarthy face was attractively lean, his eyes sharp and magnetic, and his shoulders broad and powerful-looking in his well-fitted evening coat. Her smile widened, her dimples very much in evidence, and her eyes shone with a look of supreme confidence in her ability to coax an answering warmth from any gentleman on whom that smile was bestowed. "I must have caused you extreme discomfort and embarrassment," she insisted. "I'd been so looking forward to seeing my dear cousin again that I suppose I was overeager." She extended her hand. "I most sincerely regret my error."

The tall stranger did not respond to her smile with an answering one. Nor did he take the proffered hand. Instead, he raised his quizzing-glass and looked at her with cool scrutiny. Unaccustomed to such a reaction, Sophia felt herself blush. She suddenly became aware of a sense of embarrassment at the daringly low décolletage of her dress and its too-bright color. Her hand dropped awkwardly to her side. The gentleman dropped his quizzing-glass, bowed politely and turned away.

The blood drained from her cheeks. She'd been given

the *cut direct*! The snub was unmistakable. Never in her life had she been rebuffed, and *this* had been done with such cold finesse! She clenched her fists to keep the world from noticing her trembling fingers.

Beside her, Bertie was watching the group move away from them as the rest of the onlookers turned away, grinning. "Hummmph!" he muttered. "Not a very friendly fellow, that."

"No, not very," she answered with a laugh that was compounded of equal parts of shock and chagrin. "Was it a very dreadful scene I made?"

"That fellow must have found it so," Bertie shrugged. "But let's not bother our heads about him. Everyone will have forgotten the matter by tomorrow. Now, let me look at you." He surveyed her admiringly. "I say, Sophy, you've grown up to be a regular out-and-outer."

"Thank you, Bertie," she smiled, but as she took a last, quick glance at the stranger who was disappearing with his friends into one of the card rooms, her expression changed. "But it appears," she said ruefully, "that not everyone is in agreement with you."

"Never mind him," Bertie insisted, following her eyes. "Most any man would agree with me, whatever that fellow thinks. You cut a regular dash!"

Sophia couldn't help grinning. She turned her full attention to her cousin. "And you, Bertie," she said with affectionate bluntness, "why, you've become a veritable butter-box. Oh, Bertie, I *am* so glad to see you! Let's find a quiet corner where we can sit down, and you can tell me *everything* that's happened to you in the last eleven years."

"Nothing I'd like better," Bertie agreed amiably, "but perhaps we'd better find Grandmama first. I haven't seen her yet."

The rest of the evening flew for Sophia. She and Bertie found time for a comfortable coz behind the potted palms, and she and Lady Alicia went down to supper on his arm. After supper, when the dancing resumed, Sophia found herself surrounded by more than her usual number of admirers asking for her hand for the few dances that were left. Correctly attributing her rise in popularity to the attention she'd received for the little scene she'd caused earlier in the evening, she nevertheless enjoyed herself hugely, flirting and laughing and cavorting on the dance floor with more than her usual animation.

Bertie, escorting his grandmother and cousin to their carriage at the end of the festivities, remarked, as they walked down the curved stairway, that their little Sophy had taken the shine out of all the females in the room. "She made more conquests than anyone else, I'd warrant," he said proudly.

Lady Alicia, who had been a witness to the entire episode of mistaken identity and knew that it was only a brief and vulgar notoriety that had caused the flurry of popularity for her granddaughter, merely grunted. At that moment, they arrived at the bottom of the stairway and came face to face with the stranger whom Sophy had so embarrassed. She met his eye and blushed to the roots of her hair. The gentleman's lips seemed to tighten; he nodded briefly and went quickly out the door. Sophy threw a nervous glance at her grandmother, who was frowning at her disdainfully. "Well, Bertie," Sophia laughed uncomfortably, her eyes on the stranger's retreating back, "you'll have to admit that I didn't make a conquest *there*."

Chapter Two

LADY ALICIA EDGERTON had a few choice words to say to her granddaughter before they retired, and she delivered them in a voice whose vigor and venom were not in the least impaired by her advanced age, the lateness of the hour, or the fact that the servants (those that might be lurking about outside the drawing room door) could have, if they tried, heard every word. She told her granddaughter without any roundaboutation that the incident had been a humiliating one for all concerned, and that it had been brought about by Sophia's heedlessness, her impetuosity and her inexcusable lack of good manners.

"But Grandmama," the girl protested, "it was only a little mistake—"

"One needn't make one's mistakes on quite so grand a scale," her grandmother declared icily. "Surely you knew that everyone's eyes were on you when you made that grand entrance in that dreadful red dress—"

"You said you *liked* the dress when you saw it earlier!" Sophia cried in understandable annoyance.

"That was before I realized that you intended to make one of your scandalous entrances in it. When you lifted your skirts and ran across the room crying Bertie's name, no one could *miss* you. You should have *seen* Martha gape. And Gussie Derwent's eyes nearly popped from her head. I was so ashamed I didn't know where to look."

"I'm truly sorry I embarrassed you, Grandmama, but—"

"There can be no 'but.' Your behavior was *inexcusable*. You rushed headlong into a shocking scene without giving the least thought to what you were doing."

"But I was so *sure* the gentleman was Bertie—!"

"*Bertie*, ha! Have you any idea whom you accosted in that vulgar way?"

Sophia shrugged. "They called him Marcus, I think," she replied, "but that's all I know about him. Except, of course, that he's quite the rudest, most top-lofty coxcomb I've ever—"

"That 'coxcomb,' I'll have you know, is none other than Marcus Harvey, Earl of Wynwood, a gentleman of impeccable character and laudable reputation, whose mother, Charlotte Harvey, happens to be one of my dearest friends."

"Charlotte Harvey? Do you mean *Lady Wynwood*? The same Lady Wynwood who's invited us all to spend a fortnight in her home in Sussex?" Sophia asked incredulously.

"The very same. And how we are to face her now, I shudder to imagine."

There was a moment of silence. "Well, I, for one, don't intend to hang my head," Sophia said bravely, holding up her chin as if to demonstrate the manner in which she intended to face Lady Wynwood. "I've done nothing so very terrible to her son, after all."

"Only made him a laughingstock," her grandmother reminded her.

"I made *myself* a laughingstock. He was just the . . . er . . . recipient . . ."

"It is my understanding, young lady, that Lord Wynwood is extremely well-bred, and not the man to enjoy any sort of unwarranted notice or public scrutiny, both of which you forced upon him in good measure."

"If he is so high in the instep as to be disturbed by a petty little incident at a private party, I have no sympathy for him."

"A petty little incident at a private party indeed! There were three hundred people present who saw you fling your arms around the neck of a perfect stranger—a man who then had to remove himself from your clutches by sheer force!"

Sophia whitened. "Remove himself—? Oh, Grandmama, was it as bad as that?"

"Every bit of it," her grandmother declared coldly.

Sophia's eyes filled with shame. Lady Alicia's anger melted at the look in her granddaughter's face, but she didn't permit the softening to show in her expression. The girl must be made to see that her rash behavior could have painful consequences.

Sophia stared at her grandmother, blinking away the tears that had welled up in her eyes. "Well, I don't see what g-good it will do to stand here and . . . and review the matter," she said, her chin quivering. "I admit that I made a mistake. I thoroughly embarrassed myself . . . and you, too. I'm s-sorry. But it will do no good to t-talk about it."

"Very well, then, I'll drop the subject. You may go to bed. But I hope that the incident will teach you to be less impetuous in future."

The subject was destined to come up again, however, the very next morning. No sooner had the ladies sat down to breakfast when they were interrupted by the arrival of Bertie's parents, Sir Walter and Lady Isabel Edgerton. Lady Alicia's son and daughter-in-law could wait no longer to pay their respects to the parent whom they hadn't seen for eleven years. Sir Walter, Alicia's younger son, was a stocky, florid-faced man who was often described as blunt. From the top of his short-cropped hair to the tips of his square fingers, the adjective applied. His disposition exactly matched his physique, for Walter was incapable of subtlety. He said what he thought with unblinking directness.

His wife, on the other hand, felt that it was her mission in life to soften the effect of her husband's directness on the world. Soft, round and placid herself, she could not believe that people could like to hear her husband's flat, honest statements. She held that roundaboutation was the kindest way to put a point across.

The greetings between the couple and their mother, so long separated, were voluble and as warm as could be expected from the acerbic Lady Alicia, who didn't wait ten minutes before remarking to Isabel that she'd put on too much weight. Sir Walter, who'd picked up a plate immediately on being invited to sit down at the table and was now digging in to his coddled eggs and ham with gusto, guffawed loudly. "*Told* you Mama would have something to say about your weight," he chortled.

Poor Isabel colored, stirred her tea and mumbled something vague about the amount of oil used in Indian cookery.

"I don't know why you're laughing, Walter," his mother said as bluntly as her son would have. "You could drop a stone on two yourself."

Now both visitors were silenced, and an awkward pause ensued. Although the lowered eyes and strained atmosphere bothered Lady Alicia not a whit, Sophy jumped into the breach and asked for Bertie's whereabouts. "Why didn't he come with you?" she asked her aunt and uncle.

"He's gone to look up a fellow he met in India," Walter said.

"His name is Lawrence Dillingham," Isabel amplified. "You remember the Berkshire Dillinghams, don't you, Mama? Their boy resides in London now. He and Bertie became great friends before the Dillinghams returned to England, and Bertie is most eager to renew acquaintance." Aunt Isabel's explanation was made in a rush of words, the purpose of which was to fog over the awkward effect of her mother-in-law's earlier slur.

"By the way," Walter put in, happily returning to his coddled eggs, "we were told about the to-do at the Gilberts' ball last night. It must have made quite a scene." He chuckled as he reached for a second biscuit.

"What Walter means, Mama," Isabel interjected in her usual mollifying way, "is that we heard a bit of mild gossip. Nothing very critical, you understand. Just slightly amusing."

"I know what Walter means, Isabel. You needn't explain my son to me. It was a completely reprehensible incident, Walter, and should not be the subject of levity," his mother told him quellingly.

Isabel nodded in agreement. "That's just what I told

him myself, Mama. Lord Wynwood must have been horribly embarrassed.''

"If the fellow tells his mother the tale," Walter suggested, "we shall have a cool reception in Sussex next month."

"Then perhaps we shouldn't go," Isabel offered worriedly.

"I don't like houseparties anyway," Walter put in promptly. "We can go to Wiltshire instead and spend a comfortable time at Edgerton."

"Nonsense! We're already promised to Lady Wynwood," his mother said firmly. "Besides, Edgerton is no longer a comfortable place to visit, now that your brother has taken an Evangelical shrew for a wife."

"An *Evangelical*?" Isabel exclaimed, shocked. "You cannot mean it. I had heard that Lady Edgerton's nature is not conformable, but no one mentioned her religiosity."

"I can't believe my brother would marry a religious," Walter exclaimed. "He has never shown the slightest interest in the church."

Lady Alicia picked up her teacup with a shrug. "Ask Sophia, if you think I exaggerate."

"She is certainly an Evangelical," Sophy said in vehement agreement, "and much worse than a shrew. I warn you, my dear Aunt and Uncle, that a visit to Edgerton these days will not be at all pleasant. And in any case, I fail to see why the plans to go to Sussex should be changed."

"Well, *really*, Sophia—" Isabel began.

"If you are going to refer again to that ridiculous incident at the Gilberts' ball, I shall have an attack of the vapors! It was nothing but a small misunderstanding. A little mistake! If Lord Wynwood were not so puffed up with his own consequence, the entire matter would not have caused comment. There is no cause whatever for us to hide from the world—or from Lady Wynwood either. I say we should visit Lady Wynwood just as we'd planned. If she brings the matter up, I shall not hesitate to tell her that nothing at all occurred to cause her son to raise such a dust."

"Hear, hear!" Sir Walter cheered appreciatively. "The girl has pluck, I'll say that for her, Mama."

Lady Alicia snorted. "Since Lord Wynwood is hardly likely to repeat to his mother anything concerning a matter that he no doubt considers beneath his attention, it is highly improbable that Sophia's pluck will be put to the test. And as for *you*, Miss Prattlebox, may I remind you that Lord Wynwood did *not* raise a dust. He said not a word throughout the whole humiliating incident. Whatever dust was raised was entirely your own doing." And with that, Lady Alicia put down her teacup and rose from the table, thus indicating that the breakfast, the subject and the visit were at an end.

Later that afternoon, Bertie presented himself at his grandmother's house in Russell Square, his friend Dillingham in tow. Lawrence Dillingham was a tall, gawky youth who had not yet become adept in the techniques of flirtation and courtship. He took one look at his friend Bertie's attractive cousin and was instantly smitten. "Close your mouth," Bertie whispered to him when the boy gaped adoringly at Sophia from across the room as soon as they'd been introduced. "You look like a moony fish."

Sophy laughed. "Don't tease your friend," she admonished her cousin. "Mr. Dillingham doesn't in the least resemble a fish."

Dillingham blushed. "More like a beanpole, I'm afraid," he said with a shy smile, shaking her hand awkwardly.

Bertie watched with growing disgust as the stricken Dillingham ogled Sophy adoringly. When they took their leave, he stopped on the street and fixed an accusing eye on his friend. "I thought you said you ain't in the petticoat line," he said contemptuously. "How do you account for the way you gaped at my cousin?"

Dillingham blinked. "Oh . . . er . . . did I gape?"

"Like a blasted conniwobble."

Poor Dillingham kicked at a pebble embarrassedly. "It's just . . . that she's such a deucedly pretty little thing . . . all eyes and dimples and little dark curls . . . Are you angry with me?"

"Disgusted, more like," Bertie said bluntly.

Dillingham chewed at his underlip worriedly. "Are you . . . ? You're not . . . taken with her yourself?"

"Who, *I*?" Bertie gave a disdainful snort. "You must be a bigger beetlehead than I supposed. I told you that I ain't disposed to dangle after females just yet. I don't want to get leg-shackled for *years*. Besides, the girl's my cousin. Known her since she was a brat. She ain't the type I'd have in mind to court, even if I *had* a taste for that sort of thing."

"Then why did you take me to meet her?" Dillingham asked.

"Because she's such a jolly good sport. I thought we could all be *friends*. How was I to know you'd turn up sweet?"

Dillingham walked alongside his friend in thoughtful silence. "I don't see why you're upset," he remarked after a while. "Why can't we all *still* be friends?"

"We can't if you're going to act like a damned mooncalf every time we see her. She wouldn't like it any more than I would. You ain't the sort that a female like Sophy would care to encourage in a flirtation."

"No, I suppose I'm not," Dillingham acknowledged with a deep sigh.

"Well, you needn't fall into the dismals. We *can* all be friends if you'll only promise to be sensible."

Dillingham nodded manfully. "Very well, I promise," he said bravely.

It was noticed (by those who watched) that Sophia behaved with some restraint for the next few days. But the incident at the Gilberts' ball was not sufficiently disreputable to set tongues wagging for very long, and by the end of the week it was all but forgotten. Sophy's confidence and good spirits quickly reasserted themselves, and her old behavior returned. Lady Alicia heard from several acquaintances that her granddaughter had been seen riding in the park with Bertie and his friend Dillingham with uninhibited speed and noise; that she'd danced with Sir Tristram Caitlin three times in succession at a ball given by Lady March; and that she was heard during a play at Covent Garden to laugh out loud at a line which no lady should have admitted that she understood. By the end of the second week, her grandmother was more disgusted with the girl than ever.

Lawrence Dillingham, had he been aware of it, would not have agreed with Lady Alicia's assessment of Sophy's character. The young man had been deeply struck by Sophy's charms and would have called to task anyone who maligned her in his presence. Painfully smitten, he took every opportunity to join Bertie when he went to call on her. The three were often seen together, riding in the park, strolling through the Pantheon Bazaar or visiting the shops on St. James Street.

They made a jolly, lively threesome. To Sophy's surprise, Bertie, although a year her senior, now seemed younger and far less sophisticated than she. His friend was content merely to follow along and laugh at the pleasantries of the other two. Sophy enjoyed their company, for they seemed like two younger brothers; the relaxed intimacy which they developed was different from her friendships with the knowing young ladies and the practiced, artful gentlemen with whom she usually associated. Two or three times a week, Sophy indulged herself by permitting her lighthearted cousin and his shy young friend to squire her about.

One morning, three weeks after the incident at the Gilbert's ball, Sophy induced her young escorts to accompany her to Hookham's library in Old Bond Street. The bookstore was large and very popular with the *ton*, stocking all the new and most talked-about novels and books of poetry. Here was *The Absentee*, by Maria Edgeworth, who had made such a stir with a novel she had written some years before called *Castle Rackrent*; there was *The Giaour*, a lurid verse-romance by Lord Byron, whose poem *Childe Harold's Pilgrimage* had made his name a household word just a year before.

Hundreds of books and periodicals were displayed on the tables which were arranged in two neat rows down the length of the store. The bookstore was bustling as well-dressed ladies and elegant gentlemen sauntered through the

aisles, pausing to examine a leather-bound volume through
a quizzing-glass or to leaf through a current issue of the
London Magazine with gloved fingers. Sophy and her
escorts were soon separated by the throng, but, momentarily
distracted by her fascination with the opening verses of
Byron's poem which she'd begun to peruse, she was not
aware that she'd been left alone. She looked up from her
copy of *The Giaour* to find herself staring into the eyes of
the stranger of the Gilberts' ball, Lord Wynwood himself.

His lordship's expression was puzzled, and Sophy
immediately guessed (when their eyes met, and he quickly
looked away) that he'd forgotten who she was. It was
obvious that he couldn't place her almost-familiar face.
She quickly realized why. She didn't look much like the
girl at the ball—her rather shocking cherry-colored ball
gown had now been replaced by a dove-gray walking
dress, and her noteworthy auburn hair was now covered by
a *bergère* hat tied in place with a modest lilac ribbon. No
wonder he couldn't place her.

Unable to resist an impulse to set the arrogant, forgetful
Lord Wynwood at a loss, she made a deep bow and said
sweetly, "Good day, Lord Wynwood." She was gleefully
aware that, although she'd learned *his* identity, he'd never
learned hers. He would therefore be at an awkward
disadvantage. The imperturbable, cold Earl of Wynwood
was in an embarrassing position, and she would have the
pleasure of watching him squirm.

There was, however, no trace of awkwardness in the
Earl's manner or his expression. "Good afternoon, ma'am,"
he replied smoothly, with an answering bow.

Sophy had no intention of letting him off so easily. She
decided to continue the conversation and force him to
acknowledge his ignorance. But she noticed that a young
woman who'd been standing near his lordship had looked
up from her book with a questioning glance. She was
evidently in his company, for she put down her book and
took Lord Wynwood's arm. The lady was a tall, elegant
creature with dusky-gold hair, a swan-like neck and alabaster
skin. Although she looked vaguely familiar, Sophy didn't
bother to identify her. She was occupied with an amused

sense of triumph: the Earl would *have* to introduce them.
She would have him *now*!

"May I present Miss Bethune?" Lord Wynwood murmured, his brow wrinkling as he desperately tried to
remember who this girl was. "Iris, this is . . . is . . ."

Miss Bethune put out her hand. "Miss Edgerton, is it
not? I believe we met last year at Lady March's birthday
fete. How delightful to meet you again. I didn't know you
were acquainted with Miss Edgerton, Marcus."

"Well, I—" Lord Wynwood gestured helplessly, still
unable to jar his memory.

"I say, Sophy," Bertie called from across the aisle,
"take a look at *this*." He waved a book at her as his riding
boots clumped across the floor. "It's called *A Wicked
Lady,* and it's absolutely *shock*—Oh!" He stopped short,
stared at Lord Wynwood and his face flooded with color.

"Good heavens," Lord Wynwood muttered, his eyes
lighting in recognition, "it's *Bertie!*"

"Bertie?" Iris Bethune asked, turning to the Earl with
her eyebrows raised.

Lord Wynwood smiled, both relieved that he remembered
and amused at Miss Edgerton's obvious embarrassment.
"Forgive me, my dear," he explained to Miss Bethune,
"but I suddenly recalled where Miss Edgerton and I had
met. It was at the Gilberts' ball. On that occasion, Miss
Edgerton took me for Bertie here."

"Took you for—?" Miss Bethune stared at Bertie
nonplussed. "I don't understand . . ."

"Never mind," Lord Wynwood said firmly. "It's much
too long a story, and we shall be late for our luncheon with
Stanford. Good day, Miss Edgerton. Good day, Bertie, old
fellow. I do hope you'll excuse us from the amenities. We
must be off." And with a smooth but hasty efficiency,
Lord Wynwood nodded to them both and turned Miss
Bethune toward the door.

Lawrence Dillingham hurried up to Bertie and, in what
was meant to be a whisper, asked, "I say, who's the Bond
Street Beau? I've never *seen* such a magnificent coat!"
His voice, even in his attempted whisper, had a penetra-
ting quality which carried throughout the store. Up and

down the aisles, heads turned and eyes glinted in their efforts to obtain a glimpse of the Bond Street Beau in the magnificent coat. Sophy could see Lord Wynwood's back stiffen as he steered Miss Bethune to the door with quickened steps. "Really, Mr. Dillingham," she hissed in a furious undervoice, "couldn't your remarks have waited until we were alone?"

She turned away from her escorts in disgust and humiliation, leaning against the table in an attempt to compose herself. To her intense dismay, the table gave way, and the dozens of books displayed upon it tumbled to the floor with a thunderous crash. She jumped back, uttered a little scream and looked quickly towards the door. *Let him be gone,* she prayed with a desperate earnestness. *Please let him be gone. Let him not see what I've done.*

But Lord Wynwood had heard the crash just as he was stepping through the doorway, and he turned around instinctively. He stared at her with his eyebrows raised. Ignoring the goggling eyes and disdainful murmurings of everyone else, she could feel only *his* eyes on her. Her cheeks burned, and she couldn't bear to meet his look. But his expression of distaste was so apparent that a spark of anger flared in her breast. How dared he look at her so? She lifted her chin and stared back at him challengingly. His lordship's lips twitched in barely-perceptible amusement; he shook his head in barely-expressed disbelief, bowed briefly and disappeared into the street.

Although the proprietor of the shop was very kind, and despite the fact that her escorts found the scene uproariously funny, Sophia left the bookstore in a state of almost unbearable chagrin. Bertie's company was suddenly insupportable, and Mr. Dillingham's asininity seemed to have markedly increased. She insisted upon being taken home. Ignoring their attempts to tease her out of the doldrums, she walked along silent and withdrawn. The memory of Lord Wynwood's expression at that last, deplorable moment was etched on her inner eye. *I don't care what he thinks of me,* she repeated to herself firmly as the mortifying scene played over and over again in her imagination. But each repetition made the incident appear more odiously vulgar, and the state of her emotions made it quite clear that she cared very much indeed about what his lordship thought of her.

She dismissed her escorts on her doorstep and entered the house quietly, wishing only to creep up to her bedroom and hide away from the world. Her spirits utterly depressed, she didn't want to face her grandmother. Lady Alicia, as soon as she learned the details of the morning's fiasco, would be sure to blame the whole debacle on Sophy's impetuosity. Sophy therefore hurried up the stairs on tiptoe. But she'd only reached the first landing when her grandmother's voice stopped her. "Is that you, Sophy?" her ladyship called from the sitting room.

Lady Alicia only called her "Sophy" when she was in a very good mood, so it was evident to the girl that the news of the incident had not yet found its way to her grandmother's ears. In some relief, she went down to the sitting room. "Good afternoon, Grandmama," she said from the doorway.

"I've had a letter from Lady Wynwood," Alicia told her, looking up from the closely-written sheets of paper she'd been reading. "She writes that our visit to Sussex is to be even more festive than she'd planned. It seems that her son is to be married, and he's requested his mother to make the announcement at Wynwood Hall to a small, select group of friends and relations, ourselves included."

Sophy's breath caught in her throat. "Do you mean . . . ? Are you saying that Lord Wynwood will be *staying* at Wynwood Hall . . . at the very time when *we'll* be there?"

"Yes, my dear, that's *just* what I'm saying."

Sophy stared at her grandmother in wide-eyed horror. "But . . . but you never *told* me that he would be present—!"

"I didn't know it, you peagoose. But you needn't look so alarmed, my love. If your concern is caused by the recollection of the to-do at the Gilberts' ball, you may put such thoughts aside. Perhaps I made too much of the incident when it occurred. The matter can be of no moment to Lord Wynwood—certainly not after all this time. With a marriage in the offing, you may be sure he has more important matters on his mind. I shouldn't wonder if his lordship doesn't remember you at all.''

"You would have been right, if this were yesterday," Sophy said glumly.

"What do you mean?" Lady Alicia asked, her complacent expression fading.

"He'll remember me *now*. I made an *indelible* impression on him today.''

"Today?'' her grandmother asked apprehensively. "What happened *today*?''

"I . . . never mind. It was of no importance. But you may as well understand, Grandmama, that I have no intention of going to Sussex if *he's* to be there.''

"But . . . why not? You're *expected*!''

"Expected or not, I shan't go. I couldn't face that man again.''

The old woman stared at her granddaughter for a moment and then closed her eyes as if to shut out a horrifying image. "Sophia, what have you done now?''

"I don't want to talk about it, Grandmama, please.''

Lady Alicia opened her eyes and fixed them on her granddaughter lugubriously. "As bad as that, eh? Well, if you don't want to talk about it, I'm sure I don't want to hear about it. I'm much too old to subject my nerves to the shock of dealing with another of your hairbrained misdeeds. So don't tell me. I will merely say that you *will* accompany me to Sussex whether you like it or not.''

"Never!'' Sophia said roundly. "You can go in the company of Aunt Isabel and Uncle Walter. You don't need me.''

"Of course I don't *need* you, you little ninny. But I can't leave you here alone. So, will-you, nill-you, you will go.''

Sophia drew herself up to her full height and faced her grandmother dramatically. "You don't understand,'' she declared tremulously. "I *can not* go. You can leave me here alone, send me back to Papa, or do whatever else you will with me. But, Grandmama, there's nothing on *earth* which could prevail upon me to go to Wynwood Hall. I

won't face that man for anyone or anything in the world!''
She ran to the door, throwing her grandmother a backward
glance. "And that," she said with her most histrionic
tremor, "is my *final word* on the subject!"

Chapter Three

ALL THE EDGERTONS but Sophy were eagerly anticipating their visit to Wynwood Hall. Each had his own specific reason for desiring the fortnight in Sussex. Isabel knew that an invitation to Wynwood was a rare prize and put one high in the esteem of the *ton*. In addition, she looked forward to a respite from the active social whirl of London. Her husband, Sir Walter, merely yearned for the smell of country air. Since his return from India he had done nothing but complain about the offensive stench of the London streets. Bertie had learned that Wynwood possessed a superb stable and that the hunting was excellent. And Lady Alicia, of course, was eager for a reunion with her dear old friend Charlotte. As the time for departure drew near, the prospect of the sojourn in Sussex grew more and more inviting, and it increasingly became the subject of conversation when the family came together.

Not one of the family, however, was able to persuade Sophy to change her mind and make one of the party. Lady Alicia harangued her repeatedly on the problems her stubbornness was causing. The old lady could not permit her granddaughter to remain in London with no one but the servants. She finally agreed, with great reluctance, to send the girl back to her Wiltshire home for a fortnight's stay. The fact that Sophy agreed to this unpleasant expedient was ample proof to her grandmother that, to Sophy's mind at least, *anything* (even the prospect of living with her stepmother) was preferable to facing Lord Wynwood again.

As the day of departure grew closer, it was apparent to everyone that Sophia's spirits were declining. Even the companionship of the good-natured Bertie, the devoted Dillingham, or her newest swain, Sir Tristram Caitlin, did nothing to lift her out of the dismals. Sir Walter, who was usually quite oblivious to the vagaries of female emotions, noticed the girl's moodiness and was touched by it. To everyone's delighted surprise, he offered to escort the entire family to Drury Lane to see Sarah Siddons perform Shakespeare. Isabel was so pleased by her husband's unwonted thoughtfulness that she promptly invited the family to take dinner at her house before the play.

Sophy, realizing that her family was taking elaborate pains for her benefit, resolved to do her part to make the occasion a success. On the evening appointed for the theater expedition, she put on her favorite gown (a graceful swirl of green lustring which brought out the glints of red in her hair), pinched a good color into her cheeks and put on her widest smile. When she set off with her grandmother to Sir Walter's residence, Lady Alicia complimented her most sincerely on her appearance. Lady Alicia herself was quite in her best looks, wearing a new lavendar crape roundgown and her favorite diamond brooch. When one knows one is looking quite up to the mark, it is hard to be downcast, and the pair arrived at Sir Walter's residence in almost excellent spirits.

The dinner did nothing to dampen their mood. In fact, it made a delightful beginning for the evening. Isabel was an over-anxious but generous hostess, and when Lady Alicia deigned to compliment her on the dinner (refraining for once from making her usual caustic comments on the blandness of the menu or the toughness of the beef), Isabel beamed with relief and pleasure. Bertie made them all howl with laughter at his humorous account of his friend Dillingham's first appearance in evening clothes. (He had urged Dilly to order a dress suit, and it had arrived from the tailor's the day before. Bertie had made his friend model it for him. His description of Dilly's stiff-legged walk in his new black silk breeches—which made his thighs look even longer and thinner than they were—gave a vivid verbal picture of a crow in a white neckcloth.) And Sir Walter spent the better part of the dinner hour imbibing generous amounts of wine to fortify himself against the onslaught of culture which he was about to endure at the theater, and he was, by the end of the meal, in a very mellow mood indeed.

It was therefore a merry group which climbed into Sir Walter's most commodious carriage for the ride to Drury Lane. On their arrival, Sir Walter and his party were ushered up to one of the very best boxes. A number of acquaintances in the boxes nearby nodded or waved, and many eyes turned up to them from the pit to admire the elegance of their attire and the cheerfulness of their spirits. They settled into their chairs with satisfied sighs and prepared to attend the play.

Sarah Siddons, the most renowned actress of the century, was making one of her rare appearances, recreating her role as Volumnia in *Coriolanus*. Her first appearance was greeted with cheers and applause, and Sophy, enchanted by the woman's unmistakable magnetism, leaned forward on the balustrade to watch the performance. Mrs. Siddons was tall, imposing and commanding, her advancing years only enhancing her talents. When her rich voice rang out with:

> "... *Away, you fool! (Blood) more becomes a man Than gilt his trophy. The breasts of Hecuba,/When she did suckle Hector, looked not lovelier/Than Hector's forehead when it spit forth blood/At Grecian sword* ..."

Sophy felt a little, thrilled shiver over her skin. Mrs. Siddons's short scene breathed awesome life into a play of ancient political intrigue. Sophy had always enjoyed reading history, her grandfather (an expert on military history) having instilled in her a sense of its grandeur when she was a young child, and the story of Coriolanus was quite familiar to her. What surprised her was the interest of the rest of the audience. Their attention was rapt, and Sophy was impressed by the fact that so many listened with such fascination to the re-creation of events which would have faded into oblivion centuries ago had not Shakespeare and these performers made them live again.

She was about to return her attention to the stage when her eye was caught by a familiar profile. Across the theater, in a box almost directly opposite, sat Lord Wynwood. Her heart gave a little lurch, and something in her throat constricted in fear. Why, she asked herself, had that detestable man such power over her emotions? Why was she afraid of him? Why did she feel it necessary to win his good opinion? Why, in fact, did she concern herself with him at all?

She could find no logical answers. Her reaction to seeing him was beyond what was reasonable. She must exercise control over such inordinate sensations. She turned her eyes to the stage and forced herself to concentrate on the play.

By the time the third act had ended, she was fully caught up in Coriolanus's dilemma. Volumnia's cold-bloodedness froze her blood, and Coriolanus's pride, when he spoke the lines:

> ". . . I would not buy
> Their mercy at the price of one fair word . . ."

quite moved her to tears. When the intermission lights were lit, she was caught wiping the corners of her eyes with the tip of a gloved finger and was unmercifully teased for her softheartedness by Bertie, who said bluntly that as far as he was concerned, the play was a deuced bore.

Lady Alicia frowned at her grandson indignantly. "I have as little patience with sentimentality as anyone," she declared roundly, "but remaining unmoved by these remarkable performances, Bertie, shows you to be sadly undiscerning, and to find Shakespeare a bore says little for your education and your taste."

Bertie, thus chastized, promptly made his exit from the box with the excuse that he would fetch a glass of champagne for each of the ladies.

Sophy brought to her grandmother's notice the fact that her crony, Lady March, seated several boxes away, was attempting to send a message to Lady Alicia by means of some indecipherable hand-signals and eye-blinkings. "What on earth can the woman be trying to tell me?" Alicia muttered irritably. "Run over there, Sophy, and find out what she wants."

Obediently, Sophy left the box and hurried down the corridor toward Lady March's location. To her intense dismay, she saw that, far down the hallway, two men were approaching, one of whom was the disturbing Lord Wynwood. The men were engrossed in conversation and probably had not yet noticed her. She looked about desperately for somewhere to hide. At her left was the open door of a box. A quick look showed it to be empty. Sophy darted inside and closed the door. She leaned against it, trying over the beating of her heart to listen for the two gentlemen's passing steps. But she could hear nothing. After an interminable moment, she opened the door just a crack and peeped out.

In the restricted view the narrow opening provided, she could see a few people milling about a waiter who carried a tray loaded with glasses of champagne. Lord Wynwood and his friend walked into her line of vision, approached the waiter and each took a glass. Horrified, she watched as they stood sipping their drinks just outside the door behind which she'd hidden herself. She ground her teeth in frustration.

"Filthy stuff," she heard Lord Wynwood's friend mutter in disgust.

"Well, Dennis," Lord Wynwood answered pleasantly, "one can hardly expect the best champagne at Drury Lane. This is not Prinny's table, after all."

The man called Dennis laughed and nodded, drinking the champagne with apparent gusto despite his criticism of it. "But to return to our subject," he said, "I mean no criticism of Iris (who is a divine creature, I assure you) when I say you are making a mistake."

"A mistake? To marry?" Wynwood asked calmly. "Are you against marriage on principle? I'm very much afraid,

Dennis, that your development has been arrested somewhere at about nineteen years of age. There comes a time, old fellow, when one must face up to one's responsibilities.''

"Responsibilities? Have we a responsibility to settle down like old codgers snoozing before the fireside of life?''

Wynwood laughed. "You phrased that very poetically, I must admit, but not very logically. We're past thirty. It's more than time we settled down to raising families, overseeing properties, attending to politics, and facing all the other concerns of maturity.''

"Faugh! Marcus, you sound quite like my father. You must do as you see fit, of course, but as for me, I intend to spend ten years more at least on chasing females, gambling recklessly and wasting my time at all the more reprehensible pursuits.''

"Do so, by all means. I'm not your father, however much my views may resemble his. If you wish to behave like an over-aged schoolboy, I haven't the least objection. Only don't expect me to join you.''

"Too bad,'' Dennis sighed with exaggerated disappointment. "What great fun you'll miss. But it's not yet too late. At least *tonight* you're still free. The night is charged with promise. What say you, Marcus, old man? Look at that ladybird down the hall standing with Hester Delafield. Isn't she a beauty?''

"Yes, she is, indeed. I've no objection to your departing from my side to try your hand with her.''

"No, no, I meant her for *you*. *I* have my eye on the girl I pointed out to you in the box. The one in the green dress, Now, *there's* a filly who's *something like*! Don't you think so?''

"Green dress? I don't seem to recall—''

Dennis made an impatient gesture. "Of course you do. I pointed her out to you earlier. She's the one who threw herself at you at the Gilberts' ball.''

Sophy gasped. Those dreadful men were talking about *her*! She had a strong desire to throw open the door, fix them both with an icy stare and leave them in humiliated astonishment. But Lord Wynwood was about to respond to his friend's question concerning his opinion of her, and she could no more resist eavesdropping on his answer than she could refrain from breathing. She put her ear close to the tiny opening in the door and listened.

The old adage that eavesdroppers never hear good of themselves proved again to be quite true. "You mean Miss Edgerton, I collect," Lord Wynwood was saying. "She's a pretty-enough little thing, I grant you, but I shouldn't want to become involved with her sort."

"What sort is that?" Dennis asked in a tone that clearly expressed his intention to disagree with whatever it was his friend would tell him.

"The melodramatic sort," Marcus said promptly. "A shatterbrained hysteric. You know, the sort of little ninny who makes scenes, enacts Cheltenham tragedies, farcical comedies and all levels of melodrama in between."

Dennis looked at his friend dubiously. "What *are* you talking about? You met the girl only once, isn't that right? How can you jump to such conclusions from just one meeting? And *how* did you learn her name?"

"I met her *twice*, giving me quite enough time in which to learn her name and her nature. During the first meeting, you were present. You saw with your own eyes the scene she created, so I needn't review the details. During my second meeting with the silly chit, she managed to make herself and me the center of attention in a bookstore crowded with people. It took her barely five minutes to embarrass me about my manners and my coat—"

"Your coat?"

"My coat. And not two minutes later, the girl somehow contrived to overturn a table covered with books. When I last saw her, she was surrounded by a pile of debris and a cloud of rising dust, but managing to hold her head up high." He laughed at the recollection. "She was not unlike our Mrs. Siddons in that last act, declaring to Coriolanus that 'Thy valiantness was mine!' "

Dennis chuckled and shook his head. "Sounds like a Banbury tale to me. Are you bamming me, Marcus?"

"I shall allow you to decide that for yourself. In the meantime, we'd best start back. The crowd has thinned. Intermission must be coming to an end."

They turned and strolled back down the corridor, leaving behind a Sophia trembling with fury. How *dared* that beast malign her so! How dared he take a series of unfortunate mishaps and twist them into an indictment of her character! Was it her fault that the table in the bookstore had fallen over? The manager himself had admitted that the table had a weakness in its structure. And was it her fault that Dilly had made that unfortunate remark about Lord Wynwood's coat? The remark, embarrassing as it had been, had been made in admiration, after all . . .

Approaching footsteps checked her angry brooding. People were returning to their boxes. She slipped from her hiding place and hurried back to Sir Walter's box.

"There you are, girl," her grandmother declared. "Where have you been this age? What did Lady March want?"

Sophy blinked. "Lady March?" she asked stupidly.

"Yes, Lady March, Lady March! Isn't that where you went?"

Sophy had completely forgotten her errand. How was she to explain to her irritable grandmother that she'd spent the entire intermission hiding behind a door? Before she could frame a reply, the curtains rose on the fourth act.

"Never mind," Lady Alicia muttered. "Lady March's remarks are never of any consequence." And she turned her attention to the play.

But Sophy was no longer interested in the tribulations of Coriolanus and his prideful mother. Even Mrs. Siddons's magnificent bearing and reverberating voice failed to distract Sophy from her brooding over what she'd overheard. He'd called her a shatterbrained hysteric! A ninny! A silly chit! She positively trembled with vexation. Never had she felt so painfully humiliated.

She turned her eyes to Lord Wynwood's box. He was watching the play, but his friend's head was turned in her direction. The great distance between them made his face seem a white blur, but Sophia was convinced that he was grinning at her. She turned her back on him. The detestable Lord Wynwood had evidently succeeded in turning an admirer into a scoffer. She was nothing now but an object of ridicule. But why should she care? Both Lord Wynwood and his friend Dennis Whoever-he-was meant less than nothing to her!

Sophia was grimly silent on the way home, making it plain to the family that the evening they had planned with such optimism, and which had started with such promise, had failed in the end to give the girl a bit of cheer. Isabel remarked to Sir Walter, after they'd said their good-nights to Lady Alicia and the stormy-eyed Sophia, that she'd been afraid from the first that Coriolanus had been a poor choice of play. "All that ranting over honor and death— it's enough to give one the megrims," she complained.

"Don't refine on it too much, Mama," Bertie advised callously as he went off down the hall to his bedroom. "Sophy'll get over it. I've never known her to poker up for very long."

Lady Alicia, undressing for bed, was having thoughts of a similar nature. Although she would not have expressed herself like Bertie, she was convinced that her volatile granddaughter would not remain in the doldrums for very long. However, she could not be easy in her mind while the girl was unhappy. If the prospect of a fortnight's visit to her stepmother could depress the girl to such an extent, perhaps it behooved Alicia to cancel her trip to Sussex.

She dismissed Miss Leale, put a wrapper over her nightdress and padded in slippered feet across the hall to her granddaughter's bedroom. "Sophy," she asked, tapping lightly on the door, "are you asleep?"

"No, Grandmama. Come in if you wish."

Lady Alicia stepped into her granddaughter's room and peered about her in astonishment. The girl had not even undressed. Her portmanteau, which had already been packed for her trip home, was lying open on her bed. Her trunk stood open on the floor. She had evidently been rummaging through her luggage. Petticoats, shawls, dresses and shoes were scattered about in considerable upheaval. "What on earth are you doing?" Lady Alicia asked bewilderedly.

"Packing, as you see," the girl told her curtly.

"Packing? But you'd *already* packed."

"Well then, if you wish me to be perfectly accurate,"

Sophy said, ruthlessly crushing an expensive silk evening dress into a ball and tossing it into the trunk, "I'm *re*packing."

"But . . . whatever for? And *why* are you taking that ball gown? Surely you won't need it in Wiltshire."

"That's just the point. I'm not going to Wiltshire."

"Not going to—?" Poor Lady Alicia dropped into the nearest chair, groaned and put a hand to her forehead. "Sophia, you are giving me the most fearful headache. If you're not going home to Wiltshire, will you kindly tell me *where* you plan to go?"

"I'm going with *you* . . . to Sussex." The words were said with grim determination, the girl sorting out clothes with careless dispatch.

"*What*! To *Sussex*?" The old woman studied her granddaughter narrowly. "What sort of hum is this. You've been *adamant* in your refusal to set foot in Wynwood Hall. What has caused this sudden about-face?"

Sophy ceased her frenzied packing and looked down at her grandmother with a glint in her eye which Lady Alicia had not seen before. "I've changed my mind," she said, elaborately casual.

"Why?"

Sophy shrugged. "Call it a whim."

"A *whim*? Listen here, girl, I don't like whims. For days now, you have been swearing—and for no reason that I can determine—that you'll never face Lord Wynwood again. Suddenly, because of a *whim*, you make a complete reversal. How can I plan our lives on *whims*? Perhaps, when the wind changes, you'll reverse yourself again."

"I promise I shall not."

"Are you telling me that you are now willing to *face* Lord Wynwood?"

"Willing?" Sophy smiled, a slight smile that held no warmth and caused her grandmother to feel a twinge of apprehension. "I'm more than willing. In fact, there's suddenly nothing I'd rather do than face Lord Wynwood again."

Lady Alicia returned to her room, her brow creased in

thought. What had caused this shocking turnabout? That
something had happened in the theater was obvious. She
could even pinpoint the time of the occurrence: the
intermission following the third act. And of course, Marcus
Harvey, Lord Wynwood, was somehow involved. What
part had he played? Had he *cut* the girl? Was Sophy
planning a foolish revenge of some sort?

She shook her head and climbed wearily into bed. She
must give up this pointless speculation. Whatever had
occurred, it would lead to some sort of disaster—of that
she was sure. Well, she'd long been aware that Sophy's
headstrong behavior would lead the girl into trouble. It
was coming . . . the old woman could feel its approach in
her bones. But as she pulled the covers up to her neck and
snuggled into the comforting warmth, she banished the
subject from her mind. She couldn't live Sophy's life for
her. Nor could she protect the girl from the consequences
of her impetuous behavior. Sophy would have to handle
those consequences herself; there was very little a grandmother could do. Lady Alicia could only hope that the
pain would not be severe, that Sophy would learn from her
mistakes, and that she, weary old creature though she was,
would be permitted to assist in picking up the pieces.

Chapter Four

MARCUS HARVEY, the fifth Earl of Wynwood, felt no particular eagerness to attend his mother's houseparty at Wynwood Hall, even though it had been arranged at his request and was being held in his honor. The only reason he'd requested it at all was to avoid the much more ostentatious affair that his future mother-in-law had threatened to arrange. Iris's mother, Lady Lorna Bethune, had spoken of holding an engagement ball at her London townhouse for two hundred of her most intimate friends. "A mere two hundred?" Marcus had asked drily, hoping her ladyship was jesting.

"If you are implying that the number is too large, my dear boy, you may save your breath," the strong-willed dowager declared. "I couldn't invite fewer without giving offense."

Marcus quailed. "But, Lady Lorna, I couldn't—"

"Now, Marcus, be a good fellow and don't object. After all, you must understand that one's only daughter does not become betrothed every day. One likes to be surrounded by one's nearest and dearest at such a time."

The prospect of facing the congratulations of two hundred of Lady Bethune's nearest and dearest proved too much for Marcus to stomach. Hoping for aid from his intended bride, he cast an anguished glance at Iris, who was seated on the settee beside him. But Iris was gazing demurely

down at the hands folded in her lap, as if to indicate that it
was not proper for a well-bred young lady to take part in
planning for a party at which she would be the guest of
honor. Marcus rose and began to pace about the room. He
had an almost obsessive antipathy toward public display,
and he abhorred to be made conspicuous. A ball such as the
one his mother-in-law contemplated (at which he would be
at the center of a crowd of well-wishers) was utterly
repugnant to him. "But . . . my mother writes that . . . er
. . . *she* wishes to give the party," he improvised desperately.

Lady Bethune gaped. "Your mother? You mean at
Wynwood?"

"Yes," he went on, sinking deeper into deception, "at
Wynwood. Mother wants to hold a houseparty, with only
our immediate families and a few friends present."

If any of Lord Wynwood's intimate friends had overheard
the exchange, they would have understood the reason he'd
fabricated that story. They all knew him to be scrupulously
honest, so if he were concocting Banbury tales, the reason
could only be that Lady Bethune was attempting to violate
his deep sense of privacy. Lord Wynwood was known to
have a reticence in public that was beyond the ordinary.
One could see it in the subdued and modest style of his
dress and manner—a style which he consciously adopted
to keep himself out of the limelight. He hated to be
noticed. If onlookers were inclined to take heed of his
entrance into a room (and they often were), it was either
because his height and his craggy features had caught their
eyes or because his admirable reputation had preceded
him.

His friends described him as the sort who never put
himself forward. He kept his opinions to himself unless
pressed, but since he was known to be a man of sense and
considerable knowledge, his friends always pressed him
for those opinions. He would then comply, of course, but
with a soft-spoken, non-contentious manner which seemed
to suggest that the listeners could accept or reject his views
as they pleased. Those who didn't know him often asked
why a man so obviously gifted by nature and so highly

placed in the world would behave in so self-effacing a way. His intimates, however, knew that he was far from self-effacing. He was very much his own man and knew quite well how to please himself. If they could have witnessed the little scene between Marcus and his mother-in-law-to-be, they would have found it a case in point. For Marcus had no intention of subjecting himself to a grandiose pre-nuptial party which he would thoroughly dislike, and if a small deception were necessary to extricate himself from the situation, why then it was a price he was willing to pay.

So he had invented the story of his mother's letter, and Lady Bethune had been caught up short. She'd choked, and her mouth had dropped open. In fact, she'd almost goggled. "At Wynwood?" she'd repeated, awed. "You don't mean it!"

She had fallen back against the back of her chair and closed her eyes. What a dilemma the boy had faced her with! She was quite aware that invitations to Wynwood Hall were very much prized by the *ton*. There were two reasons for the value set on those invitations: the first was that Wynwood was one of England's great estates, and the second that invitations to visit there were offered only rarely—and then only to Lady Wynwood's most special friends. Lady Bethune's mouth fairly watered at the prospect of having her daughter's betrothal announced at Wynwood. On the other hand, she had quite looked forward to parading her daughter's "catch" (for it was universally agreed that the Earl of Wynwood was a very big fish indeed) before half of London society. If the affair were held in Sussex, the number present would be very small.

Lady Bethune had never met the mother of her prospective son-in-law, but she looked forward to the meeting with an eagerness bordering on awe. For Lady Wynwood was a somewhat legendary figure among the Londoners of her generation. Charlotte Harvey, Lady Wynwood, had been a great beauty in her youth. She'd been described as having "enchanted" eyes, an ethereal expression and an aloof manner. Even in those days, she'd kept the world at bay, permitting only a select few to enjoy her company. Thus her reputation for exclusivity had begun. When she'd married the taciturn Earl of Wynwood, a man fifteen years her senior and more at home on horseback than in a drawing room, she had set society's tongues wagging. Lord and Lady Wynwood had ignored the comments, had retired to the country and had lived there in apparent contentment. They were seldom in London. The few close friends who were invited to Wynwood Hall came back to town with tales of lovely surroundings, warm hospitality, lavish meals, good sport and stimulating conversation, and those who were not privileged to share in those pleasures listened with growing envy. And the value of an invitation grew. After the old Earl died, the invitations became even more rare and more desirable.

All this was quite well known to Lady Bethune. Although she had not yet set foot in Wynwood Hall, her friends already envied her. From the moment she'd whispered (to a mere eight or nine of her closest friends) that a match between her daughter and the desirable Earl of Wynwood was a settled thing, she had seen it in their eyes. If she could tell them now that her daughter's betrothal was to be announced at a small, select party at Wynwood Hall, they would be positively green.

Marcus had watched in unholy amusement as Lady Bethune's face reflected her inner turmoil. Her lust for a large ostentatious ball battled with her desire to mingle with the elite society of Wynwood. Elitism (as Marcus expected it would) had won the day.

Marcus had quickly taken his leave, inwardly sighing with relief. He'd immediately written to his mother to confess what he'd done. Lady Wynwood had responded in her usual, unworldly style. *My dearest boy,* she'd written, *you needn't apologize at all. I should have thought of having a party for you myself. I shall be most delighted to hold a house-party on such an occasion. I am quite looking forward to it, especially to meeting your young lady. How exciting that you are betrothed! I have no doubt at all that I shall love Miss Bethany—or is it Miss Battersea?—on sight. And Marcus, dearest, you must invite anyone you wish, but don't forget to ask your uncle Julian. He would be quite put out if he were not included. Which reminds me that I myself have invited a few friends down for the fortnight in question, but I'm sure they will all blend in very well with your people. We shall have a very merry time of it, I assure you. Oh, by the way, do you think you should invite your cousin Elvira? She is a bit garrulous, I know, but she would be so pleased to be part of the festivities. Of course, if you do, we shall have to have the entire Fitzhugh branch, so perhaps you'd better not. I suppose we might ask Henry and Constance, too, for they are always pleasant to have by when one needs extra hands for cards. I leave it all to you, my dearest. You are so much better at making such decisions than I. À bientôt. Your loving Mother.*

The letter, while it made him laugh out loud at the first reading, soon filled him with misgivings. How many friends had his mother already invited? And did she really want him to invite Henry and Constance? They could scarcely be called immediate family, no matter how skilled they were at cards. Didn't his mother realize that more than a dozen people would be horrendous? Every time they'd sit down to a meal, it would be like a damned *banquet*!

It was clear that, if the party were not to get out of hand, he would have to take control himself. Decisively, he ordered his valet to pack a bag. While that was being done, he paid quick visits to Miss Bethune, Dennis Stanford and his uncle Julian. Those errands done, he tossed the bag into his curricle and set off for Sussex.

It was early evening when he entered the gates of the estate. With the smoke and din of London far behind him, and the smell of spring filling his nostrils, Marcus found his mood brightening. Although he had not made his home at the Hall for several years, he loved the place better than any other on earth. His first glimpse of the house, whenever he'd been away from it for long, always filled him with pleasure. Wynwood was approached through a large, oak-studded park, over a balustraded stone bridge which spanned a bubbling rivulet with fern-covered slopes, and round a bend in the road which brought one face to face with the main buildings. The house, which had been built by the first Earl in the seventeenth century, was a lovely, three-storied block with an imposing six-columned portico, to which a pair of beautiful, curved wings had been added a century later, but with such tact that no one could see they'd been an afterthought. Even the outbuildings, the stables and the greenhouses seemed to blend in a pleasing coherence. As Marcus rounded the bend, he saw that the setting sun had sent sparks of radiance to dance on the bowed windows of the west wing and the greenhouses. He drew his horses to a stop and sat for a moment in admiring contemplation of his Sussex home, the view driving from his mind the annoyances that had brought him here.

But an hour later, after the affectionate greetings between mother and son had been exchanged, and his travel-weariness had been dispelled by the indulgence in a lavish tea prepared by Mrs. Cresley, the housekeeper, in honor of his arrival, the problems of the forthcoming festivities returned to his mind. He pushed aside his teacup and faced his mother purposefully. "I say, Mama," he began, "did you mean it when you said you don't mind having a houseful of guests descend upon you?"

"Of course I don't mind, dearest," she assured him with her customary serenity. "I shall enjoy every moment. What better way could I find to celebrate my only son's betrothal?"

Marcus rose and went to her chair. "Thank you, my dear," he said, leaning over and kissing her cheek affectionately. "I'm more grateful than I can say. I've come a week early so that I can help you with the preparations."

"There was no need for that, silly boy," she said, patting his hand, "although I'm delighted to have you here. Mrs. Cresley and the butler can handle all the details, you know."

Marcus winced. It was just like his mother to expect things to fall into place without any effort on her part. She had an unshakable faith that everything she undertook would turn out right. Any efforts she would make, she believed, would merely interfere with the smooth workings of Providence. Since *Providence* would provide, there was no need for *her* to exert herself. "It might be of some help to Mrs. Cresley," Marcus suggested mildly, returning to his chair, "if we worked out some menus together."

Lady Wynwood was having some difficulties with her shawl which kept slipping from her shoulders. "Very well, if you think we should," she agreed absently while she fiddled with it.

"And we could plan a few outings. You know . . . to keep the guests happy and busy during the days. Things like riding, sightseeing, that sort of thing . . ."

"What a very good idea," she acknowledged, looking up from her shoulder with a smile.

"And bedrooms," Marcus persisted. "We should think about where to put people, don't you agree? We want to make them comfortable, you know. By the way, how many have you invited so far?"

"No one, dearest," she replied, still occupied with her shawl. "I told you I would leave all that to you."

"But you wrote that some friends of yours were coming down—"

Lady Wynwood looked up at him, wrinkling her brow in concentration. "I don't remember writing . . . Oh, yes! You mean Alicia. Yes, of course, Alicia is coming. She's my best and oldest friend—we must have *her*."

"Oh? Is she the only one coming?" Marcus asked hopefully.

"Well, there's her granddaughter, of course. One couldn't expect Alicia to leave her behind. And Walter and Isabel—"

Marcus sighed. "Walter and Isabel?"

"Yes. Alicia's younger son, you know, and his wife. They've been away for years . . . India, I believe . . . so I thought, as a sort of welcome—"

"That makes four. Well, I suppose four can be managed." He fixed his eyes on his mother's face and asked firmly. "Are there any more? *Think* now!"

"Let me see. I think . . . I'm almost certain that Walter and Isabel have a son. He'll be coming too, I expect," Lady Wynwood murmured and turned her attention to her shawl again.

"Confound it, that makes five! Are you sure that's all?"

Lady Wynwood pressed a finger to her lips thoughtfully, causing the wayward shawl to slip from her shoulders again. "Well, I . . . I *think* that's all. Or . . . did I ask the Carringtons too?"

"The *Carringtons*? Good Lord, Mama, there are *six* of them!" Marcus groaned in anguish.

"No . . . no, wait. The Carringtons are not coming this month. I think they said they'd be abroad 'til summer."

"Whew!" Marcus breathed in relief. "That's a bit of luck. So that leaves five, then. With Julian, the Bethunes, Dennis and us, we'll be just under a dozen. That won't be too bad. Are you sure you haven't forgotten anyone else? That you've asked only those five? By the way, Mama, who *are* these people? Do I know them?"

"The Edgertons? Well, I really don't remember if you've met them. Except for Alicia, of course. Surely you've met my friend Alicia Edgerton."

"Edgerton? Edger—? Oh, Lord . . . *no*!" Marcus stared at his mother in dawning apprehension. "Is her grand-daughter named *Sophia*?"

"Yes, I believe that's her name. I haven't seen her since she was a tiny baby, but . . ." His mother's voice trailed off as she smiled in misty recollection. "Yes, that was it . . . little Sophy . . ."

"Good God!" Marcus exclaimed, appalled. "You haven't invited *Sophia Edgerton*! I can't believe it!"

But Lady Wynwood didn't seem to hear. She was smiling at a distant memory. "Little Sophy . . . oh, you should have seen her, dearest. She was the most adorable little thing . . . so pink and plump, with a shock of carrot-red hair—"

"Mama, must you be woolgathering at a time like this?" her son cut in curtly. "Do you realize what you've *done*?"

"Done?" she asked, smiling up at him innocently. "What have I done?"

"You've probably turned this affair into a *disaster*!" he replied glumly.

Lady Wynwood smiled at him condescendingly. "Don't

be so silly, love. How can I have done that? Just by asking little Sophy?''

"Your little Sophy is no longer a plump and innocent babe, you know, Mama. She's a grown woman—''

"Well, of *course* she is! I know *that*. I sent her some pearls for her come-out, if I remember rightly. But what does that signify? You wouldn't want her here if she were a child, would you? Children can be so trying when a house is full of guests.''

"She'll be more of a nuisance than a *dozen* children, I'm afraid,'' Marcus predicted grimly.

"Alicia's little Sophy? I don't know what you're talking about. I've been told she's a most charming young woman.''

Marcus snorted. "Yes, I suppose she is. But she carries disaster around with her like . . . like that shawl you keep struggling with. It surrounds her . . . like a cloud.''

Lady Wynwood shrugged, dismissing her son's statement as mere nonsense. She rose and wandered over to her son's chair. "I cannot imagine how you came by such a notion, dearest,'' she said putting a gentle hand on his shoulder, "but I'd put it out of my head, if I were you. What can a mere slip of a girl do to spoil your party?''

"I don't know,'' Marcus muttered, trying to prepare himself to face the inevitable, "but it will be something deplorable. She'll spill hot soup at dinner and scald somebody. Or she'll fall down the stairs and break her neck. Or burst into tears at some unintended slight. Something of the sort.''

Lady Wynwood gave a tinkling laugh. But when her son turned around and glared up at her, she restrained her amusement. "Oh, dear,'' she murmured apologetically, "I suppose one shouldn't laugh. Is she *really* that sort of girl?''

Marcus nodded numbly.

"That *is* too bad,'' his mother remarked sympathetically. "Poor Alicia must have her hands full.'' She wandered unconcernedly toward the door. "Well, we'll do what we can to see that they enjoy themselves anyway. Don't worry about it, love.'' And she drifted placidly out of the room.

Marcus stared after his mother in a kind of admiring dismay. "Of *course*, Mama," he muttered ironically, "you are quite right. Why should I *worry*? I shall be the host at a party which might explode at any moment. It could become a *shambles* . . . Miss Sophia Edgerton will see to that! A complete shambles. So what have I to worry about, eh? What on earth have I to worry about?" And he threw up his hands in a gesture of dismissal, shrugged his shoulders and went off to dress for dinner.

Chapter Five

"I DON'T SEE why I can't come along," Dilly complained when Bertie stopped at his lodgings to say goodbye. "I've heard the place is enormous. They'd surely have room for one more person."

"You're the most crackbrained clunch I've ever known," Bertie told him flatly. "You ain't been invited. You surely don't want to put in an appearance where you ain't been invited, do you?"

"Yes, I do. How could I have been invited when Lady Wynwood don't know me? But if I was to show up at the door, she'd *have* to—"

Bertie made a disapproving face. "You sound like a regular *sponge*! It just ain't *done*, you know that! If I didn't know better, I'd think you was cast away. You didn't dip into the brandy, did you?"

"Don't be a gudgeon. Don't even like the stuff. I just . . ." He hung his head.

"Just what? You can manage without me for a fortnight, can't you?"

"No . . . it's not *you* . . ."

"Not me? Then what—?" The answer suddenly dawned on Bertie, and he glared at his friend in disgust. "Do you mean to stand there and tell me that all this is because *Sophy* will be going?"

Dilly nodded gloomily. "It's for an entire fortnight, you see. A *fortnight*!"

"Damme if I've ever known such a nodcock! What *difference* does it make? I've told you and *told* you she ain't for you."

Dilly kept his eyes lowered shamefacedly. "Not now, perhaps . . . but someday . . ."

"Humbug!" his friend said bluntly. "You haven't a prayer. Besides, what has that to say to the matter at hand?"

"Well, you see, a great deal could happen in a fortnight," Dilly explained worriedly. "She could go away and come back *betrothed*!"

"What rubbish! Who'll be there for her to fix on? Me? Wynwood, who's betrothed already? You're addlebrained."

"I've known it to happen before, Bertie. *Really*. A girl leaves her usual surroundings, and the next thing you know, she's wed! It's the strange air or something. Happened to my own sister!"

"You don't say!" Bertie shook his head in bewilderment. "Females! There's no accounting for 'em. But strange air or no, she can't become betrothed if there's no one there to attach to. She'd much more likely hook a fish right here in town."

Dilly shook his head stubbornly. "There'll be a house *full* of guests at Wynwood Hall. You can't be *sure* there won't be an eligible in the bunch. If she was here in town, I could at least keep an eye on her."

"You're besotted," Bertie declared unsympathetically. "If you insist on spending the next two weeks torturing yourself with these wild imaginings, there ain't a thing I can do." And he clapped his beaver on his head and made for the door.

"Wait, Bertie! If you won't let me go with you, then will you do something else for me?" Dilly asked urgently, catching his arm.

"What?"

"Keep an eye on her? Don't let anyone dangle after her . . .!"

Bertie shrugged the hand from his arm. "Don't be a worse gudgeon than you already are. I ain't the sort to interfere in my cousin's life. And if you weren't so bubble-witted, you wouldn't ask it of me.''

Dilly clutched his arm again, his eyes desperate. "Then will you at least *write* to me? Let me know who's there, and if there's any danger of . . . of . . . you know!''

"Write to you! I should say not! You'd only read all sorts of nonsense between the lines and upset yourself over nothing.''

Dilly dropped his hand and turned away in frustration. "Very well, *Mr. Edgerton*,'' he said in a voice that he tried to make cold but which trembled with emotion, "if you won't even d-do that one little thing for me, you needn't bother to come here when you get back. I won't be sp-speaking to you!''

Bertie snorted. "Ha! A likely tale. I don't credit it for a moment. When I get back I shall no doubt find you sitting on my doorstep.'' And without another word, Bertie Edgerton took his leave of his best friend.

Within the hour, a haggard-looking Lawrence Dillingham appeared at Lady Alicia's door. He found the hallway full of luggage and the two footmen busily darting in and out, loading the carriage which stood waiting at the door. Not one of the busy servants took the least heed of the gangling young man who stood in the doorway except to glance at him in annoyance when they found him in their way. At last he plucked up his courage and approached Miss Leale who, already dressed in her travelling cloak and a bonnet crazily askew, was attempting to supervise the preparations. "May I see Miss Edgerton, please?'' he asked diffidently.

Miss Leale favored him with a brief, harried glance. "Oh, it's *you*, Mr. Dillingham. Sorry, lad, but Miss Sophy's about to leave for Sussex. She won't 'ave time for callers today.''

"But I only want a moment,'' he pleaded urgently.

Miss Leale shook her head and turned to the small hall mirror on the wall near the door. "Look at that hat, will ye now?'' she muttered. "I can't make it stick on straight.'' Then she turned back to Mr. Dillingham. "Go along now, like a good lad," she said with motherly firmness, "or ye'll be gettin' in the way."

"But, ma'am," the hard-pressed Dilly begged, "you don't understand. I *must* see Miss Edgerton on a matter of the utmost impor—"

At that moment, Sophy appeared at the top of the stairs. She was magnificently attired in a rose-colored pelisse and a straw bonnet with an enormous poke and a captivating bunch of silk roses pinned to the crown. "Dilly!" she exclaimed. "What on earth are you doing here now?"

"Oh, Sophy!" he breathed in relief. "I mean, Miss Edgerton! How glad I—I mean, it's lucky that . . . I mean, I had so wished to . . ." Quite tangled in his explanation, he floundered into silence.

Sophy came down the stairs. "Yes, I understand, Dilly, but you can see that I've no time to talk to you now. If you'd care to drop by when I get back . . ."

"Sophia, stop dawdling!" came her grandmother's command from the top of the stairs. The old lady came marching down the stairs exuding nervous impatience. "We're more than an hour behind schedule. Leale, where's the large hat-box? And Sophia, will you carry this jewel case for me? Good heavens, child, why are you wearing that *dreadful* hat?"

"I *like* that dreadful hat," Sophy replied saucily.

"Well, suit yourself. Now, as for you, young man, you are decidedly in the way."

"Yes, ma'am. I mean . . . I just wish a moment with Miss Edgerton—"

But Lady Alicia had brushed by him without another glance and swept out the door. Miss Leale, throwing him a look of impatience, ran out hurriedly after her mistress, babbling about the large hat-box having already been stowed aboard.

"Well, goodbye, Dilly. We shall be seeing you soon," Sophy said purposefully, urging him out the door ahead of her.

"But Miss Edge—Sophy, you *must* let me speak! I only want you to promise me something—"

"*Sophia*!" her grandmother barked. "Are you going to

dawdle there all day? Come down here and help us find the large hat-box. I packed all my powders and medications in it, and I will not stir a step unless I have them with me."

Sophy started down the stone steps, but Dillingham caught her arm. "Sophy, you *must* promise me—!"

"I'm coming, Grandmama," she called. "Really, Dilly, you are becoming the greatest nuisance! What *is* it?"

"Only promise me that you won't . . . won't . . ."

"*There* it is m'lady," Leale squealed in relief. "Right there beside Miss Sophy's trunk, see?"

"Good," Lady Alicia grunted and allowed herself to be assisted into the carriage. "Sophia," she called threateningly over her shoulder, "come down *immediately*, or we shall depart without you!"

"Won't what, Dilly?" Sophy asked him curiously, ignoring the hysteria below.

"That . . . that you won't go and do anything hasty . . . like getting yourself buckled," he urged desperately.

Sophy stared. "*What*? What are you *talking* about?"

"Buckled. You know . . . leg-shackled. Wedded. Or even . . . betrothed. *Promise*!"

She gave a light laugh and shook her head. "Wedded? Betrothed? Don't be a fool, Dilly! I don't know why the matter should concern you, but you needn't worry. I haven't the least inclination in that direction." Her eyes took on a distant, almost-militant glitter. "My mind shall be occupied with other matters entirely."

"Other matters?" Dillingham asked, confused.

"*Sophia*!" came a stentorian cry from the carriage.

"Please, Miss Sophy, hurry," Miss Leale pleaded warningly. The abigail stood waiting at the carriage door impatiently, the fingers of one hand clenching and unclenching nervously while her other hand held her trying bonnet in place on her head.

"What other matters?" Dillingham repeated.

"Never mind," Sophy flung back as she ran down the steps. "Suffice it to say that finding myself a husband is the very *last* thing on my mind!"

With the roses on her hat bobbing, she jumped into the

carriage, Miss Leale quickly following. The footman shut the door, the coachman flicked his whip, and the carriage lumbered off down the street, leaving behind a breathless and sad-eyed Dillingham. The boy had had her promise, but he felt not in the least reassured. For the first time in his life, he realized that the protestations of females, being only words after all, do not carry enough conviction to ease the pangs of jealousy that eat into a lover's heart.

Chapter Six

THE DAY THE guests were to arrive at Wynwood dawned fine. The end-of-May sunshine was gently warm, the sky a clear amethyst blue, the air crisp and the breeze playful. It seemed a ploy of nature to lure Marcus into a false sense of optimism and security concerning the success of the festivities. But it was not long before he reverted to his customary pessimism, for as the day wore on he was beset with several surprises, all of them bad.

The first arrivals were Iris and her mother. Iris looked as lovely as a spring lily and greeted Lady Wynwood with just the right combination of warmth and diffidence. But Lady Lorna Bethune was overly effusive, rhapsodizing over every shrub and stone with such ardent indiscriminacy that she quite set his teeth on edge. To make matters worse, she was accompanied by her sister, a Mrs. Maynard, and her sister's three muffin-faced progeny, none of whom had been expected. And since Mrs. Maynard did nothing but echo her sister's sentiments, Marcus could not convince himself that her presence would be an asset.

Sir Walter Edgerton and his wife Isabel were the next arrivals. For some reason which Marcus couldn't explain (except that the fuss over this event had thickened his brain) it had not occurred to him before that the Edgerton's son would turn out to be the notorious *Bertie*. He managed to conceal his surprise and to greet the fellow with proper warmth, but he was quite disconcerted nevertheless.

Then his uncle Julian arrived, jovial and boisterous as usual. He brought with him two cases of what he described as the most magnificent French brandy ever to be smuggled into the country. He found an eager audience in Sir Walter, and the two gentlemen disappeared into the library, not to be heard from again all afternoon except for occasional outbursts of raucous laughter.

Dennis Stanford's arrival gave Marcus a momentary lift, for his friend had come alone (as he'd promised) and promptly offered to help in any way that he could. Marcus took him at his word and immediately sent him to squire a group of the ladies on a tour of the gardens and greenhouses.

But before he had a chance to breathe a sigh of relief, another carriage arrived at the door, bearing, of all people, the Carringtons! All *six* of them! *And* their Blenheim spaniel! Marcus noted that his mother looked not the least discomposed as she floated out to greet them on her son's arm, trailing clouds of the finest silk tulle from the billowing sleeves and the enormous flounce of her graceful gown. While the two youngest Carrington offspring, both boys, tumbled from the carriage with noisy hilarity, Lady Wynwood greeted their mother. "Cora, dearest, how lovely to see you. And Horace! Such a pleasant surprise!"

Horace Carrington squinted at her fuzzily. His eyesight was weak, but his vanity kept him from wearing his spectacles on social occasions. "Surprise?" he murmured in some confusion. "Were we not expected?"

But Lady Wynwood had turned to greet his eldest daughter. Fanny Carrington, just turned seventeen, stepped from the carriage with the excitement and eagerness natural to a young lady arriving at her very first houseparty. Her large gray eyes shone as she paused on the bottom step of the coach and surveyed her surroundings. "Lady Wynwood, how beautiful everything is!" she breathed.

Cicely Carrington, her sixteen-year-old sister, whom everyone called Cissy, followed her out of the coach. "Look, Mama," she said cattishly, "the boys are teasing Shooshi!"

While Mrs. Carrington turned to reprimand her sons and rescue the plump, white-haired spaniel from their hands,

Mr. Carrington fumbled for the pince-nez which hung on a cord around his neck. "We *were* expected, were we not?" he repeated worriedly.

Marcus, his mood hovering somewhere between dismay and amusement, waited for his mother's response with wicked pleasure. But there was no trace of embarrassment in Lady Wynwood's innocent smile. "Of course you're most welcome," she assured Mr. Carrington blithely. "I'm completely delighted that you've returned from the continent in time to join us."

Mr. Carrington affixed his pince-nez to his nose, as if by clearing his eyesight he would also clear the fog from the bewildering situation. "Returned from the *continent*?" he asked, looking from Lady Wynwood to Marcus in confusion. "Whatever gave her that idea?"

"Mama had the impression you were fixed abroad until summer," Marcus explained.

"Fixed abroad? We haven't *gone*! Never intended to, while Nappy's still at large."

"Well, of course, we *did* speak of taking a trip *next* year, if Wellington's successful," Mrs. Carrington said to Marcus with a bland smile that revealed her complete lack of awareness that a problem existed.

But her husband was not so simple-minded. "Good heavens, Charlotte, my dear . . . does this mean we really are *not* expected?" he asked, aghast.

Marcus wanted to laugh out loud. It was just like his mother to muddle the details. It took all his tact and his mother's charm to convince Mr. Carrington that the misunderstanding did not matter a whit. "You shall have the green bedroom, just as you always do when you stay here," Lady Wynwood assured them airily. "We can put the boys in the west wing in the old nursery. And Fanny and Cissy can have the room right next to yours. That will serve perfectly well, won't it, Marcus?"

Marcus mentally tore to shreds the elaborate plans he had drawn up for the assigning of bedrooms. "That will be fine, Mama," he assured her recklessly. "Just fine."

Everyone would now have to be given rooms in the completely haphazard way his mother would have done if he hadn't been there at all. And probably everything would turn out well enough. Mrs. Cresley would undoubtedly manage to arrange for enough food to feed ten extra mouths. He'd been a fool for wasting his time trying to organize things.

The Carringtons, their hosts, their children, their boxes and their dog had moved into the entrance hall when Lady Alicia's coach drew up to the door. "Sophy," the old lady hissed before allowing herself to be assisted down from the equipage, "take off that hideous hat before Charlotte sees us. I can't think why you wore such an abomination."

"I *like* it," Sophy said stubbornly.

"Nonsense. I've never seen you wear such a thing before. It makes you like like . . . like a damned *actress*!"

"Yes, doesn't it?" Sophy agreed with a wicked gleam. "That's just the effect I intend."

Lady Alicia's eyebrows drew together suspiciously, and she opened her mouth to pursue the matter when she saw her friend Charlotte approaching. Instantly, the matter of Sophy's hat flew from her mind. "Charlotte!" she chortled, hopping down from the carriage with the agility of a youngster, "you are a *witch*! I don't believe, in the years since I last laid eyes on you, that you've aged a *day*!"

As the two friends embraced and laughed and admired each other, Lord Wynwood offered his hand to assist Sophy to alight. "Welcome to Wynwood, Miss Edgerton," he said with a cautious smile.

"Thank you, my lord," Sophy answered grandly, offering her hand to be kissed. "The edifice of your house is every bit as impressive as I had heard."

Marcus couldn't help smiling at her imperious manner. "But not as impressive, I'm sure, as your bonnet, ma'am," he said smoothly.

"Do you really think so?" Sophy responded indifferently. "Grandmama thinks it would be more suitable on Mrs. Siddons."

"It could be no more suitable on anyone than it is on you," Marcus said reassuringly. But his compliment fell on deaf ears, for Sophy had turned to greet his mother.

The party moved into the entrance hall, where the

Carringtons still lingered. The group from the garden also came indoors at this moment. The hall was as crowded as an inn courtyard, with children darting about, footmen carrying baggage, friends greeting each other, and the Carringtons' spaniel waddling about and barking hysterically. Sophy paused in the doorway and took in all the details. Then her eyes narrowed, she took a deep breath, stepped over the threshold and gave a piercing scream.

"Good Lord, Sophy, what's wrong?" the startled Lady Alicia cried. Everyone in the room stood stock still and stared.

"The *dog*!" Sophy gasped, one hand clenched to her bosom, the other dramatically pressed against her forehead. "That dreadful *beast*! Take it away!"

"Dog? What's wrong with the dog?" her grandmother asked bewilderedly.

"*Please!* Someone take it away!" Sophy shrieked.

"But my dear, it's only Shooshi," Mrs. Carrington said deprecatingly, approaching the quivering girl. "She's perfectly harmless, I assure you. Really, she's the most dear little darling. Here, you may pet her if you wish. She won't bite."

"No, *no*! Take her away this *instant*!" Sophy insisted hysterically.

Marcus stepped forward to take matters in hand. "May I have your permission, Mrs. Carrington," he asked gently, "to have . . . er . . . Shooshi . . . taken for a stroll? Then, when we have everyone settled in, you and I can confer about suitable quarters for her."

"Well, of course." Mrs. Carrington, with a pitying glance at the still-trembling Sophy, obligingly handed the dog to her host. "But there's really no need to be afraid of Shooshi. No need at all."

While Marcus arranged for the removal of the offending animal, Bertie, who had come in to greet his cousin, crossed the hall to her side. "I say, Sophy, has the ride addled your wits? What's wrong with you?"

"Ssssh!" Sophy hissed from the corner of her mouth.

"But you ain't the least afraid of dogs," Bertie persisted.

Sophy covered her face with trembling hands. "Mind

your own business!" she whispered from behind her fingers. "Just come here close to me and pretend you're comforting me." She clutched at his coat, drew him close beside her and buried her face in his shoulder.

The dog having been removed from the premises, Marcus came up to her. "There, Miss Edgerton, you can look up now. The monster has been removed."

Sophy turned her face timidly from its hiding place in Bertie's coat. "Is . . . Is she truly gone?" she asked fearfully.

"Yes, my dear. You may feel quite secure again. If you are up to it, I should like you and all the others to come out on the terrace for a light refreshment."

"Thank you, my lord," Sophy said weakly, "but I'm afraid the incident has quite overset my nerves. I'm terrified of dogs, you know. Terrified."

"I *say*, Sophy—!" Bertie began, but a fist pressed cruelly into his stomach stilled his tongue.

"If you don't mind, sir," Sophy continued in a shaking little voice, "I should like to be excused. Will you ask one of the servants to show me to my room?"

Marcus made an acquiescent bow and turned to make arrangements with one of the footmen. Lady Alicia, meanwhile, glared at her granddaughter suspiciously. "What mischief are you up to, my girl?" she whispered. "Overset your nerves, indeed. You *haven't* any nerves."

Sophy, about to answer, saw that Lord Wynwood was approaching again. "Don't worry about me, Grandmama," she said in the affectedly-weak little voice she'd used a moment ago. "I shall recover soon. I need only to lie down for a bit." And while everyone's eyes followed her, she made a bow and followed the footman up the stairs.

Once she was out of sight, Marcus was able to encourage his other guests to move through the hallway to the terrace. As the assemblage drifted out, Marcus breathed a sigh of relief. His friend Dennis came up behind him and clapped him sympathetically on the shoulder. "That was quite an opening scene," he teased.

Marcus nodded ruefully. "I dread to imagine what the *rest* of this fortnight's performance will be like. What do you think of your Miss Edgerton now?'' he asked with a sudden grin. ''It seems that my assessment of her character was right on the mark.''

''She's the melodramatic sort, all right,'' Dennis agreed, ''but I shan't let that deter me.''

''Deter you from what!''

''From attempting to arouse her interest. The girl's enchanting, whatever you may feel. Despite her tantrums, she's a regular out-and-outer. As far as I'm concerned, the prospect of this fortnight's rustication (which you and your betrothed have wished upon me) has been considerably brightened by her presence.''

Marcus shook his head in mock dismay. ''My grandfather used to say, 'Every man hath a fool in his sleeve,' but *you* seem determined to show your foolishness quite openly. Well, if you're determined to play the fool by pursuing the girl, I'll not attempt to deter you.''

''You couldn't deter me if you tried, old fellow,'' Dennis grinned, ''so save your breath and lead me to the refreshments. I sincerely hope, after my exertions in your gardens—playing the gallant to half the ladies in this assemblage—that you intend to reward me with some liquid libation more potent than lemonade.''

At the same moment, Lady Alicia had detained her hostess at the door which opened out to the large stone terrace where a table had been laid with tea sandwiches, fruits, champagne and other delectables the housekeeper considered suitable for an alfresco luncheon. ''Don't go out just yet, Charlotte,'' Alicia said in a low voice. ''First let me apologize to you.''

''Apologize? Whatever for?'' Charlotte asked in surprise.

''For my granddaughter. That she should have seen fit to create such an upset fills me with dismay.''

''Nonsense, my dear. What upset?''

''Come, Charlotte, you know quite well. The upset over the dog! I cannot imagine what maggot has got into the girl's head. She's not in the *least* afraid of dogs.''

Charlotte dispensed with the entire matter with an airy wave of her arm. ''Oh, pooh! It was nothing. I think the child is charming, absolutely charming." She took her friend's arm and led her out to the terrace.

Marcus and Dennis had come up to the doorway in time to overhear the exchange. "See?" Dennis chortled in a mocking undervoice. "Even your mother agrees with me." Without further ado, he headed straight for the champagne.

But Marcus remained staring after Lady Alicia with knitted brows. *Not afraid of dogs*? If the chit was not afraid of dogs, what was the meaning of the little scene she'd created? Marcus had no idea of what the girl was up to, but whatever it was, it boded no good. But there was no time to brood on the matter. He had to rearrange bedrooms, talk to the cook, and arrange for a governess to take care of five unexpected children. He squared his shoulders, put on a smile and went out to play the happy host.

Chapter Seven

BERTIE KNOCKED ANGRILY on Sophy's door. As much as he would have wished to join the others on the terrace and fill his hungry stomach with a good share of the delicacies he'd glimpsed on the table, his curiosity had got the better of him and led him to her room. "Open up, Sophy," he ordered firmly. "It's only me."

"Are you alone?" she asked cautiously from behind the locked door.

"Of course."

She opened the door and let him in. To his surprise, she looked perfectly composed. She'd removed her hat and pelisse and evidently (since she still held the brush in her hand) had been brushing her hair when he'd knocked.

Bertie glanced around the room. It was very pleasant, painted a cheerful white except for the window alcoves which were covered with a blue flowered paper in a style called 'chinoiserie.' His own room, on the floor below, was somewhat more impressive with its walls of polished wood panelling and its red silk draperies, but this one was brighter and more feminine. The draperies were of a sheer white dimity embroidered all over with the Chinese blue flowers, matching charmingly with the bed hangings and the wallpaper. Sophy had drawn the draperies aside and opened the windows to let in the spring breeze. From far below, the sounds of laughter and gay conversation floated up to them. "Do you hear that?" Bertie asked. "Every-body's having a fine time at luncheon. If we had any sense, we'd be down there, too."

"Well, why *aren't* you down there? I didn't ask you to come here, you know," she responded sourly.

"I just came to find out what your game is. You don't fool me, you know, screaming about being terrified of dogs. You wouldn't be terrified of *tigers*! You're up to something smoky."

"I don't see what business it is of yours."

"Don't take that tone to *me*, Miss," Bertie said with unwonted severity. "I'm related to you, you know, and you've made the whole family ashamed that you're one of us."

"That is regrettable," Sophy answered indifferently, turning to the little dressing table between the window alcoves and resuming her brushing.

"Do you mean to say that you don't *care* that you made a scene?"

"Not in the least. You'll see me make a few others before this visit is over."

"A few *others*? What gammon is this?" he demanded, alarmed.

"Never mind."

"What are you about, Sophy? Are you trying to ruin your reputation?"

"I don't care a fig for my reputation."

"Well, *I* do. I don't want people saying my own cousin is addled in her wits."

"That's not any worse than what they say of me now," Sophy muttered sullenly to her reflection in the glass. "*One* person, anyway."

Bertie looked at her sharply. "Is someone telling rappers about you?" he asked, taking her by the shoulders and pulling her around to face him. "Tell me."

Sophy shrugged him off. "I don't want to talk about it."

"You *must* talk about it," he insisted angrily. "I won't have anyone telling whiskers about my own cousin!"

"It's none of your business, I tell you."

"It *is*, if you're going to make a spectacle of yourself. I don't understand, Sophy. If someone *is* spreading tales about you, why do you want to provide him with more? If you insist on acting like a loony, you'll only make things worse."

"I don't care! I swore to myself that I'd get even by making a catastrophe of his houseparty, and I will!"

Bertie stood stock still in shock. "What are you saying? That it's *Wynwood* who's maligning you? I don't believe it!"

"You may believe what you choose," Sophy said coldly, turning her back on him.

"Dash it, Sophy, how *can* I believe it? His lordship ain't the sort to go about brewing scandal-broth like any gabble-monger!"

"No?" his cousin cried vehemently, jumping to her feet, her hands clenched in suppressed fury. "How do *you* know what sort he is? I tell you, underneath that veneer of smiling politeness, Lord Wynwood is a . . . a . . . ."

"A what?"

"A . . . top-lofty, smug, stuffy, contemptuous, censorious *prig*!" Sophy burst out, her knees trembling and her cheeks paling. To Bertie's acute dismay and her own surprise, she burst into tears.

"*Sophy*, don't!" Bertie uttered miserably. "I didn't mean to . . . I wouldn't for the *world* make you cry!" He led her to the bed, sat her down and patted her back awkwardly. "If that man has done something unkind to you, I'll . . . I'll call him out!"

There was the sound of a hiccough as a little laugh broke through Sophy's sobs. "Oh, B-Bertie, don't b-be such a c-clunch!" she managed.

"I mean it!" Bertie insisted. "What did the blackguard *do* to you?"

Sophy took a handkerchief from her bodice and blew her nose, her sobs subsiding to little sniffs. "He . . . he called m-me a . . . a shatterbrained *hysteric*!"

Bertie blinked, nonplussed. "He *did*? Well, that was quite rude, I suppose, although I don't see that it's anything worth crying over. When did he say that to you?"

"He didn't say it to *me*. That's just the point. He's been saying it to everyone else behind my back!"

Bertie cocked a suspicious eye on her. "What rubbish! How can you think that?"

"Because I overheard him saying those very words to Mr. Stanford, the other night at the theater."

"Overheard?" He narrowed his eyes shrewdly. "You mean you were eavesdropping."

Sophy hung her head. "Well, I suppose I was. It was completely accidental, I assure you. And it doesn't alter the fact that he described me as a silly chit, melodramatic, hysterical and shatterbrained!"

Bertie shrugged. "And so you are."

"*Bertie!*" Sophy jumped to her feet furiously. "If that's how you feel about me, you can take your leave!"

"Oh, don't get on your high ropes. You know you tend to be dramatic. But no one says it's a crime. I think you're making too much of all this. His lordship only said those things to his friend. I'd go bail he didn't say it to anyone else."

"That he said it even *once* is too much for me," she retorted. "Since he gave me the name, I'll give him the game!"

"Do you mean to say you're going to spend this fortnight behaving like a . . . an overwrought loon?"

"I intend to take every opportunity to make scenes, create disturbances, and cause havoc."

Bertie shook his head helplessly. "You *are* shatterbrained. What do you suppose Grandmama will say when you begin turning things upside down?"

"Everything will look completely accidental. She won't be able to do anything about it. And if she *does* suspect—"

"*If* she suspects? I'd lay odds she suspects already, after that dog business. She ain't a fool, you know."

"Even if she does, she won't be able to punish me until we return home. I'm quite prepared to face her wrath, once I've accomplished my purpose."

"Well, your 'purpose,' as you call it, is positively *addled* in my opinion. I've heard of a 'woman scorned' but this is the first time I've seen one. It's enough to drive a man to *drink*!'' He went to the door, shaking his head in disgust, ''If you persist in going ahead with your idiotic scheme, don't look for any help from me,'' he warned. ''You can play your little game alone.'' And he slammed the door behind him.

A party of sixteen sat down to dinner in the softly-lit, gracious dining room of Wynwood Hall that evening, the five youngest members of the assemblage having been fed earlier and taken by a maid (whom Marcus had assigned to act as governess) to play in the nursery. The dinner was a most enjoyable one for all but Bertie. The poor fellow could barely attend the conversation or savour his veal in his apprehensive anticipation of the catastrophe about to be generated by his vengeful cousin, although he had not a clue as to the nature of the disaster she was planning. For the others, however, the food was memorable and the conversation engrossing.

The table talk centered on the news from abroad—of the French reverses since Napoleon's fatal withdrawal from Russia. Even the women were fascinated by the lively argument in which Julian and Horace Carrington supported Dennis in his sanguine expectations of a British victory before this year of 1813 had passed; while Sir Walter and Marcus, on the other hand, contended that Napoleon's victories at Lutzen and Bautzen proved that the French general still had surprising strength and recuperative powers, and that even the outstanding strategies of Wellington could not lead to a quick or easy victory.

The latter argument drew support from two of the ladies. One was Iris, whose remarks, while not especially insightful in themselves, nevertheless drew admiring smiles from the listeners because of the devoted loyalty they revealed to the man whose intimate relationship to her had not yet been announced officially. The other speaker in Marcus's behalf was Lady Alicia, whose spirited comments about Napoleon's shrewdness at the battle of Bautzen showed her to have a surprising understanding of modern warfare. ''Are you interested in military strategy, Lady Alicia?'' Marcus inquired in some surprise.

"My late husband encouraged my interest years ago," Alicia explained.

"Yes, my father was considered quite an expert," Walter added. "He even wrote on Marlborough, you know. Made us all read history when we were small."

"So your interest has persisted during all these years, Lady Alicia?" Horace Carrington asked. "I must say, I find that admirable in a woman. I cannot seem to make Cora take an interest."

"Well, I'll have to admit that my interest lapsed after my husband's death. It was Sophia who roused it again. She has a positive fascination for the subject."

"Is that so?" Julian asked, directing a smile at the girl. "That's quite unusual in a young woman, is it not?"

"Her grandfather had her reading history in the schoolroom. She quite hangs on news of Wellington, these days," Alicia said proudly, grateful for the opportunity to present her unpredictable granddaughter in a good light after the turmoil of the afternoon.

"How very interesting," Marcus remarked, his eyebrows raised. "I had no idea, Miss Edgerton, that a fashionable young lady like you would occupy herself with such pursuits."

Sophy had been biting her lip in chagrin throughout her grandmother's encomium, but at his lordship's remark she glanced up at him, her eyes glinting coldly. "My grandmother exaggerates, my lord," she said. "Military strategy is much too complicated for a shatterbrained ninny like me."

For a moment there was a shocked silence. Marcus stared at the girl in surprise. Her tone made him feel that he'd been given a sharp set-down. What on earth had he done to anger her?

Before he could frame a rejoinder to her challenging remark, his mother rose from her chair. "*All* the ladies are shatterbrained for remaining here at the table during this talk of warfare and battles. Come, my dears, let us withdraw and leave the gentlemen to their port and their arguments. *We* shall have music."

But after the ladies had gone, Marcus did not re-enter

into the discussion. He found himself brooding about the
Edgerton creature. The chit had an unfathomable talent for
disconcerting him. Marcus had an uncomfortable feeling
that the girl harbored some deep resentment towards him,
but he couldn't imagine what he'd done to inspire it.
Despite the fact that she'd subjected him more than once to
deeply humiliating experiences, he had treated her with
impeccable politeness. Why had *she* taken *him* in dislike?

The matter continued to irritate him as the gentlemen
left the table to rejoin the ladies. They found them gathered
in the music room. Mrs. Carrington was singing a charming
Dutch lullaby, with Iris accompanying her on the piano.
The gentlemen tiptoed to their seats, Marcus taking a place
on the piano bench beside his betrothed, to help her turn
the pages. Iris looked up at him with a thankful smile. She
looked particularly lovely in the glow of the eight-branched
candelabrum on the piano. He was a fortunate fellow
indeed, he realized, to have won so beautiful and gracious
a girl for his bride. Suppose it had been Miss Edgerton to
whom he was betrothed—what an ordeal *that* would be!

The song ended to enthusiastic applause and appreciative
comments. Mrs. Carrington blushed with pleasure but would
not be cajoled into an encore. "Perhaps Miss Edgerton will
sing for us," Dennis suggested with what Marcus thought
was insidious flattery. "Do you sing, Miss Edgerton?"

"My voice is quite unexceptional, I'm afraid," Sophy
responded pleasantly, "but I'd be happy to play something on the piano, if you wish."

This suggestion was happily approved by the obsequious
Dennis and seconded by the others, and Iris surrendered
her seat at the instrument to Sophy. While Marcus escorted
his lady to the sofa and took a place beside her, Sophy sat
down at the keyboard, adjusted her skirts gracefully about
her and flexed her fingers. Bertie, suddenly noticing a
slight smile which seemed to play dangerously at the
corners of Sophy's mouth, tensed himself for the crisis to
come. He *knew* that smile—he had seen it on her face
often in their childhood, when she was plotting some
mischief.

But Sophy played a little rondo with quite commendable

skill and charm. Perhaps his cousin had had second thoughts and had given up her foolish scheme, he thought in relief, when she'd finished her selection without incident. Then Sophy rose to bow in acknowledgement of the appreciative applause. A slight movement of her hand caught Bertie's eye, and his blood froze. *Oh, my God*, he thought in horror, *what is the little idiot doing*?

The piano was covered with an embroidered, fringed scarf. As she rose from the bench and grasped her skirt to make her bow, Sophy had also grasped a bit of the fringe which hung from a corner of the scarf. As she stepped forward, smiling complacently and taking her bow, she pulled the scarf along with her, causing the candelbrum to topple over. "Look out!" Mr. Carrington shouted.

But it was too late. Sophy, ostensibly unaware that the fringe was still clutched in her hand, continued to pull the scarf with her as she jumped, startled, out of the way of the falling candles. The ladies screamed as the candelabrum fell to the floor, the flames igniting the scarf which flared up at once.

Marcus snatched a cushion from the sofa behind him, jumped up and beat out the flames without much difficulty. Within a moment, the candelabrum was restored to its place, the candles re-lit, and the ruined scarf dispatched to the rubbish heap. But Sophy was inconsolable. "Oh, Lady Wynwood, I'm so *sorry*!" she cried to her hostess.

"But my dear, it was nothing," Lady Wynwood assured her placidly. "Please don't trouble yourself about it for a single moment."

"Never liked that thing very much, myself," Uncle Julian said with a hearty laugh. "Just forget it."

"Quite right," Lady Wynwood agreed. "I didn't like it either. Come, let's have some more music. Would you care to play again, my dear?"

"Play?" Sophy asked tremulously. "*Play*? I shall never touch the piano again as long as I live!" With that impassioned pronouncement, the girl fled from the room.

Bertie, who recognized the histrionics in her voice, winced. Sir Walter and Isabel, who did not, exchanged puzzled glances. Lady Alicia, in complete amazement,

stared at the door her granddaughter had slammed behind
her. "I don't know what has afflicted that child!" she
muttered.

"It's nothing but nerves," Lady Wynwood said calmly.
"She has sensitive nerves, like a true artist. Go after her,
Marcus, and assure her that we want her back. She'd done
nothing wrong, the poor dear, nothing at all. Meanwhile,
Miss Bethany, will you play for us again?"

"Bethune, Mama, Beth*une*," Marcus corrected, giving
Iris's hand a squeeze and obediently heading for the door.

Before he could leave, he found Dennis blocking his
way, an amused grin lighting his eyes. "Let *me* go to
console Miss Edgerton," he whispered slyly. "I'd be
happy to relieve you of that chore."

"Step aside, you skirter," Marcus whispered back, "and
control your libertine propensities. Why you want to pursue
that skittish little zany is a mystery to me."

"If your eyes won't tell you, then I can't. But come, let
me take your place."

"Not a chance. A man must do his duty. So step aside,
old fellow, and let me do mine. Just be thankful that I'm
saving you from the snare of that disastrous female."

By taking the stairs two at a time, Marcus was able to
catch up with Sophy on the second-floor landing. "Wait,
Miss Edgerton, please. There's not the least need for you
to be so upset. Mama wants you to come back."

Sophy kept her face turned away from him and shook her
head. "Thank your mother for me, my lord, b-but I cannot
show my face again this evening. I'm too ashamed."

"What is there to be ashamed of? It was nothing but an
accident."

"Yes, but . . . it quite ruined the evening! Everything
was going along so . . . so pleasantly . . . and I . . . I
spoiled *everything*!"

"Nonsense. You must learn not to overdramatize, my
dear."

There was a quick turn of her head toward him and as
quick a turn away again. But the motion was not swift
enough to keep him from catching a glimpse of an odd
look in her eyes. Those eyes were neither tearful nor

remorseful (as one had a right to expect them to be) but seemed instead to cast a challenging look at him. "*Do* I overdramatize?" the girl asked. "You'll have to admit that I almost set the house afire."

"I doubt that a few candles could have accomplished *that*," he assured her with a laugh.

But she did not respond to his levity. If he could have made any sense of it, Marcus would have described her expression as somewhat disappointed. Good heavens, did the girl *want* to burn the house down?

She was adamantly tugging at the restraining hold he'd kept on her arm. "Please permit me to retire, my lord."

"Won't you take my word that the incident was too slight to deserve this self-punishment?" There was no answer. "Look here, my girl," he ordered, reaching out and taking her chin in his hand, "I promise you that . . ." But the reassurances he was about to phrase faded from his mind. Her face, tilted up at him, had an arresting poignancy. Her curly hair was tousled, her cheeks flushed, her lips trembling. And her eyes, dark and misty, gleamed with that unfathomable, unexpected expression. The look held his attention—it was a puzzle that he felt compelled to solve. It was a look of distress, yes, but behind it there lurked a glimmer of amusement. Was this irritating creature *laughing* at him?

There was something decidedly feline in those dark eyes. He wanted to look away from them, but something held him. He became aware of a completely unfamiliar feeling of constriction—a fear that this girl would leave some sort of mark on him . . . that he might never be the same.

He had no idea how long he'd remained staring at her when she spoke. "I *have* ruined your evening, haven't I?" she asked softly. There was no apology at all in her tone; in fact, it seemed to have in it a tinge of triumph.

Before he could answer, she wrenched herself free of his grasp and ran up the stairs. He was left with a quite-unexpected feeling of disappointment. He didn't want her to go! The sense of emptiness which seemed to flow in her wake was a sensation utterly new to him. The little wretch!

Had she cast some sort of spell on him? He shook his head, as if to ward off these disturbing emotions, and walked slowly down the stairs. The girl was certainly in the right about one thing at least—she *had* ruined his evening!

Chapter Eight

THE MORNINGS AT Wynwood Hall were relaxed and completely free of regimentation. A guest was at liberty to rise at whatever hour best suited him. Breakfast would be waiting in the sunny breakfast room overlooking the rose garden, or (as many of the ladies preferred) the morning meal could be brought to one's bedroom and consumed while one lolled against the bed-pillows in luxurious comfort. Several of the gentlemen, however, preferred to rise early and take advantage of the opportunity to ride one of the Earl's famous horses across the Sussex downs.

By mid-morning, on the day after the music-room fire, Marcus found himself suddenly relieved of his duties as a host. The ladies all seemed to be still abed, and he had already taken most of the gentlemen (his uncle Julian, Mr. Carrington, Sir Walter and Bertie) to the stables and seen them suitably horsed and on their way. Dennis was still in bed; he would probably sleep til noon. So it now seemed that Marcus would have a couple of hours of peace before the guests gathered for luncheon. Taking advantage of the respite, he repaired to his study to apply himself to some matters of business which required his attention.

He had no sooner spread out his papers and prepared himself to attack them when he was distracted by the sounds of a skirmish on the lawn outside his window. In some annoyance, he went to see what the trouble was. There in the spring sunshine, Lady Bethune's three nephews were noisily and determinedly pummelling the two youngest Carrington children who, outnumbered and outweighed, were shrieking loudly for help. The inexperienced maid who had been assigned to supervise them did not even try to separate them—the five wriggling bodies seeming to her to be too hopelessly entwined. She did nothing but scream and wring her hands.

Marcus, about to step over his window-sill to intervene, noticed Miss Edgerton come into the scene. She had evidently been visiting the greenhouses and been distracted, as he had been, by their noise. "I say," she called pleasantly to the children, "is there anyone who would care to play Prisoner's Base with me?"

Five smudged faces immediately turned in her direction. The Carrington children eagerly agreed to the change in activity, the others joining in shortly afterwards. In a twinkling, the rules were reviewed and the game begun, with Miss Edgerton and the maid both taking an active part. Marcus watched the proceedings with an appreciative smile. The sight of Sophia lifting her skirts and running across the lawn with surprising agility and grace was a delight to the eye. It was not her dexterity alone that caught his attention—it was the attraction of a very pretty pair of ankles glimpsed below the raised skirts that could not be ignored. So engrossed was he in admiration of the wantonly-displayed limbs that he didn't hear the knock at his door. It was not until Miss Bethune entered and came up behind him that he became aware of her presence. He started almost guiltily. "Oh, Iris! I didn't hear—"

She smiled at him archly. "Good morning, Marcus. I was afraid I'd be interrupting you at your work, but I see you are already distracted."

"Yes, I am. The children were so noisy that I got up to see what they were about. But as for you, you may interrupt me at any time you wish, my dear."

She gave his arm an affectionate squeeze and looked at the children. "They seem to be having a very merry time. Good heavens, is that Miss Edgerton playing with them?"

"Yes, indeed. It was she who started the game."

"How astonishing. She seems quite adept at it, too."

"So I notice. It *is* astonishing—she hasn't tripped or fallen once. I thought she'd have broken an ankle by this time."

Iris laughed. "Perhaps she's more suited to the outdoors than to dining halls and drawing rooms and bookshops."

"Perhaps she is," Marcus agreed with a wide grin. "Then, if we could only find a way to *keep* her outside. . .!"

Iris giggled, and the two smiled at each other with comfortable understanding. But a shout from outside (one of the boys had been tagged) turned their eyes back to the game. "I used to love to play Prisoner's Base when I was a child," Iris remarked wistfully.

"*Did* you? So did I. I don't suppose . . .?" Marcus looked at her, a small, hesitant smile turning up the corners of his mouth.

"Are you suggesting that we *join* them?" Iris asked, shocked. Then she smiled back at him. "Oh, Marcus, *let's*! It would be such fun."

Marcus leaned over and kissed her cheek. "Iris, you're a great gun!" he said appreciatively and took her hand. He helped her over the sill, and they ran out across the lawn.

Sophy was quite startled at their arrival, but she readily agreed to permit them to join the game. "The more the merrier in Prisoner's Base," she said gaily.

"Then may I be permitted to play also?" called a voice from above them. They looked up to see Dennis Stanford leaning out of his bedroom window.

"Come down," Marcus answered jovially, "and join the rest of the infantry."

They had not quite finished choosing up new teams when Fanny and Cissy, the Carringtons' elder daughters, came round the shrubbery and begged to be allowed to participate. With the game thus expanded, it was not many minutes before the air rang with the laughter, shouts and cries of the players as they chased wildly across the lawn, taking prisoners or fleeing from pursuers. When Fanny, after an energetic chase punctuated with much giggling and heavy breathing, managed to capture the elusive Dennis and lead him to the prisoner's base, Dennis was glad of a moment's respite. He dropped down on the grass, breathless. Standing above him, Marcus, the only other prisoner at the moment, chortled vindictively. "Caught," he teased, "and by a mere child—and a girl at that!"

"Yes, but a most determined one," Dennis said defensively, looking after the retreating figure of the seventeen-year-old girl in some consternation. "If that child were a year or two older, I'd swear she had designs on me. But, to change the subject, Marcus, I must compliment you. This game was an inspiration. I haven't been so well entertained since you dragged me here from town."

"I'm glad you're enjoying yourself, old fellow. I might have known this sort of juvenile activity would suit you. But the game wasn't my idea. Miss Edgerton initiated it."

"*Did* she, by Jove! Good for her. Makes up for upsetting everyone in the music room last night, I'd say."

"Yes, I quite agree," said Marcus, just as a little nine-year-old urchin who was his teammate came up and tagged him free. With a farewell wave to his still-imprisoned friend, he started off the base.

"Perhaps she's not quite such a disastrous little zany as you thought!" Dennis called after him tauntingly.

The loudness of Dennis's voice caught Marcus up short. Good Lord, had the man no tact? He looked about for a glimpse of Miss Edgerton and spotted her halfway across the lawn. He couldn't help wondering if, from that distance, she could have heard the unfortunate remark. She was chasing the child who'd freed him, and she didn't appear to have paused in her forward movement, but her mouth was set in a straight, unlaughing line. Of course, *that* could be caused by the strain of running. *Disastrous little zany*. Dennis had been quoting Marcus's own words. Marcus bit his tongue. Had he really said such an unkind thing?

As far as the game was concerned, his ruminations were his undoing, for he had stopped running and had not noticed the boy who crept up behind him. He was tagged again, and he promptly found himself back at the prisoner's base. He sat down next to Dennis on the grass. "You gudgeon," he muttered. "What if she'd heard you?"

"Who? Miss Edgerton? Don't be silly, she couldn't have," Dennis said with a dismissive shrug.

A high-pitched, breathless cry caught their attention. It was Iris, fleeing from a determined Sophy across the lawn in front of them. "Good girl, Iris," Marcus shouted encouragingly.

"*That's* the way, Miss Edgerton," Dennis countered promptly. "Just put out your hand. You can reach her!"

Iris made a little turn to get out of the path of her pursuer and somehow tripped and fell heavily, face forward on the ground. Marcus thought he'd seen Sophy put out her foot right in Iris's path. It had been a quick little movement—he couldn't be sure. But in any case, Sophy toppled over on top of the prostrate Iris. Dennis and Marcus came running over, Dennis lifting Sophy to her feet and Marcus performing the same service for Iris. "Are you all right, my dear?" Marcus asked his betrothed.

"Yes, I . . . think so . . ." Iris answered breathlessly. "Just a bit . . . winded . . ."

"Let's make sure. Can you walk?" Marcus led her a few steps away.

Iris looked up at him with a wan smile. "I'm fine, really."

"Thank goodness," he muttered. Then he bent close to her ear. "It seems that our plan for keeping Miss Edgerton out-of-doors won't work either," he said in a rueful undervoice.

Iris giggled and turned back to the group who were watching her with anxiety. "I'm really quite all right," she announced. "See? I can walk quite well." She looked down at her feet as she spoke, and for the first time noticed that her dress had been badly stained by the grass and ripped at the hem. "Oh, *dear!*" she said in dismay. "My gown—!"

Sophy gasped. "It's ruined! *Ruined!*" she cried in horror.

"Oh, never mind the gown," Dennis said cheerfully. "So long as neither of you is hurt, let's get on with the game."

"The *game!*" Sophy echoed, looking at him in disbelief. "I *couldn't!* Forgive me, Miss Bethune. Forgive me, everyone." With a little sob, she turned, ran across the lawn and disappeared into the house.

With Sophy's disappearance, the jolly mood that had been inspired by the game quickly dissipated. Iris followed after Sophy, explaining that she had to change her dress. The other players, too, started to drift back to the house to clean up for luncheon. Only Marcus and Dennis remained. Marcus stood just where Iris had left him, staring thoughtfully ahead of him at nothing in particular. Dennis studied him moodily. "Dash it all, Marcus, you win," he admitted reluctantly. "You were right—the girl is a veritable calamity."

Marcus glanced at his friend but held his tongue. Yes, he was in complete agreement: Sophia Edgerton was a troublesome nuisance. But he was beginning to suspect that the disastrous occurrences which she seemed to generate with such accidental innocence were not what they seemed. Could it really be possible that the havoc she created was *calculated*? Could she be doing these things on *purpose*? If so, what *was* her purpose? What sort of game could the girl be playing? It made no sense at all.

But there was a luncheon to supervise. He had no time to meditate on the matter. He started toward the house, Dennis trudging alongside. They maintained a gloomy silence until they almost reached the door. "I suppose I shall be forced to continue my pursuit of the girl, in any case," Dennis said finally, "since there are no other fish in this rural backwater. If you'd been a truly considerate host, you would have provided me with one or two other females on whom to exercise my wiles."

Marcus grinned. "You are forgetting Fanny Carrington. You should have an easy time there, you know. As you yourself pointed out, she has designs on you already."

"Fanny Carrington!" Dennis snorted. "You are *too* generous. Only *think* how delightful it will be. I can spend my evenings playing at spillikins with her in the nursery. Thank you, my lord. Thank you very much." With an ironic bow, he stalked off to his room.

Lady Alicia did not learn of Sophy's latest mishap until tea time. The fact that Sophy had not joined the guests here in Lady Wynwood's favorite sitting room didn't trouble her unduly—the girl often skipped her tea. But when she heard Fanny Carrington (who had followed Dennis Stanford all around the room and finally accosted him just behind the sofa where Alicia was seated) refer to the morning's game "which had so disappointed me when it was spoilt," Alicia couldn't help but perk up her ears. Fanny Carrington amused her; the girl's pursuit of the very sophisticated Mr. Stanford was beginning to provide an entertaining diversion for one or two of the more perceptive observers.

"I *so* enjoyed it," Fanny went on. "I would have liked to play all afternoon."

"I'm sure you would," Dennis answered, his dry tone not lost on the eavesdropper. "You children have so much energy. We *old folks* were quite glad to call a halt."

Fanny giggled flirtatiously. "Oh, Mr. Stanford, *really*! Old folks, indeed. You know very well that you yourself begged Miss Edgerton to go on with the game."

At the sound of her granddaughter's name, Alicia stiffened. But Dennis did not reply. The only sound that reached her ears was the irritated clink of his spoon against the cup as he stirred his tea. Fanny, however, was not daunted. "Wasn't it dreadful," she chattered on, "the way Miss Edgerton ran off crying like that?"

Alicia was startled. Had there been another scene? She sat frozen in her place, straining to catch every word of Stanford's answer.

"It was not dreadful at all," Dennis responded coldly. "Miss Edgerton was quite naturally agitated because of having damaged Miss Bethune's gown. I'm sure that any tenderhearted young lady would have behaved in the same way." With that reproof, he turned on his heel and sauntered away.

Under ordinary circumstances, Lady Alicia would have found much to amuse her in observing the flirtatious child's response to Stanford's setdown, but now she could only feel keen agitation. Her granddaughter had made another scene. It was almost more than she could bear. She rose unsteadily and started toward the door. She would march up to Sophy's room this instant and give the girl the dressing-down of her life.

But before she could leave the room, she was stopped by her hostess. "You are surely not leaving already, Alicia?" Lady Wynwood inquired from her place behind the tea tray. "Come and sit down beside me for a moment. Everyone seems to have wandered out to the terrace and I am quite deserted, even by Lady Bethany or whatever-her-name-is, who has been dogging my steps all day. I've been longing to find a moment to chat with you, and now is our chance."

Alicia couldn't gracefully refuse such a request. Reluctantly, she pulled a chair close to Lady Wynwood's and perched on it. "Very well, Charlotte, if you wish," she said distractedly, "but only for a moment. I must soon be on my way. I have an urgent matter to take care of."

"Is something wrong, my dear?" Charlotte asked affectionately.

"Yes. My maddening granddaughter. I've just learned that the child had made yet *another* scene!"

"Are you referring to the incident on the south lawn this morning? A mere trifle, I assure you."

"To you, a raging *hurricane* would be a trifle!" Alicia grumbled. "I have never known anyone like you, Charlotte, for imperturbability. A wild wind could rage around you, and you'd call it a zephyr."

"Well, you know, dear, that I've always been even-tempered. It seems to make life so much easier," Lady Wynwood said complacently.

"Hummph! That's probably what an ostrich would say to justify its tendency to avoid facing up to the dangers around it," Alicia said bluntly. "A hurricane is a hurricane, and your calling it a breeze doesn't keep the roof from flying off."

Lady Wynwood laughed. "If you're comparing the incident this morning to a hurricane, you quite off the mark. The only thing that happened was that Miss Bethany's dress was torn."

"Beth*une*, Charlotte, Bethune. Why can't you remember

the name of the girl who's about to become your daughter-in-law?''

Lady Wynwood waved aside the interruption indifferently. ''Yes, of course, Bethune. Anyway, the dress is nothing to trouble over. My dressmaker is repairing it.''

''It's not the dress,'' sighed Alicia, troubled. ''It's my Sophy. I don't know what's come over the girl. She's always been skittish and impetuous, and to an extent which gives me some little concern, but she's never been like *this*!''

''Now, Alicia, are you sure you're not making too much of all this? Perhaps you are my opposite. While I make zephyrs of hurricanes, you make hurricanes of zephyrs.''

''Three disquieting incidents in less than two days do not make a zephyr,'' Alicia said glumly. ''They feel like the beginning of a hurricane to me.''

''Oh, rubbish! I have eyes in my head, even if I *am* imperturbable. Your Sophy is a lovely child. You've nothing to worry about.''

''Haven't I? I wish you were right. But you see, I suspected the silly chit was up to something even before we left London. I think she took it in her head that Marcus . . .'' But thinking better of the matter, Alicia decided not to go on.

Charlotte gave her friend a long, piercing look. ''What about Marcus?''

''I'd best not discuss it. It probably doesn't signify.''

''Come now, Alicia, it won't do to poker up now. Had my son any dealings with your granddaughter? Was there some difficulty between them?''

Alicia shrugged. ''I'm not quite sure. There was a rather amusing misadventure at the Gilberts' ball, when Sophy mistook Marcus for her cousin Bertie—too silly to bother to explain the details to you—and I believe they've met once or twice since. But nothing to explain her taking him in dis . . .'' She stopped herself again and bit her lip.

''In dislike? Sophia disapproves of my Marcus?'' Charlotte inquired with unruffled interest.

''I think so. She called him a . . . well, let's say that she didn't describe him favorably.''

Charlotte leaned back in her chair, her eyes thoughtful. "What you were about to say was that she called him a prig, or words to that effect." There was a brief pause, during which Alicia watched her friend's face with awakened interest. "She was quite right, you know."

"Sophy?" Alicia blinked in surprise. "In saying Marcus is a *prig*? How *can* you, Charlotte? You cannot mean it. Marcus is everything fine and proper, and you know it!"

"Yes, of course he is," Charlotte agreed, but there was the merest ghost of a cloud in the serenity of her expression. "However, I've been noticing of late that he has a tendency to withdraw from life. And a . . . certain rigidity . . . He gets it from me, I expect. It's that reticence, you know. That tendency to cling like a barnacle to one's privacy. It makes one seem priggish when one finds one's self under public scrutiny. But I cannot like the tendency. A man like Marcus shouldn't hide himself away forever from the crowd. He has the brains and ability to do something useful with his life . . ."

"Yes, I know what you mean," Alicia said with quick understanding. "He's the sort who should take an active role in Parliament one day."

"Exactly. But I don't know how he's to accomplish that unless he overcomes his reluctance to take chances . . . to face the limelight . . . to do so many things he is loath to undertake. Every decision he makes seems to be in the direction of . . . withdrawal. Even his choice of bride . . ." She shook her head. "But I go too far. I should not have said it."

Lady Alicia gave her hand an affectionate squeeze. "Never mind. I understand completely. But I think you are mistaken if you believe that Miss Bethune would not make a suitable wife for a man in public life. She is as lovely and well-bred as one could wish."

Charlotte eyes lowered. "Yes, of course she is. But she won't be the one to shake Marcus from his . . . No, I mustn't talk like this. It doesn't matter that *I* find her somewhat colorless. It's Marcus's choice, of course, not mine."

"Whatever you may feel, you at least may console

yourself that she is so well-behaved. I wish my Sophy were more like her," Alicia said, sighing in the sudden recollection of her *own* troubles.

"No, I don't agree with you. Your Sophy is full of vitality, excitement, exhuberance. You mustn't spoil that." She leaned forward and took her friend's hand. "Promise me that you won't scold the girl."

"Do you expect me to ignore the matter? Say not a word to her?"

"Yes, I do."

Alicia shook her head dubiously. "But . . . then there will probably be more of the same. *Something* should be said to the wretch—"

"I'll talk to her, if you like."

Alicia looked at her friend in pleased surprise. "*Would* you, Charlotte? You know, that may be the very thing! With your equanimity and composure, you'd make the *perfect* model for my wayward granddaughter!"

Charlotte smiled tranquilly, gathered her flowing skirts about her and rose gracefully. "Very well. Consider it done," she promised, and moved with her fluid step toward the terrace.

"But, when?" Alicia asked insistently.

"Soon. Very soon."

"Really, Charlotte, must you always be so vague? When, exactly?"

Charlotte was disappering into the dimness of the summer evening. Her voice came floating back to her impatient friend. "One of these days," she said placidly. "One of these days . . ."

Chapter Nine

LADY ALICIA WAS inclined to believe that Charlotte's advice had been sound when Sophia appeared at dinner time in a modest, demure little blue lustring gown and demeanor to match. She spoke when spoken to, her answers were pleasant and polite and her manners were unimpeachable. Another elegant dinner passed without incident, and the party was entertained in the music room with a few more songs from Mrs. Carrington without the least disturbance from the volatile Miss Edgerton. Sophy steadfastly refused to leave her seat or even unfold the hands clasped in her lap. When teased by the ever-present Dennis Stanford about her puritanical demanor, she merely smiled coyly and said she was taking no chances on causing any sort of upset.

Only one little incident occurred to mar the peacefulness of the evening. It occurred a short while after the music had ended and Lady Wynwood had ordered the card tables set up. Three tables were organized, with only Sophy, Dennis and the two Carrington girls refraining from the games. Dennis had brought his chair close to Sophy's and was entertaining her with a steady stream of flattering remarks. Fanny was standing at the window, throwing jealous glances toward the insensitive couple whose murmurings and giggles caused her such anguish. Cissy, oblivious to the entire drama, had her nose buried in a copy of *The Castle of Otranto* which she'd found in the library. Suddenly, there was a loud scream from Fanny. "A *face*!" she cried. "I saw a face looking in at us!"

Everyone turned to the window, but nothing was there. Fanny nevertheless kept insisting that she'd seen a man's face looking in through the window . . . a face she'd never seen before. "Balderdash, child," Julian laughed boisterously. "Peeping Toms don't go peering into music rooms. There's nothing worth seeing. It's *bedrooms* they prefer, y'know."

This made poor Fanny quite hysterical. "A Peeping Tom?" she shrieked, horrified. "Will he come looking in my bedroom, then?"

"Just because you were standing at the window don't mean he came to look at *you*, you know," Bertie pointed out. But somehow Fanny did not find any comfort in that remark either.

Marcus and Dennis went out on the terrace and peered into the darkness, but there was nothing to be seen. After a while, Lady Wynwood calmed Fanny, and the games resumed. This time, however, Bertie convinced Dennis to take his place at the card-table while he sat down to chat with his cousin. "Was that one of your schemes?" he asked her in a disapproving whisper.

"What do you mean?" she asked, offended. "The man in the window? Don't be daft."

"Well, how do I know what queer starts you're apt to concoct," he muttered. "You've given me no reason to credit you with any sense."

"I've enough sense not to do anything like *that*!" she declared haughtily. "Did you think I'd go out and hire a Peeping Tom?"

"I don't know *what* you'd take it in your noggin to do."

Sophy made a face at him. "You know, Bertie, your eleven years in India have spoiled you. You used to be much more fun when we were children."

"So were you," he retorted promptly. "You used to *do* things, then. You'd race, or you'd ride, or you'd go exploring. You didn't spend your days making up wild schemes to embarrass yourself.''

"I *don't* spend my days making up wild schemes," she declared outraged. ''At least, not before now. It's only here and now . . . because of the special circumstances . . .''

"Well, you're spoiling a very good opportunity to have a rollicking good time," he said sullenly.

"I'm not spoiling *your* good time, am I?"

"Yes, you are, in a way. Why didn't you come riding this morning? It was great sport, but I missed you. I had no one to joke with.''

Sophy was touched. It was the first kind word she'd heard in a long time. "Did you really miss me? Well, I'll go riding with you tomorrow, if you'd like."

"Do you think you can spare the time?" he taunted. "I wouldn't want to lure you away from your important 'purpose.' Don't you have any mischief to concoct?"

She made another face at him. "If that's the lively sort of conversation I can expect from you this evening, I think I'll take myself to bed." And without further ado, she did just that.

The gentlemen had already gathered in the stables the next morning when Sophy made her appearance there. Her dark blue riding costume, topped by a cocky little plumed hat worn at a rakish angle, gave a clear indication that she intended to ride. "I didn't know you're a horsewoman, Miss Edgerton," Marcus said in some surprise.

"There's not much you *do* know about me, Lord Wynwood," she retorted saucily.

"So it seems," he said drily and turned to find a suitable hack for her.

The horse he chose, a mild little mare, was a well-shaped animal, but to Sophy's chagrin she proved to be completely spiritless. Try as she would, Sophy could not manage to push the horse into a gallop. She was forced to lag far behind the others, for the horse did nothing more energetic than to plod listlessly along the bridle path. Bertie soon came galloping back to see what had become of her. "Having trouble with the animal?" he asked sympathetically.

"Trouble?" she fumed. "I can't arouse any *movement* from this deplorable slug! Our irritating host didn't believe I could really ride!"

Bertie laughed. "He's probably afraid that you're too skittish to control a good horse. Can't say I blame him. A girl who's terrified of spaniels ain't likely to be able to handle a prime bit o' blood. He's afraid the horse'd run off with you."

Sophy, who'd learned to ride before she could walk, glared at him, jabbed her spurs into the mare's side and wheeled her around. She would have loved to ride off in a burst of speed, but the mare would not respond. As she plodded off homeward, Sophy could hear Bertie's mocking cackle for much longer than she felt was at all necessary.

She returned to her room and threw off her riding coat furiously. She felt much abused. For one morning she'd attempted to behave in a normal fashion, to enact a truce, to put aside her grudge. And what was the result? His High-and-mightiness had insulted her *again*! How dared he assume that she was incapable of handling herself on horseback? That infuriating man had merely *looked* at her and judged her to be cowhanded. What was there about her that made him jump to the conclusion that she was a dotard at everything?

Bertie, if he'd been privy to her thoughts, could have answered her. He would have told her that if she insisted on *behaving* like a jingle-brain, she would be *judged* a jingle-brain. But Bertie was not there. And the turmoil of her feelings did not permit logical reflection. At the best of times, Sophy permitted her passions to rule her judgment, and as far as she was concerned, this was a far cry from the best of times. That she could be quite as much at fault as Lord Wynwood did not even occur to her. She paced back and forth in her bedroom like a caged tigress, fanning the sparks of her fury into a bright flame. She would get back at him! Just wait!

Marcus, who liked things to be orderly and well-planned,

had organized an outing for the afternoon. There was a beautiful, fifteenth century church in a little village not very far away, and he announced at luncheon that he'd made arrangements to take those of the party who were interested to visit the place.

The children, as well as the not-quite-out-of-the-schoolroom Cissy, turned up their noses at the prospect of going out just to see a church, its impressive antiquity notwithstanding. Isabel, Cora Carrington and Fanny, however, expressed immediate interest. Uncle Julian just as promptly declined. "I'm for a nap, my boy," he said without the slightest embarrassment. "A man like you, who *claims* to be civilized, ought to know better than to suggest such vigorous exertions in the *post-meridian*. Afternoons are meant for relaxation."

"Hummmph!" Lady Alicia grunted, poking him meaningfully on his protruding midsection. "What fustian you speak, Julian. If you'd exert yourself a little more, either *post* or *ante-meridian*, you'd have a little less girth to carry about with you."

"You're quite right, dear lady, quite right," Julian agreed jovially, "but since it has taken me many years to acquire this impressive girth—"

"Impressive it certainly is," Alicia assented with a snort.

"—I should be loath to lose it capering about in an old church tower," he concluded, quite without having taken the least offense.

Sir Walter guffawed. "Well said, old man, well said. I'll stay behind with you, if our host has no objection. We'll have a game of chess before *siesta*."

Marcus had not the least objection. He turned his attention to those who had not yet responded to his invitation. Lady Bethune and Mrs. Maynard had hesitated. Secretly, they were in complete sympathy with the sentiments expressed by Julian Harvey. Taking a nap in the afternoons was a favorite pastime of both sisters. But as soon as it had become clear that Lady Wynwood was to be part of the expedition, Lorna Bethune couldn't resist going along. To become an intimate of the illustrious Lady Wynwood was an ambition dearly cherished in her bosom, and she would lose no opportunity to accomplish that goal. Mrs. Maynard, being by nature a follower, couldn't bear to be left to her own devices, so she joined her sister in expressing willingness to go. Deep down, however, she took no pleasure in the prospect of climbing towers and marching down sleepy village lanes in the heat of the afternoon.

As for the others, they all assented to making the trip. And if the enthusiasm of their response was somewhat less than Marcus had wished, he could console himself with the hope that, since their expectations were not overly great, the fulfillment of those expectations would more easily be achieved.

Marcus had made very careful plans—so careful that he was sure nothing could go amiss. The party would be taken (in three carriages driven by his own coachmen) to the picturesque little village of West Hoathly, only an hour's distance. There they would disembark. They would wander freely down the village's one street, visit the Church of St. Margaret with its fifteenth century tower and its graceful, shingled spire, walk through the gardens of the half-timbered cottage called the Priest's House (considered one of the loveliest buildings of its type in the country), and, in short, drink in the atmosphere of a Sussex locality which had been in existence for the past twelve centuries.

After they'd all taken in the sights, admired the flowers along the lane and rhapsodized over the lovely, rural cottages roofed with the Horsham slabs so characteristic of Sussex, they would all climb back into the carriages and return to Wynwood in plenty of time for tea. He didn't see how anything could go wrong. But of course, he had reckoned without Sophia Edgerton.

From the very beginning, matters did not proceed as planned. Marcus had arranged for the first and largest of the carriages to carry five passengers and the other two to carry four each. But the maneuvering for "advantageous" seats threw his plans awry. First, Mrs. Bethune and her sister (who could not be separated) requested seats with his mother, who had already taken a place beside Lady Alicia and Isabel. And since Lady Alicia had specifically saved a place in the carriage for Sophy (who had not yet made her appearance) the large coach would be overcrowded. Then Fanny refused to be coaxed into a carriage until she saw where the waiting Dennis would take his place. And Bertie begged to be allowed to sit on the box with one of the coachmen, in the hope that he would be permitted to handle the ribbons.

Sophia finally emerged, looking calm and restrained. She wore a becoming little walking dress of pale green cambric and a modest straw bonnet tied with a green ribbon. No one, not even Bertie, could detect behind her shy smile and discreet manner that she still seethed from the morning's "insult." Marcus, by promising Bertie that he could take the ribbons on the trip home, inveigled the boy into escorting his cousin to the third coach (where he and Iris would be seated and where he could keep an eye on his troublesome guest) and to keep her company there. Thus the harried host was able to assure Lady Alicia that her granddaughter was properly taken care of, and room could be made for Lady Bethune and Mrs. Maynard in the first carriage.

With the first carriage full, and Bertie, Sophy, Iris and Marcus taking up the third, it was obvious that Dennis and Fanny would have to take their places with Mr. and Mrs. Carrington in the second. Dennis threw Marcus a number of looks of indignation and appeal, but Marcus could do nothing but shrug and grin. Dennis desperately walked about checking the bridles of all the horses, trying to delay the inevitable, but since the girl trailed after him while he procrastinated—a situation every bit as distasteful as being forced to sit beside her—he at last surrendered and took his place in the carriage.

Marcus signaled the driver of the first carriage that they were ready to start and jumped aboard the third beside his betrothed. Just as they started to move, a desperate Dennis thrust his head inside Marcus's vehicle. "I say, Edgerton," he said urgently to Bertie, "you wouldn't consider changing seats with me, would you? I have an aversion to . . . er . . . to laudalets."

Marcus gave a shout of laughter and nodded his

acquiescence to the amiable Bertie. "I can still take the ribbons later, can't I?" Bertie asked suspiciously.

"Yes, of course you can," Marcus assured him. Dennis helped Bertie down, watched him climb aboard the second carriage, and then jumped up beside Sophy with a blissful sigh of relief. Marcus, meeting his eye, couldn't keep back his laughter. He leaned back and roared. Dennis, turning quite red in embarrassment, soon joined in. Iris and Sophy looked at each other nonplussed, but neither Marcus nor Dennis was in any condition to enlighten them. "What on earth has amused you so?" Iris demanded. Gentlemanly honor prevented them from responding, but Marcus did whisper to Iris that, if she wanted to be entertained that afternoon, she would do well to keep her eyes on Dennis when they alighted.

When they arrived at West Hoathly, the sight of Dennis being relentlessly pursued by the unshakable seventeen-year-old provided Marcus with so much amusement during their rambles through the village that he forgot to concern himself with Sophy. It was not until the various charms of the tiny hamlet had been duly admired, and the members of the party were ready to return to Wynwood that it was brought to his attention that Sophia was not anywhere in evidence.

Marcus quickly strode up the lane and around the churchyard to find her, but she was not there. Meanwhile, Mr. Carrington and Bertie combed the grounds around the Priest's House, and Dennis climbed the tower. When they returned to the waiting carriages and reported to Marcus that they hadn't found her either, his lordship did something quite uncharacteristic: he uttered a sharp and vulgar epithet. *I might have known,* he thought, gnashing his teeth in frustration, *that the infuriating Miss Edgerton would get herself lost*!

Chapter Ten

IT WAS QUITE impossible for anyone to get lost within the tiny confines of West Hoathly. Everyone agreed on that. But Sophy was indeed lost.

"*Lost*?" cried the long-suffering Lady Alicia. "How can she be lost?"

"Oh, pooh, she's *not* lost," Charlotte said optimistically.

"She just sat herself down in some corner of the church and fell asleep," Mrs. Carrington theorized.

"Irritating chit," Lady Bethune muttered under her breath to her sister. "First she sets fire to the music room, then she rips Iris's dress, and now this!"

Marcus walked to the edge of the road and looked over the landscape. Sophia was not asleep in the church—he and Dennis had made sure of that. And she couldn't be anywhere in the village—even asleep—and not have heard them calling her. It was therefore logical to assume that she'd wandered out of the village. But where? To the east lay a wide expanse of Sussex downs, on which no movement could be discerned. There was nothing there to attract anyone, either. It seemed to him that there were only two possibilities: either Sophia had wandered in a northerly direction up the road on which they'd come, or she'd ventured into Ashdown Forest which surrounded West Hoathly on the south and west. If she'd gone up the road, the home-bound carriages would catch up with her. If, on the other hand, she'd gotten lost in the forest, they were in great trouble.

But he couldn't alarm the ladies with his fears. In order to minimize their alarm and to proceed with a search in an organized manner, Marcus decided to send most of the party home in two of the carriages. The third would be retained for the search party. A brief conference with Dennis, Mr. Carrington and Bertie resulted in a plan: Bertie and Marcus would make up the search party; the rest would travel home in Mr. Carrington's charge. If the homeward-bound carriages were to find Sophia along the road, Dennis was to take one of the horses and ride back to West Hoathly to inform Marcus.

When the ladies were requested to climb into the carriages, Lady Alicia, in acute distress, begged to be permitted to remain with the searchers. She could not bring herself to leave without her beloved Sophy. But Charlotte gently coaxed her into her seat, assuring her of Marcus's competence to handle the situation and convincing the worn-out, distracted old woman, by the calm sincerity of her manner, that Sophy would be found so quickly that Marcus's carriage would catch up with them before they even reached home.

It was a depressed and silent band who gathered in the lane, and a depressed and silent Marcus who assisted them to climb aboard. When Iris came up beside him, he took her hand. "I'm so sorry I shan't be riding back with you," he whispered.

She squeezed his hand comfortingly. "So am I. I hope you won't be long."

"I hope not." he smiled at her ruefully. "You must be wishing you'd never agreed to this party. Your mother's ball for two hundred would have been far less troublesome."

"Not at all. Don't tease yourself on my account. Everything has been lovely so far. And even this will be something to laugh about when you've found Miss Edgerton and have come back home."

Marcus smiled at her gratefully. "As I said before, my dear, you are a great gun."

As soon as the carriages had left, Marcus and Bertie set about their task. With West Hoathly as their starting-point, they agreed to walk in opposite directions along the edge of the woods for half-an-hour. They were then to return to the village and, if they'd had no luck, they would reassess the situation.

As Marcus hurried along, peering through the trees and calling Sophy's name over and over, he began to feel something akin to terror. Although there would be three hours or so of daylight, the depths of the forest already looked forbiddingly dark. If the girl had lost her way in those quickly-deepening shadows. he very much doubted that they could find her before nightfall. A group of experienced searchers might manage to find a lost girl in a patch of woods at night by using torches, but Ashdown was a *forest*, thick, deep and widespread. The chances of locating her within its depths were slim, and the dangers which a defenseless girl might have to face within its bounds were many. And they were dreadful to contemplate.

When Bertie and Marcus met at the carriage and looked at one another, their eyes were frightened and their lips set. "If this is one of her tricks," Bertie muttered, "I'll *throttle* her!"

Marcus looked at him curiously. "Tricks? What do you mean?"

Bertie colored. The words had just slipped out because of his fear for her safety. He hadn't intended to give her away. "I . . . I only meant . . . she used to like to play this sort of trick on me when she was a child," he improvised embarrassedly.

"I see." Marcus scrutinized the young fellow shrewdly. Sophy *had* been up to something these past few days, that much was clear. And Bertie was privy to it. But he looked too pale and frightened to have any information *now* that she was playing a game. They must find her, and quickly. "I think we'd better face the fact that the forest is too big for us to cover on our own. Let's see if we can get some help from the locals."

The coachman pointed out that a woman in a cottage right near their present location was peering out at them through a little, leaded window. Marcus tapped at her door and told the aged, bright-eyed woman who answered what the problem was. The woman clucked sympathetically. "I th'ot 'twas somethin' o' the sort," she said. "Been watchin' ye fer an hour or more." Her son would be glad to help, she said, when he came in from the fields, but in the meantime she suggested that his lordship go to see Old Andrew, who lived in the last cottage in the lane. Andrew was said to know the forest better than anyone.

While the coachman walked the horses, Bertie and Marcus hurried to the cottage the woman had indicated. But there was no answer to their knock, and when they peered into the house (the door not having been locked), they found it empty. "Old Andrew must have gone out," Bertie said, discouraged.

Marcus kicked at the pebbles in the path in chagrin. "Damn it all, I can't stand around here waiting. I'm going to search Ashdown myself. You wait for this Andrew and bring him in after me. You'll hear me shouting—just follow the sound."

Despite Bertie's protests that he'd get himself lost as well, Marcus strode off toward the forest without another word. But as he came round the back of the cottage, he noticed an old man walking in his direction from the woods. He carried a huge bundle of twigs on his back. When they were close enough to speak, Marcus asked, "Are you called Old Andrew?"

"That's who I be," the man answered. "Are you wantin' me for somethin'?"

"I'm told you know the forest very well, We've lost a member of our party who may have wandered in there. Will you help us search?"

"There ain't nobody in there now . . . leastaways, not hereabouts. I been wanderin' about in there fer the last hour and didn't notice no tracks."

Marcus gestured helplessly. "Are you sure? Where else could she have gone?"

"*She*?" Old Andrew gave Marcus a sharp look, then set his bundle on the ground. "This lost party . . . it's a *female*?"

"Yes. Why do you ask?"

"Pretty little thing, with reddish hair an' a green dress?"

Marcus felt his heart leap. "Yes! Have . . . have you seen her?"

"Yessir, I have. But she ain't in the forest, that I kin swear to."

"Well, then, where *is* she? Speak up, man!"

The old man cackled. "I ain't sayin' as I know where she *is*. All I know is she ain't back in there."

Marcus groaned in impatience. "If you don't know where she is, how can you be sure she's *not* lost in Ashdown?" he demanded.

" 'Cause no one could ride a horse in there nohow."

"A *horse*?" Marcus was beginning to feel that the conversation was taking place in a dream. Nothing was making sense. "No, you don't seem to understand. The lady we're looking for was not on horseback. She was on foot."

Old Andrew grimaced at the impatient gentleman with disgust. "I know *that*," he said in a tone he might have used for an idiot child. "I giv'd her *mine*."

"What? You gave her a *horse*?"

"Well, I din't *give* it exac'ly. She paid me a yellow-boy to let her ride him."

Marcus shook his head in utter bewilderment. "Perhaps we'd better start at the beginning," he said, mustering up what patience he could. "How did she happen to ask you for your horse?"

"Well, sir, y'see, I was rubbin' ol' Thunderer down, there in front o' the shed where I stable him, when the young Miss comes walkin' up the lane and stops to watch me."

"This 'young Miss'—you say she had a green dress and auburn hair?"

The old man nodded. "All curled, it was. An' her bonnet . . . it was tied on wi' shiny green ribbons—"

"Yes, that's the girl. Well, go on."

" 'That's a fine roan,' she says, friendly-like. 'Thank ye, Miss,' I say, givin' me forehead a knuckle. Then she nods 'n comes up to ol' Thunderer an' pets his nozzle. Ol' Thunderer, he takes to her amazin'! She has a real way wi' horses, she has. Then she asks me can she ride him fer a bit. I can't think what to say to that, 'cause Thunderer, well, he's a bit huge fer a wisp of a lass like her. But she takes out this here yellow-boy from her—what do the ladies call 'em?—reticule. E'en so, I hold back. But she says as she's a bruisin' rider—those 're her very words, 'I'm a bruisin' rider,' she says. So I let her have 'im.''

Marcus, straining to follow the gist of the old fellow's account, was unaware that Bertie had come up behind him and was listening to the tale with open-mouthed attention. It was Bertie's snort of laughter which made Marcus look round. "Did you hear all that, Bertie?" he asked in a kind of stupefied amazement. "She's gone off *riding*!"

"If that ain't just like her!" Bertie marvelled, a tinge of reluctant admiration for the girl coloring his tone.

"Can you tell me what *isn't* like her?" Marcus snapped. "Is there *any* impropriety, any indiscretion, any outrage which that infuriating little madcap would not perpetrate?" He turned and stomped furiously back across the field. Bertie, stung by Marcus's tone and the injustice of his words, ran after him. "That's not quite fair, you know, my lord," he shouted indignantly. "Not fair at all."

Old Andrew watched them for a moment, shaking his head at the inexplicable tempers of the gentry. Then he calmly picked up his bundle, shifted it onto his back and trudged after them.

Marcus continued across the field, each step pounding the ground heavily, as if the force of his footfalls would in some way dissipate his rage. He'd been misused—abused, rather!—by that abominable girl. He had come to spend a fortnight in the country with a few intimates, to celebrate a special occasion in his life, and she had completely cut up his peace. And her witling of a cousin dared to say that he was *unfair*!

Without warning, he wheeled on the unfortunate Bertie, who was coming up behind him. "Unfair, am I? In what way am I being unfair? There has not been a day since we arrived that your goose-witted cousin hasn't made some mischief. And now she's taken a horse and ridden off to God-knows-where, to return God-knows-when! And you have the temerity to call me unfair?"

Bertie, so unexpectedly attacked, turned pale, colored at the ears and looked embarrassedly at the ground. "I only meant . . . I know Sophy's been behaving badly . . . but . . ."

The boy's look of acute discomfort softened Marcus immediately. "I'm sorry. I was shouting at you, wasn't I? Forgive me. Your cousin's behavior should not be laid at your door. But you cannot be trying to make *excuses* for the girl. There can be no excuse for what she's done this afternoon. You know as well as I do what turmoil her little escapade has caused."

"I didn't mean to make excuses for her," Bertie said miserably. "I only wanted to suggest—how can I say this?—that perhaps . . . Sophy is not *entirely* at fault." He took a deep breath and went on bravely. "I beg your pardon if I'm . . . stepping beyond the bounds to say this, my lord, but . . . you, yourself, may have had a bit to do with this, you see."

"I? *I*? I'm afraid I don't see that at all."

"Well, you *did* offend her this morning, you know."

Marcus peered intently at the red-faced boy through the gathering gloom. "Did I? In what way?"

"Do you remember, at the stables, that you gave her that slug to ride? Sophy's been riding since she was a babe, and she couldn't be expected to be pleased that you thought her incapable of handling anything better."

"Oh? A really good horsewoman, is she?" Marcus asked. Bertie's nod made Marcus add in a defensive mutter, "Hang it all, Bertie, how was *I* to know the chit could ride?"

"You might have asked."

This simple response caught Marcus short. He bit back the cutting retort that sprang almost automatically to his tongue. The boy was obviously sincere in his suggestion that Marcus had been thoughtless and rude. Could the fellow be right? Could *he*, Marcus Harvey, have been guilty of discourteous behavior towards a guest? "Did Miss Edgerton complain to you about this?" he asked.

Bertie did not know how to respond. He was sure that Sophy wouldn't wish him to repeat their conversations about Lord Wynwood. "About the mare?" he asked evasively. "No, she didn't. Not directly. I saw her trying to coax the mare to gallop, and I could tell she was . . . er . . . somewhat displeased."

"I see. And you think she undertook this little stratagem to show me my mistake?"

"I can't say, my lord. It ain't my place to speak for her."

Marcus nodded. The fellow was not such a simpleton as Marcus had judged him to be when they'd first met. The boy had a strong sense of loyalty, an observant eye and blunt honesty that Marcus couldn't help liking. In an unspoken apology, he put an arm about the boy's shoulder. "I wish you'd stop calling me 'my lord' in that punctilious way. I'm Marcus to my friends. Now, let's see what's become of Old Andrew. Perhaps he can give us some inkling of when our impetuous horsewoman intends to return."

But Andrew, who had returned to his cottage and begun to light his evening fire, had no clues to offer. The young Miss had promised to return in just a little while, he told them. He certainly had no idea that she intended to stay out until dusk.

But dusk was rapidly becoming dark, and the two gentlemen, sitting on the little stone wall which edged the cottage garden, could discern no movement on the deeply-shadowed downs. Bertie watched Marcus's face apprehensively as, with the passing minutes, his eyes narrowed and the creases around his mouth deepened. *Damn the girl, had she no sense?* Bertie wondered. If she took much longer, his lordship—Marcus—would be as furious as he'd been before Bertie had softened him up.

Bertie's fears were quite justified. As the sky darkened, so did Marcus's mood. At length he ordered Bertie to take the carriage and return home. "Lady Alicia will be distraught by this time. You can relieve her distress by telling her that her granddaughter and I will be following closely behind."

"But if I take the carriage, how will you—?"

"I'll keep one of the horses. Come on, let's help my man unhitch him."

"Marcus, why not send your *man* home on horseback? That way, I can wait with you, and we can drive the curricle back ourselves when Sophy gets here."

"Because, my boy, what I have to say to your Sophy, when she gets here, will not be fit for you to overhear."

Bertie sighed. "That's what I was afraid of. Very well, I'll go if I must." He climbed gloomily into the curricle and the coachman clucked at the horse. Just as the carriage began to move, Bertie stuck his head out. "You won't be too hard on her, will you?" he asked worriedly.

"Hard on her?" Marcus said between clenched teeth. "I'm going to *wring her neck*!"

The sky became black. Nothing could be seen but the stars, a quartermoon, and the dim lights from the cottage windows, and still Sophy had not come. Old Andrew, who had come out a few times to mutter that he hoped the lass had not made off with his horse, had callously gone to bed. Marcus's mood had progressed from impatience, through raging fury to abject terror. This was more than sport, more than a girl's game. No one with a grain of sense would keep a horse out after dark, especially on strange terrain. The girl must have been thrown and was lying somewhere unconscious. Dead, perhaps. He alternately paced up and down the lane or sat stock still on the wall listening for the sound of hoofbeats. Added to his agony was the awareness that there was nothing he could do but sit and wait.

His anticipation of the satisfaction of wringing her neck had long since given way to quite another feeling. He yearned, he longed, he *prayed* for the sound of those hoofbeats. If only she were not harmed, not unconscious, not dead . . . he would forgive her everything. He would be patient with her, kind, thoughtful, understanding. Anything! Everything! If she would only . . .

There was a slow clip-clop from the far end of the lane. He held his breath. Yes, he could hear it quite clearly. His heart jumped joyfully into his dry, fear-frozen throat. It must be she! He peered intently down the lane and saw a moving shadow in the faint, faint moonlight. Leaping

eagerly from the wall, he raced down the lane. "Sophy?
Sophy, is it *you*?" he cried.

"L-Lord Wynwood . . . ?" came a frightened little voice.
And in another moment the horse was at his side, and
Sophy was sliding from the saddle into his waiting arms.

For a moment, unconscious of what he said and did, he
held the girl against him muttering "Thank God," into her
hair, so intense was his relief. But the feeling spent itself
almost immediately and was replaced by the most violent,
inexplicable rage. All the feelings he'd suffered throughout
those harrowing hours came flooding back. He had no
awareness of the girl's trembling limbs, her tear-streaked
face, her frightened eyes. Like a mother who viciously
slaps her beloved, lost child the moment after she finds
him safely restored to her, Marcus seized the girl by her
shoulders and shook her furiously. "Damn you, woman,"
he hissed, "where the devil have you *been*?"

For Sophy, this was the worst and most difficult
development in a very bad and difficult day. "P-Please,
l-let m-me go!" she stuttered, appalled at the ferocity of
his anger. "You're *h-hurting* m-me . . ."

"Hurting you? I'd like to *strangle* you! Do you realize
that I've been sitting on the wall, picturing you lying in a
pool of your own blood, for almost *four hours*?"

"I . . . I'm sorry. I l-lost m-my way . . ."

"Sorry? You're *sorry*? That meaningless word comes
very readily to your tongue, doesn't it? Is that supposed to
be a sufficient explanation for your thoughtless, calamitous
behavior?"

They glared at each other breathlessly. Sophy's spirit,
which had flagged completely under Lord Wynwood's
startling attack, began to stiffen. Now that she was no
longer lost and alone, her courage reasserted itself. "If
you'll stop b-bruising my arm and give me a chance to
explain—" she managed to gasp.

Guiltily, he loosened the hold on her arms. It was not
until this moment that he realized how cruelly he'd been
grasping them. "What is there to explain?" he growled.
"You wanted to teach me a lesson for underestimating
your horsemanship. Well, you've succeeded. If you managed

this enormous animal for all this time, you must be a very talented horsewoman indeed. I compliment you.''

Sophy turned on him a pair of very startled eyes. "How did you—? What makes you think—?"

"Bertie told me." He turned away and fumbled for the horse's bridle. "I'm sorry I offended you this morning, but couldn't you have made your point with a little less drama? Did you have to put me . . . us . . . through this protracted torture?"

"I didn't mean to . . . surely you don't think I *intended* to do anything like this! I meant only to take a short ride, and then gallop back to the carriages while everyone was getting ready to leave. In that way, you would all see how well I—"

"A likely tale," he said with a sneer, wheeling around to her. "You needn't have ridden off to the downs to accomplish *that*!"

Sophy hung her head. "I suppose I needn't have done that. But once I'd climbed on the roan's back and felt his power, I longed to race him. The downs at this distance seemed more level and flat than they turned out to be. By the time I'd passed over a few hills, I looked back and couldn't see the village. Not even the spire! I rode back, but I must have mistaken my direction, and before I knew it I was hopelessly lost. I'd gone miles out of my way before I found anyone to ask, and then I . . ."

"Then you what?"

She looked up at him defiantly. "You won't believe it, but I was misdirected and became more hopelessly lost than ever."

"Oh, I believe it. You have a talent for getting yourself embroiled in these unbelievable coils. It's quite like you."

Sophy drew in her breath. "Quite like me? How *dare* you! What gives you the right to make assumptions about me on the basis of a mere brief acquaintance?" she asked haughtily.

He gave a bitter laugh. "Brief acquaintance? My dear girl, in the few days I've known you, you have managed to put me through more turmoil than anyone else could have done in *years*! I think that what I suffered tonight *alone* gives me the right to make certain assumptions—''

"You *suffered*? What a bit of gammon!'' she said scornfully. "As if you cared if I lived or died!''

Marcus, whose inner trembling over her safety was only now beginning to abate, raised a derisive eyebrow. "Listen here, Sophy, what sort of man do you think I am? Not *care*? What do you think caused me to lose my head when you turned up just now? You surely don't believe that I *normally* greet my friends by falling into a frenzy and shaking the life out of them.''

"You seemed upset, I grant you, but you cannot make me believe that it was over *my* welfare. I know what you think of me. Your only concern was the success of your houseparty! If I had met with an unfortunate accident, it would no doubt have somewhat damped the proceedings.''

Marcus stared at her in disbelief. "Don't talk like a fool!'' he said curtly. Could she—or anyone—have failed to notice the tell-tale signs of the extent of his concern? Why, his hands were *still* trembling! This wretched girl seemed to believe he had no *feelings*!

In the dim moonlight, he could see her lift her chin proudly, although she tried to hide its slight quiver. "Then perhaps, since I'm talking like a fool, we'd be well advised to stop,'' she said. "I would like to g-go home.''

The little stammer smote him like a blow. "Of course,'' he said quickly. "We'll return Andrew's horse and be on our way.'' Damnation, why had he been so curt with her? He had promised himself that, once she came back, he'd be kind.

He had an almost overwhelming urge to take her in his arms, to comfort her and tell her that he hadn't meant to scold. But he couldn't very well do that, being neither her parent nor her lover. He wasn't even a friend. He sighed and reached for the horse's bridle and started up the lane, the girl following dejectedly. A quick glance at her over his shoulder showed a woebegone, rumpled creature, her bonnet hanging limply from the ribbon round her neck, her hair dishevelled, her face streaked. He looked away quickly, feeling like a beast. But *why* he should feel so culpable he didn't in the least understand.

He led the horse to Old Andrew's shed, covered him with a blanket and set him a bucketful of oats. Then he took the crestfallen girl to the place where he'd tied up his own horse, lifted her upon it and jumped up behind her. "Why don't you lean back against me and go to sleep?" he suggested gently. "We won't be home for an hour or more. I'll have to go slowly in this darkness."

But she shook her head. He felt a stab of disappointment. He would have liked her to lean against him and nestle her head in his shoulder. It would have made him feel forgiven, although he wondered (for the second time) why—for what crime of omission or commission—he should seek her forgiveness. But the girl sat stiffly erect, as if any contact with his body would be a contamination, and they exchanged not another word or look during the long ride home.

Chapter Eleven

SOPHY TRIED TO brace herself to face the wrath of her grandmother and the subtle scorn of the other guests, but she could not. She was exhausted in mind and body, and her emotions seemed stretched to the point of snapping. If anyone should even look at her askance, she knew she would burst into tears. *Real* tears. For the past few days, she had taken enormous satisfaction in her ability to upset the placid tenor of the Wynwood establishment by her *false* tears, but somehow the thought of bursting forth in real ones was humiliating to her. It was a strange paradox. She had really caused chaos today, and that success gave her no satisfaction at all.

By the time she and Lord Wynwood returned, dinner had ended. The guests, the butler informed them, were all gathered in the drawing room awaiting them anxiously. Sophy tried desperately to steel herself to face them, but the prospect sent a tremor all through her body. "Would you prefer to go right up to bed?" Lord Wynwood asked with what Sophy felt was most unusual concern.

"Do you think . . . would that be too cowardly?" she asked. "I daresay I . . . ought to face them and explain—"

"There's not the least need for you to do so. You can leave the explanations to me. I'll send for your abigail at once and have her take you right upstairs."

He turned to say something to the butler. She threw him

a quick, dubious look. Would it be better, she wondered, to face them all now and get the matter over with, or to do as his lordship suggested and postpone the ordeal for the next day?

As if he read her mind, Marcus smiled at her reassuringly. "You have my word that no one shall plague you about this. You may trust me to set everything right."

The tears which hovered just beneath the surface threatened to spill over. "Th-Thank you, my lord. You are v-very k-kind."

"That's not quite how you described me earlier, is it?" he reminded her ruefully. "I came to my kindness a bit late, I'm afraid." He took her hand in his and fixed his eyes on hers. "Can you forgive me?"

Accustomed to expect nothing but polite disdain from Lord Wynwood, Sophy was thrown off balance by this gentle and self-effacing behavior. Her tears spilled down her cheeks. Humiliated by this display of emotionalism when she specifically wanted to be able to control it, she snatched her hand from his grasp and ran to the stairs. Halfway up, she met the relieved and overjoyed Miss Leale, who clasped her in an affectionate and completely uncritical embrace and led her off to her room.

Murmuring endearments, Miss Leale bathed and undressed the girl. Just as she was tucking her into bed, there was a tap at the door. It was a footman, bearing a tray. His lordship had sent his compliments and would be pleased if Miss Edgerton would partake of this bit of supper. On the tray were five covered dishes and a silver vase containing a single pink rose. "Thank his lordship for me," Sophy said, "but I'm not hungry." The footman bowed and was about to withdraw when Sophy stopped him. "One moment," she said, padding across the room to him. She took the rose from the vase and waved him off.

Under Miss Leale's curious eye, she casually tossed the flower on her nightstand. But in the darkness, after the abigail had withdrawn, she cupped the bloom in both her hands, sniffed it tenderly and placed it on the pillow beside her. Then, with a sigh of self-pity, she snuggled down into her pillow and fell into an exhausted sleep.

But even in sleep, the events of the day wouldn't leave her mind. She dreamed she was on the back of a sluggard horse, riding over the downs. Far in the distance was a tall church spire which she was trying to reach. But the horse would scarcely move, and the spire kept disappearing and re-appearing in unexpected places. She turned the exasperating animal hither and thither, but the spire remained agonizingly distant.

Then there came a rumble of thunder, and, in a rush of wind, an enormous roan horse came galloping over the hill, ridden by a tall, shadowy figure she knew to be Lord Wynwood. Without slowing his pace, he snatched her up to his chest. She had to cling tightly to him to keep from flying off into the wind, so great was the speed of his animal. She could feel Lord Wynwood's heart beating. There was a slight tremor in the arms he clasped tightly around her. His lips were on her hair, and she imagined (although the noise of the wind was so great she could not be sure) that he was murmuring "Thank God" over and over into her ear. She drew back her head to look at his face. In a flash of lightning, she saw that he was grinning in hideous sarcasm. "Well, you hysterical shatterbrain," he asked cruelly, "how do you like the ride?"

She woke to find that a storm was brewing and that the rain and wind were blowing into her open window. A flash of lightning recalled to her mind the pale, sardonic dream-face of Lord Wynwood, and she shuddered. She jumped out of bed and slammed the window shut. Shivering, she crawled back under the bedclothes and tried to drive that face from her mind. Another lightning flash illuminated the room, and she saw the rose still lying on the pillow where she'd so lovingly placed it. What a silly fool she was, to be sure. Lord Wynwood was absolutely right in his assessment of her. Angry at herself, she reached out, grasped the little flower and threw it across the room, sticking her finger with a thorn as she did so. "*Confound* him!" she muttered, sucking the blood from the stinging wound.

She flung herself down on the pillows, drew the coverlets up to her neck and shut her eyes. If she was to get any rest

that night, she had to banish him from her thoughts. But
the lightning continued to crack and the thunder to growl,
and she couldn't fall asleep again. Unbidden, the memory
of her return to West Hoathly came flooding back to her.
She had ridden into the village in frightened hesitancy, not
sure she'd come to the right place. Everything had looked
so nightmarishly unfamiliar in the faint moonlight. And
then, miraculously, she'd heard him calling her name.
She'd slid down from the horse into his arms with a
feeling of such joyful relief it had felt like . . . well, like
love. Or at least what she imagined that awesome,
mysterious emotion must be like. And when he'd clasped
her to him with what had seemed to her to be the same
feeling of relief, the same joy she was feeling, her heart
had leapt into her throat in amazement. She'd given no
thought to the significance of any of it, but had simply
clung to him in a blissful fog. She'd felt his heart pound
and his arms tremble as they'd tightened around her—the
always-so-cool, always-so-critical, always-so-aloof Lord
Wynwood! His lips were on her hair, and she heard him
murmuring, "Thank God, thank God . . ."

But she would really be the fool he thought her if she
attached any significance at all to the incident. She rolled
over on her back and opened her eyes. She didn't at all
like the direction of her thoughts. "Get hold of yourself,
my girl," she muttered aloud. "This sort of emotional
indulgence will not do," she said in a perfect imitation of
her grandmother's voice. But in this case, her grandmother
would be perfectly right. Anyone with sense would say the
same. This kind of thinking would not do . . . it would not
do at all.

The following morning the storm had passed, and the
beautiful June sunshine tempted many of the guests to
stroll out of doors. Breakfast was served on the terrace, a
game of quoits was organized on the south lawn, while on
the east slope, Dennis gave instruction to Bertie, the oldest
Maynard boy and the ever-present Fanny on the method of
hitting a ball with an oddly-shaped stick. This was to
prepare them, he explained, to play a fascinating game

which he'd learned in Scotland—a game he called "gowf."

In none of these activities was Sophy taking part. She'd sent Miss Leale with a message to her hostess, in which she assured everyone that she was quite well but would spend the day resting in her room. Many of the party, however, were not satisfied to accept Miss Leale's word that all was well with Sophy, and thus the embarrassed girl had to welcome several visitors to her bedside.

The first was her grandmother. To Sophy's surprise, the old lady greeted her with a pleasant smile instead of the expected scowl. Lady Alicia bent down and kissed the girl's cheek. "You're looking a bit peaked," she remarked after studying her granddaughter with her keen, bird-bright eyes, "but no worse than what one would expect in the circumstances. I'll have Leale bring you some hot broth."

"Thank you, Grandmama," Sophy said meekly. Then she grinned up at her grandmother with weary mockery. "Is that all you're going to say? If you don't give me a scold, I shall be forced to believe that *you're* the one who needs hot broth."

Lady Alicia surveyed her shrewdly. "I don't think you'll need a scold this time. From the look of you, I'd say you've brought on yourself the disaster I've been predicting."

Sophy threw her grandmother a quick look and lowered her eyes. "Perhaps not quite a disaster," she said quietly, "but close enough."

"Good," her grandmother said unsympathetically. "The experience may therefore be salutary enough to keep you from tumbling into a complete one."

Her next visitor, her aunt Isabel, found her stretched on a chaise enjoying the sunshine streaming in her window. Aunt Isabel brought with her a dish of sweetmeats which she unwittingly nibbled at herself during the quarter-hour she sat at Sophy's side.

Then came Bertie, having had enough "gowf" to last a long while. "It is a completely exasperating game," he told his cousin, "in which one is supposed to hit a ball with a stick that's utterly inadequate for the purpose."

"I don't want to talk about gowf," Sophy said pettishly.

"I want to know why you betrayed me to Lord Wynwood."

"Betrayed you!" Bertie bellowed, outraged. "I *never* betrayed you."

"You told him *something*. He accused me of hiring old Thunderer to get back at him for giving me the mare to ride."

"Well, I had to offer him *some* explanation for your shocking behavior. If I hadn't made him feel a bit responsible for your misconduct, he would have wrung your neck for sure."

Sophy made a moue. "He as good as wrung my neck anyway. Are you sure you didn't tell him anything else?"

"What do you take me for?" Bertie demanded, rising in offended dignity.

"Very well, I apologize. Don't get on your high ropes, Bertie. I'm not myself today."

"I'm not a bit surprised. Serves you right, though. Hope you've learned a lesson from all this."

"Oh, shut up, will you?" Sophy snapped irritably. "You sound like Grandmama."

"I take that as a compliment. Seems to me that old tartar has some good sense. I hope Sophy, that you've come to *your* senses at last. You're not going to continue with your silly schemes to upset things, are you?"

Sophy shrugged. "I suppose not. The whole thing suddenly seems a bit pointless."

"Humph!" Bertie snorted. "Isn't that just what I've been telling you?"

Sophy's fourth visitor was Lord Wynwood himself. He came in early in the afternoon, carrying a tray. "I've brought you the luncheon myself," he explained, "to make sure you don't send it back uneaten, as you did last night."

"Th-This is very kind in you," Sophy said shyly. "I promise to eat something. I'm quite famished, I assure you."

"Then let me see you dig in. I don't intend to leave until every morsel has been consumed." And to make good his threat, he placed the tray on her lap and drew up a chair. Under his watchful eye, Sophy timidly picked up a fork and made a little stab at a plate of cold salmon. "Come, come," he urged, "you must be able to do better than that."

"I'm not an invalid, you know," Sophy ventured with a small smile, but she proceeded to eat with more enthusiasm.

"I know that," he said, leaning back in his chair and watching her with satisfaction, "but since you touched nothing on the tray last night but a rose—and I presume you didn't eat that—I'm determined to see you take some nourishment."

At the word "rose," Sophy blushed furiously, and the hand holding the fork faltered. "You are carrying your duties as a host too far, my lord," she said in a brave attempt to hide her confusion.

"I think we can dispense with the 'my lords' by this time, don't you? And we might also dispense with your mistaken interpretation of my motives. If I show you some solicitude, it is not *entirely* because you are my guest."

"Indeed, sir?" Sophy asked, putting her fork down and keeping her eyes carefully lowered. "What other motive could you possibly have?"

Marcus leaned forward, his brow knit in perplexity. "How can you ask such a question? Don't you believe that I can have feelings of friendship and affection for you? What have I done to make you think I hold you in dislike?"

Sophy raised her eyes briefly to his face. Then she lowered them again but would make no answer.

"I thought," Marcus sighed, "that when you took the rose last night, it was a gesture of forgiveness. But I see now that the explosion of bad temper with which I greeted you on your return from the downs remains unforgiven."

"You mistake me, sir. There was nothing in your behavior last night that requires my forgiveness. As you pointed out to me, anyone who knew the circumstances would agree that your response was nothing more than I deserved."

"I don't agree," he said, rising and coming to stand over her, "but if *you* believe what you just said, why do I have the strongest feeling that I have deeply offended you? It *cannot* be that blasted mare I forced on you."

She shook her head wordlessly and kept her eyes fixed on the plate in front of her.

He bent over and lifted her chin. "Look at me, Sophy. Tell me what I've done and how to make amends!"

"I . . . It is . . . nothing, my lord."

With a discouraged breath, he dropped his hand and stepped away. "I apologize, my dear. My questions are keeping you from doing the very thing I came to encourage you to accomplish. I shall press you no further but leave you to finish your luncheon in peace." He went to the door, put his hand on the knob and hesitated. Looking over his shoulder, he asked with a tinge of embarrassment, "If you were not sending me a message of forgiveness last night, why *did* you take the rose?"

Sophy colored to her ears. "Because . . . because it was so pretty," she said with a gulp, and fidgeted with her food.

Later that afternoon, there was another knock at her door. In a swirl of filmy gauze, Lady Wynwood floated into the room. Sophia, flustered by the unexpected honor, jumped up and offered her a chair. "Sophy, my love," Lady Wynwood said in her breezy way, "have a look at the corsage I've made for you to wear tonight. Marcus tells me you like roses."

"H-How very kind," Sophy said in awkward gratitude, wondering in what context Marcus had revealed that information to his mother, "but I hadn't intended to . . . go down to dinner this evening."

"Nonsense, my dear, of course you'll come down," her ladyship answered, taking her seat with graceful nonchalance. "You cannot pretend, with that lovely touch of color in your cheeks, that you're still feeling hagged."

"No, not hagged, exactly, but—"

"I'll have no 'buts,' my love. We simply *must* have your company at dinner. It has been dull as ditchwater without you, I promise you. Last evening, for example, after we learned that you were safely in bed, Lady Bethany (or is it Bettison? I never *can* remember.) prosed on and on about what she would have been doing in London that evening, and Mr. Carrington kept consulting his pocket watch and yawning. And my brother Julian got tiddly on brandy and fell asleep in front of all of us. The most exciting thing that occurred all evening was a recurrence of that apparition in the window. But even that was only a momentary diversion, for the face appeared for just a moment and then was gone. Really, Sophy, you cannot condemn us to a repetition of that sort of evening, can you?''

Sophia giggled. "You're exaggerating, aren't you, Lady Wynwood? Besides, I don't see how *my* presence—''

Lady Wynwood fixed her eyes on the girl earnestly. "Don't you, my dear? Has no one ever told you how your presence livens up a room?''

"Oh, my *lady*!'' Sophy gasped, blushing. "You can't be serious! *My* presence?''

"Yes, my dear, yours. I mean it most sincerely.''

Sophia stared at her visitor in wide-eyed amazement. Then she shook her head and made a rueful grimace. "If what you're saying is *so*, it must be because everyone is watching for me to make some dreadful *faux pas*.''

"I don't see why you should think *that*,'' her ladyship said in honest puzzlement. "Your manners are perfectly unexceptional.''

"Lady Wynwood,'' Sophy chided, "are you trying to flummery me? You can't have forgotten the fire in the music room, and the scene when I arrived, and—''

"Really, Sophy, you are not going to harp on a couple of accidental incidents that don't signify at all,'' Lady Wynwood said with a dismissive wave of her gauze-draped arm. "What have those things to say to your manners? Now, hush, dear. I'll brook no arguments on this point. You mustn't deprive us of your company when it is such a delight and a stimulant to us all.''

"Certainly not to *all*,'' Sophy said with a troubled frown. "Your *son* would not agree with you.''

"Wouldn't he?'' Lady Wynwood asked, cocking an interested eye at the girl. "Why do you think he wouldn't?''

Sophy looked down at her fingers which she'd begun to twist in her lap. "He thinks I'm an empty-headed, clumsy, overwrought, wild-eyed *disaster*," she admitted in a sudden burst of feeling. But no sooner were the words out than she wished she hadn't said them. She darted a guilty glance at her visitor, but her ladyship was looking at her with unruffled placidity.

"*Does* he, indeed?" she asked mildly. "Poor Marcus."

"Poor Marcus?" Sophy echoed, nonplussed. "Whatever do you mean?"

"I mean, I'm afraid, that my beloved son is more of a prig than I thought."

Sophia gasped. "Oh, Lady Wynwood, no! I had no intention . . . I never meant to imply . . ."

"Of course you didn't. I wish you to understand that I adore my son as much as the most besotted of mothers, but I nevertheless know the truth. But you mustn't be too hard on him, my dear. If he has grown too fastidious and critical, the blame must be laid at my door."

"I'm sure that can't be true," Sophy declared fervently.

"But it can. You see, I raised him in the seclusion that I so much prefer to the prying eyes of society and that he, too, grew to feel comfortable with. As a result, he is not accustomed to the excitement, the turmoil, the disorder and the crises that are part and parcel of more normal lives. I suspect that his early meetings with that sort of liveliness frightened and appalled him. He conquered the fear by an attitude of disdain."

Sophy stared at Lady Wynwood in fascination. She didn't understand why she'd been singled out to receive such a confidence, but she couldn't help but be enthralled by these details of Marcus's upbringing. That Lord Wynwood could have been, in his youth, a retiring and somewhat timid boy was inconceivable to her. She longed to ask questions about his boyhood, his schooling, his preferences, his amusements, his hidden nature, but she dared not reveal to his perceptive mother the extent of her interest.

"But we mustn't permit him," Lady Wynwood went on, "to reject or disparage those aspects of life which his self-defenses tempt him to avoid. In other words, my dear, I see no reason to encourage him in his priggishness, do you?"

"No, of course not . . ." Sophy mumbled awkwardly. "That is, I don't mean that I find him priggish, exactly, but—"

Lady Wynwood laid a gentle hand on Sophy's knee. "Then you will come down to dinner and give us the pleasure of your enlivening company?" she asked with her warm smile.

Sophy nodded, blinking up at the older woman with misty-eyed reverence. "Oh, Lady Wynwood," she breathed, "no one has *ever* described me that way before. You make me feel almost . . . almost worthwhile."

Lady Wynwood rose and embraced the girl, wrapping her in a cloud of filmy silk. "Of *course* you're worthwhile, you sweet child. More than worthwhile. And I wouldn't be at all surprised if even Marcus sees it himself, one of these days."

Chapter Twelve

THE FORMAL ANNOUNCEMENT of the betrothal of Miss Iris
Bethune to Marcus Harvey, the fifth Earl of Wynwood,
was to be made at the end of the first week of the houseparty.
The announcement would be made at a very special dinner
and would be followed by dancing in the seldom-used
ballroom in the west wing. The number of guests was to
be augmented by the presence of some of the neighboring
gentry, by a dozen or more of Lady Bethune's family and
special friends who were posting down from London for
the evening, and by ten musicians who were to provide the
music. The plans for this celebration seemed to have
developed without anyone's conscious manipulation, Lady
Bethune making a suggestion here and Uncle Julian adding
a detail there. Before he knew it, Marcus was faced with a
fait accomplit, a celebration which promised to be almost
as distasteful to him as Lady Bethune's ball would have
been. But he held his tongue and accepted the inevitable
with his usual good grace.

The ballroom, the smaller of two such rooms at Wynwood
Hall, was opened, aired and polished to a gleaming sparkle.
The housekeeper and the servants polished the chandeliers,
washed the windows, removed the dust covers from the
chairs and tables, and hung floral festoons along the walls.
On the morning of the day of the celebration, the whole
household bustled. Mrs. Cresley scurried back and forth

arranging and placing huge floral masterpieces on every available surface, supervising the herculean efforts of the kitchen staff and helping the valets and abigails of the guests to prepare the costumes which would be worn that night. The servants, too, when they could take time from polishing the plate and dusting and cleaning every inch of the house, took out of their bed-chests their most formal liveries for brushing and airing. It had been many years since the Wynwood household had been the scene of such elaborate preparations. Even the guests were busy and preoccupied, having their hair trimmed, their nails manicured, their eyebrows plucked, and their feet massaged.

To escape the hubbub for as long as possible, Marcus invited Iris, shortly after breakfast, to stroll with him in the garden. At first she protested that her abigail was about to dress her hair, but the disappointment on Marcus's face made her alter her plans. Besides, in the week of her stay, she had been given little opportunity to spend time with him in private, Marcus's duties as host keeping him perpetually occupied, and she was unwilling to let this chance go by.

The June day could not have been more perfectly suited to the occasion. The sky was dotted with the merest wisps of clouds, the breeze was just fresh enough to give sparkle to the air, and the sun was modestly warm. The soon-to-be-feted pair strolled through the paths in silence, content to drink in the sights of the lush blooms and the fragrance of the air. Iris broke off a white peony bloom and, urging Marcus to a nearby stone bench, she sat down beside him and set about attaching the flower to his lapel. "There!" she said proudly. "Now you look as festive as you ought."

He grinned a bit ruefully. "Thank you, my dear, but don't you think there are more than enough signs of festivity about the place already?"

"I quite like them," she answered, looking at him with a little frown, "don't you?"

"You know I don't like fuss and feathers. These ceremonial occasions only make me uncomfortable."

"I don't see why," she said thoughtfully. "They are an agreeable change from the monotony of ordinary days.

They provide us with a bit more excitement, a touch of drama and a storehouse of memories.''

"I don't find ordinary days monotonous, and as for excitement and drama, I could easily live without either of them in my life." His own words suddenly struck him as self-satisfied and pompous. Annoyed with himself, he endeavored to change the subject. "But on the matter of unnecessary excitement, what do you think of the change that's come over our little 'dramatist' of late. It's been three whole days since Miss Edgerton has caused a furor. I wonder if she's plotting some volcanic cataclysm to overwhelm us when we've been sufficiently lulled into tranquility.''

Iris smiled dutifully, but it was plain that something else was on her mind. "Do you mind if we don't talk about the exploits of Miss Edgerton right now, Marcus? There's something I've been wishing to say to you.''

"Of course, my dear," Marcus said, noticing her worried expression. "What is it?''

"It's . . . about our betrothal. I know that our immediate circle will not be surprised by tonight's announcement, but the fact remains that until the announcement is actually made and published to the world, there is nothing really binding between us . . .''

"Iris! What are you saying?''

She put a cool hand on his mouth. "Let me finish, dear. I'm simply reminding you that it is not yet too late to draw back. If the prospect of marriage to me is in the least disturbing—''

He pulled her fingers from his lips. "Good heavens, Iris, what has brought this on? Have I given you any reason to suspect that I've changed my mind?''

"I'm not quite sure," she admitted reluctantly. "There have been a few things . . .''

"What things?''

"Well, your attitude about tonight's festivities, for one.''

"But, my dear, that has nothing to do with my feelings for you. You know that! I'm not comfortable among large groups of people, especially if I'm the center of attention. Have I been selfish?'' He looked at her in sincere dismay.

"Have my foolish complaints been spoiling your pleasure in the affair? Forgive me, I beg you. I promise to say not another word about my dislike. In fact, I'll do my best to have a rollicking good time. Does that ease your qualms?"

She smiled a little wanly. "Yes, but . . . that's not all. Are you absolutely sure, Marcus, that you *want* to go through with this?"

He looked at her keenly. "Of course I am." He took one of her hands in his. "I hope you will believe me. What else have I done to make you uneasy?"

She dropped her eyes. "They are such *little* things," she admitted with a slight blush. "You don't always approach me first when you enter a room." Her voice was low and tinged with embarrassment. "Oh, I know what you'll say to that—that you're the host and must see to your guests. I know I'm being missish. But . . . there's something else. I'm almost afraid to say it . . ."

"Afraid? I hope, Iris, that you don't think me a brute. Am I the sort who will fly into a rage at a bit of criticism? Please, my dear, say what's on your mind."

"It's just *that*—the 'my dear.' Oh, this is such a forward and unladylike thing to say, Marcus . . . I'm quite put to the blush . . . but you always call me 'my dear.' You never say 'my love'."

For a moment Marcus stared at her in surprise. Under his gaze, her eyes met his for a brief, questioning moment and then fell. She turned her head away. Her dark-gold hair, which had been hastily pinned in a careless knot at the back of her head, looked appealingly dishevelled. One thick strand had become undone and lay in pathetic loneliness at the back of her graceful neck. Lifting his free hand, he took the strand between his fingers and curled it absently. "I . . . I don't know what to say, Iris. I'm sure you've always been aware that I'm not given to . . . er . . . romantic demonstration. Surely you know my feelings without repeated protestations."

"I *think* I do," she said, not looking at him, "but we females have a need for reassurance . . ."

"Then permit me to reassure you. As my wife, you need never have a moment's concern that my devotion will flag or my eye will roam. I promise, even if I remain somewhat reticent in expressing my feelings aloud. And now, if you'll turn that lovely face to me, I'll try to reassure you still further.'' He slid his arm around her, and as she obediently turned to face him, he kissed her with what she breathlessly said was quite sufficient enthusiasm to reassure anyone. And when at length their stroll was resumed, Iris had her arm around his waist and a very becoming sparkle in her eyes.

Marcus was glad to have been able to allay her fears so easily. His own qualms were not so readily dismissed. The past week had been inexplicably disquieting to him, and not only because his customary privacy was being invaded by visitors. Playing host for a protracted length of time was not his favorite way of passing the time, but he *was* on his own territory, and the guests were, for the most part, pleasant company. No, the houseparty was not the wellspring of his depression; its source lay in deeper waters.

He had attempted to discuss the matter with Dennis the evening before, with predictable results. His friend had immediately pinpointed the source of his problem as his impending nuptials. ''I *told* you to refrain from putting on leg-shackles,'' he had said bluntly. ''No wonder you're depressed. You've given yourself a prison sentence—trading in your freedom for bed and *bored*!''

Marcus didn't even smile at the terrible pun. He'd heard it often enough before. There was scarcely a time, when groups of men gathered over their brandies, when they didn't exchange a goodly number of quips, jokes and generally disparaging gibes at the state of matrimony. Wedlock was called a prison, a horror, a curse. Even philosophers and writers were not above denigrating the 'holy estate'. Menander had called it an evil, Cervantes had called it a noose. And Boswell reported that Samuel Johnson, when speaking about a man's remarriage, had declared it to be ''the triumph of hope over experience.''

Nevertheless, Marcus wasn't taken in by what he knew was mere badinage. If a man chose his marital partner sensibly, marriage could be a source of satisfaction and security. He was a man of some maturity and responsibility, he hoped, and he had chosen a woman of beauty, good family and good sense. What could be wrong with that plan?

Dennis had been only too pleased to tell him: it was too proper by half. Where was the fun? Where was the excitement? "As I've warned you, Marcus, you'll be forced to live a life of complete predictability."

"I see nothing wrong in that," Marcus had replied staunchly. "I *like* predictability. And I don't need excitement."

Dennis had shrugged hopelessly. "It's your decision, old man, of course. I just can't help but feel that you're far too young for such an attitude. I seem to remember an old saying, 'Young men should not marry *yet*—' "

" '—And *old* men never.' Yes, I've heard it. But I'm neither that young nor that old, so if you don't mind, I'll go ahead with my plans."

He'd walked out of his friend's room with a great show of decisiveness and self assurance—Dennis's tendency to frivolous attitudes and irresponsible viewpoints always brought out in Marcus the avuncular, pompous side of his nature. But he was not so assured as he'd pretended, and the feeling of depression lingered. The little talk with Iris did nothing to ease his inner disorder; in fact, it exacerbated the problem. He began to ask himself the very questions *she* had asked—why had he so infrequently sought her company? And why had he failed to use endearments when addressing her?

He had never worried about such things before. It had never occurred to him to wonder if he truly loved Iris. Love, as Plato had said, was a grave mental disease, and he had no intention of falling victim to its disorder. When one courted a young lady, one naturally declared undying affection and the tenderest of feelings toward her—the ladies all seemed to expect such declarations—but one didn't actually *feel* them. Marcus had never heard or read that marriages were improved by the husband's possessing a wild passion for the wife. If anything, literature was full of examples of the disastrous results of such unions. A marriage partner should be chosen (as his had been) by cool, well-considered evaluation of the available, qualified females. Why, if one let one's *emotions* dictate the choice, one might very well end up wedded to someone like— terrible thought!—like Sophia Edgerton!

Therefore, he had nothing, really, to worry about. Firmly he put the matter out of his mind. During the afternoon, while the ladies were all closeted with their maids preparing for the evening, Marcus sat in his study attempting to catch up on the never-finished business matters stemming from his estates. But he couldn't seem to concentrate. After a while, he gave up and put his papers away. Wandering aimlessly about the house, he came upon his Uncle Julian dozing in the library, an open book turned over on his ample stomach. With each deep breath he took, a snore rumbled in his throat and caused his stomach to vibrate. And with each vibration the book slipped a little bit further down the mountainous incline formed by Julian's rotundity and his reclining position. To rescue the volume from the otherwise inevitable fall, Marcus reached over and gently picked it up.

Julian puffed, snorted and opened his eyes. "What—? Who—? What's amiss?" he mumbled dazedly.

"It's I, Uncle Julian," Marcus said sheepishly. "I'm sorry I woke you."

"No, no, old fellow. 'S perfec'ly all right." He sat up and reached for the watch in his waistcoat packet. "It's almost time for me to go up and get dressed, anyway."

"Don't go yet, Uncle. I'd like to talk to you, if I may."

"Certainly, my boy," Julian said pleasantly, stretching and yawning contentedly. "I'm quite awake now, so fire away."

Marcus took the wing chair opposite his uncle and leaned forward. "I was wondering, sir, why a man like you never married."

"Aha!" the shrewd old reprobate chortled. "Having misgivings, are you?"

"What makes you think that?" Marcus asked, instinctively putting up the shield behind which he hid his private feelings.

"Simple, my boy. In all these years that I've been your

bachelor uncle, you've never seen fit to ask me that question. But now, on the eve of your betrothal—''

Marcus hung his head. "Yes, you're right,'' he admitted, deeply ashamed. "I'm learning all sorts of things about myself today. I seem to be a remarkably self-absorbed creature. It never occurred to me to ask you about yourself until the subject of matrimony became vital to my *own* life. I begin to see a side of myself that is not very pretty to contemplate.''

"Rubbish,'' his genial old uncle laughed, dismissing his nephew's self-accusations with a toss of his head. "Self-interest is the most natural instinct in the world. Putting others first is all very well for saints and martyrs, but very few of us are made for such roles, thank goodness. But to return to your first question, I never married because the one woman I wanted didn't want me. And everyone else seemed too pale by comparison.''

"Do you mean to say, Uncle Julian, that you wanted to marry for *love*?'' Marcus asked in amazement.

Julian studied his nephew with narrowed eyes. "What other reason *is* there?''

"A good many reasons, I think,'' Marcus said, pursuing his argument with a kind of desperate enthusiasm. "There's the responsibility to carry on the line, for one thing. There's the obligation to maintain the solidity of the social structure by building a secure, tight-knit English family, for another. There's the comfort of stable familial values and the companionship of a sympathetic partner on one's voyage through life, for a third. There's—''

"Enough, my boy, enough! You sound like a clergyman. Your reasons are very commendable, completely unarguable and entirely inconsequential.''

"*Inconsequential*? Uncle Julian, how can you—''

"Because, when love possesses you, every other reason for marriage becomes pointless. Can't you see that? Can it be that you are not familiar with the grand passion?''

"Familiar with it? I don't even think I could recognize it,'' Marcus sheepishly admitted.

"Is that so? Then your development has been sadly arrested, dear boy. It's an experience not to be missed.''

"What is it like, Uncle? Describe it to me."

"Describe it? Impossible. Don't you read poetry? Go to the poets if you want a description, not to an old man who has no way with words and is not even sure of the accuracy of his memories."

"Oh, I've read the poets. Even the best of them make the emotion seem unreal. Like Shakespeare's 'Love is a spirit all compact of fire.' A lovely phrase, but what has it to do with reality?"

"A great deal, I think. That's a very *good* description, if you ask me. You see, my boy, the trouble is that love is like gout in one respect—you're not likely to believe in it until it strikes you."

Marcus laughed and eyed his uncle with surprised appreciation. "Uncle Julian, you have hidden depths. I should have spoken to you long before . . . before . . ." He stopped awkwardly.

"Before you got yourself entangled?" his uncle asked frankly.

Marcus shook his head. "No, no. I'm not feeling entangled, exactly . . . only a bit blue-deviled."

Julian looked at his nephew with a sympathetic frown. "It may only be the pre-nuptial quakes, you know. Every man gets an attack sometime before the wedding."

"Do you think that's it?" Marcus asked hopefully.

Julian shrugged. "I'm no expert, mind. Wouldn't want you to take *my* word. Marriage is a serious business. Bound to frighten a man . . . unless he was so besotted with the girl that nothing else mattered."

"I can't claim to be besotted, I'm afraid. Although Iris is everything I want in a wife."

"Oh, yes, yes. I quite see that. Lovely girl, Iris Bethune, lovely. Not the sort I'd choose myself, but quite a commendable creature."

Marcus looked at his uncle curiously. "What sort *would* you choose, uncle?"

"Not that the tastes of an old bachelor signify," Julian grinned wickedly, "but I'm more readily drawn to a livelier type—like the curly-haired chit who raises such a dust at the slightest provocation. What's-her-name . . . Edgerton."

"*Sophy*?" Marcus was horrified. "You'd choose her to *marry*? You're trying to cut a wheedle!"

"Not at all, my boy. Not that a girl like that wouldn't lead a fellow a merry dance. I can quite understand that *you* might not approve of such a choice."

"Approve? I'd be convinced you'd lost your *mind*!"

"Well, you needn't be so vehement about it. Besides, we're only idling with our tongues. I'm scarcely likely to change my status at this time of my life. As I said, marriage is a serious business."

"Yes, so it seems," his nephew agreed a trifly glumly.

"Do you think, Marcus," Julian suggested with a shade of diffidence, "that it might be wise to postpone tonight's announcement? Just to make sure—?"

"Oh, no. Of course not. I'm convinced you were right when you said that this is just a momentary quake. It will pass." He smiled and stood up. "Speaking of tonight's announcement, I hope you realize that you'll be the one to make it."

"I?"

"Yes, didn't you know? I should have mentioned it before, but I've been so involved with playing host I quite forgot. As my eldest male relative, you are the appropriate person to make the announcement. Do you mind?"

"Of course not, Marcus, my boy, of course not. I call it an honor. Be happy to oblige. That is, if . . ."

"If?"

Julian looked at his nephew closely. "If you're certain you want to go through with it."

Marcus instantly replied, "Of course I'm certain." But he dropped his eyes from his uncle's piercing gaze before he said it.

Chapter Thirteen

SO IT WAS THAT, a few hours later, Julian rose to make the announcement. He stood at his place near the foot of the long table at his sister's right hand, surveying the more than three dozen faces looking up at him expectantly. All the family and friends who had gathered for the evening suspected what the message would be, but they nevertheless waited in eager expectation for the words. The only sound to interfere with the hushed silence was the patter of heavy raindrops on the windows. The weather, which had been so accommodating throughout the day, had turned nasty.

The table had been set in the huge, rarely-used banqueting room in the west wing. The long board gleamed with silver and crystal. Dozens of glimmering candles lit the faces of the guests, lustrous in their evening finery and jewels. At the head of the table, his nephew Marcus sat smiling calmly at him, showing no trace of the troubled feelings he'd revealed so short a time before. At Marcus's right sat his promised bride, looking beautifully regal with a woven-gold band set on her hair like a diadem. In her cream-colored satin gown with its gold embroidery, she almost glowed in the candlelight.

Directly opposite Julian, Lady Bethune also glowed. From the top of her elaborate hairstyle (bound with a jeweled loop which held three huge ostrich feathers) to the bottom of her mauve gown, she looked triumphant. Julian's sister, Charlotte, on the other hand, was dressed in her usual, gauzy style, her blowaway hair in its customary state of controlled disarray. But there was nothing in her serene, complacent expression to give the slightest hint that she was not as happy on this occasion as Lady Bethune.

Before the silence could become awkward, Julian cleared his throat and raised aloft a glass of champagne. "Ladies and Gentlemen," he said with a twinkle, "you see me here with a glass of champagne in my hand. Obviously, I'm going to offer a toast. But before I do, I have an admission to make. I've always found champagne to be paltry stuff, so I've arranged, especially for this auspicious occasion, an alternative for those among you who agree with me."

He nodded to two waiting footmen. They stepped forward bearing trays of glasses filled with a rich amber-colored liquid. Julian went on. "A magnificent Armagnac, my friends," he said with a flourish, "eminently suitable for the toast I am about to make. I hope those of you who wish to try it will accept it with my compliments and with no embarrassing questions about how I managed to obtain it in these troublesome times."

He winked naughtily, and there was a burst of knowing laughter from the gentlemen. The footmen circled the table, providing most of the gentlemen with glasses of the smuggled brandy, although the ladies turned the offer aside and kept to their champagne.

"And now, if you are all prepared to imbibe, I shall make my toast," Julian proceeded. "In behalf of Lady Bethune and my sister Charlotte, it is my honor to announce to you all the betrothal of Miss Iris Bethune to Marcus Harvey, fifth Earl of Wynwood and my beloved nephew. To Iris and Marcus! May you have a life of domestic happiness, the only bliss of Paradise, Cowper says, that has survived the fall."

There were smiles all around, enthusiastic applause, and a cry or two of "Hear, hear!" Then the gentlemen took to their feet, everyone raised their glasses to salute the betrothed couple, the drinks were downed, and it was over. Even Marcus, if he'd been challenged, would have had to admit that the ceremony had not been much of an ordeal.

The banquet-room doors were thrown open, and the sound of music flooded in. With the leisurely contentment of well-fed cats, the assemblage made their way in twos and threes to the ballroom. At the entrance to the ballroom, Iris and Marcus stood receiving the personal good wishes of each guest. With under forty in attendance, there was no crush to surround them, and the atmosphere was easy and informal. There was a general feeling of sincere warmth, and all the kisses and blessings bestowed on the couple seemed heartfelt.

Sophy, trying to be inconspicuous, hid in her grandmother's wake as they waited to congratulate the young couple. She dreaded the moment when she would have to offer her good wishes. She only, of all the guests, had not listened to Julian's words with a feeling of good will. In fact, every word of his announcement had struck her like a hammer-blow.

Ever since the night in West Hoathly, she'd found her thoughts full of Marcus Harvey. At night her dreams were centered about him, and in the daytime she found herself brooding about him whenever she failed to concentrate her mind on other matters. She knew that this newly-born obsession was completely unjustified and utterly foolish, but she couldn't seem to help herself. He had suddenly become for her the epitome of every masculine virtue, the embodiment of all her romantic ideals. Never mind that, only a few days before, she had found him stuffy, pretentious and insufferably high in the instep. Never mind that he held her in low esteem. For no reason that she could understand, all that had changed. He now seemed to her almost knightly in his perfection.

To make matters worse, the things his mother had told her during that afternoon visit to Sophy's bedside had given her hope that the betrothal would not actually be announced. Lady Charlotte had clearly indicated that she felt the betrothal to Miss Bethune would not be the most advisable match for her son. On the basis of this very insubstantial clue, she had let herself hope that the betrothal would not be announced. She was not so befuddled as to express that hope to herself consciously, of course, but it had seeped into the back of her mind nevertheless. And when Julian had actually said the words, she'd almost reeled in dismay.

Not that the cancellation of the betrothal would have made any real difference to Sophy's expectations. Even if Marcus had *not* become betrothed to Miss Bethune, there was not the slightest indication he would turn to *her*. In the past few days, when she'd done nothing to disturb the serene tenor of the proceedings, he had completely ignored her. And she had not the slightest doubt that if she'd caused any upheaval, he would have regarded her with his usual air of resigned and ill-disguised distaste. Therefore, she told herself with perfect logic, there was no reason to hope that the betrothal would not take place. No reason at all.

Nevertheless, she found herself most painfully beset when Julian made the announcement. Logical arguments gave her no comfort. She had looked down the table at Lady Wynwood, the only other person in the room who might possibly feel as she did, instinctively seeking company in her misery. But there was not the least sign in Lady Wynwood's benign smile that anything was troubling her, and Sophy had had the additional discomfort of having to suffer alone.

Now she would have to take Iris's hand and wish her well. And she would have to tell Marcus how happy she was for him. Well, everyone considered her to be "dramatic"—an actress by nature. She would see if they were right. If she could say the necessary words without stumbling, if her lips could smile without trembling, she was an actress indeed.

Staying close behind her grandmother, she smiled and murmured innocuous compliments that evidently were sufficiently well-expressed to cause no adverse reactions. Iris Bethune thanked her warmly, and Marcus smiled at her pleasantly enough. And before she quite realized that the ordeal was over, she found herself inside the ballroom with Dennis Stanford at her side.

The younger and more energetic of the guests had already

begun to form a set for a country dance, while the others strolled about the room or sat down on the sofas to watch and chat. Dennis firmly propelled Sophy to the dance floor, refusing to accept her absently-phrased objections. He not only was determined to make some headway with the tantalizing Miss Edgerton this evening, but he hoped to make clear to the persistent Fanny that he was not the man for her. Fanny was forced to accept the company of Bertie for the dance. Neither Bertie nor Fanny looked happy to be in each other's company, for Bertie had been forced into standing up with her by the insistence of his mother. Isabel had felt so sorry for the girl that she had ordered her son to partner Miss Carrington or face her wrath. But it was painfully obvious to Fanny that Bertie had no liking for dancing or for her budding charms.

The dance began, and Dennis immediately set about attempting to ingratiate himself in the eyes of the hitherto-unreachable Sophia. "Do you know that you're the most beautiful creature in this room?" he murmured into her ear as they danced the first figure.

"What flummery!" Sophy said archly, determined to concentrate on the man at hand and forget her pain. "I care nothing for flattery, Mr. Stanford."

Before he could respond, she whirled away from him to another partner, as the figure of the dance demanded. The next time they came together, he said challengingly, "I take exception to two points in your last remark to me, ma'am."

"What two points? I don't keep a mental record of my casual remarks, I'm afraid," she responded saucily.

"I can't tell you properly now, or I shall lose count," he laughed as they made a turn. "Besides, with all the changing of partners in these dances, we shall have to part between each sentence. You must sit out the next dance with me."

She had no opportunity to answer for the next few measures. When they again came together, he asked, "Well?"

"Well what, sir?"

"Will you sit out the next dance with me?"

"I'm afraid I can't. I'm promised to my cousin."

"Confound the fellow, why can't he stay with the partner he has now?" Dennis growled, but Sophy had already passed out of his hands.

It was not until three dances later that he was able to secure her companionship. The two took seats on a sofa in the corner of the ballroom, and Sophy leaned back against the cushions with a breathless sigh. "It's good to sit down," she admitted wearily.

"I suppose there is not much use in my interpreting that remark to mean it is good to be in my company, is there?" Dennis asked wistfully.

Sophy giggled. "It would be good to sit down in *anyone's* company after three long country dances."

"Thank you, ma'am. I see you have no intention of flattering *me*, even though you accuse me of flattering you. Which brings me to what I wanted to say to you. When I told you that you were the loveliest creature in this room, I meant every word. Did you think I was offering you Spanish coin?"

"Of course I did. There are at least three ladies in the room tonight who far outshine me."

"I deny that absolutely. Point them out to me, if you please."

"First, of course, there is Iris Bethune," Sophy said promptly. "Look over at her—she is standing at the punch bowl, see? With her golden hair tied up so, and her creamy-white dress, she looks like a princess in a fairy tale."

"Oh, well, if one likes fairy-tale princesses, she is quite remarkable, I grant you, but my taste runs to ladies of the *real* world," Dennis said, looking at his quarry with brazen appreciation.

"You are being quite silly, you know. And I don't like being stared at in that way," Sophy said in an attempt to depress his pretensions.

"I beg your pardon. But please continue, ma'am. Who else do you imagine outshines you?"

"This is a very absurd conversation, Mr. Stanford, but

if you insist, I can point out Mrs. Ashley-Davies, who came with the Squire's party. I think she is quite breath-taking.''

''There is only one lady here who takes *my* breath away, and *she* rewards me for my admiration by addressing me as Mr. Stanford. My name, as you well know, is Dennis.''

''I'll make a bargain with you, sir. If you'll promise to refrain from embarrassing me with your excessively grandiose compliments and your rather leering stares, I shall be happy to call you Dennis.''

Dennis drew himself erect in offended dignity. ''What a heartless thing to say! You've completely misjudged me, and you've maligned my perfectly innocent attempts to show my sincere admiration for you. I don't know whether to accept your bargain or not.''

''Well, while you're making up your mind, old fellow, I'm going to steal the lady from you,'' came an intruding voice. Marcus was standing before them, grinning down at them. With a little bow for Sophy, he added punctiliously, ''May I have your company for the next dance, Miss Edgerton?''

Sophy's heart lurched. While carrying on the flirtatious raillery with Dennis, she'd managed to put Marcus in the back of her mind. His unexpected presence threw her off balance. ''Well, I . . . I . . .'' she stuttered.

''Go away, Marcus, or I shall call you out,'' Dennis declared in mock fury. ''Have you no manners? How dare you intrude on a *tête-à-tête*?''

Marcus looked at Sophy in quizzical amusement. ''Am I intruding on a *tête-à-tête*, Miss Edgerton? Or am I right in supposing that you are ready to be rescued from his 'grandiose compliments and leering stares'?''

Dennis jumped to his feet and reached for an imaginary sword. ''On guard, you knave!'' he cried. ''Defend yourself! For having brazenly eavesdropped on a private conversation and attempting to steal away my lady, I shall run you through!''

Marcus laughed and pushed him back upon the sofa. ''Be quiet, you cod's head, or you'll have every eye on us. I didn't eavesdrop; your voices were not lowered enough.

And as for stealing away your lady, I claim it as my right. *Droit du seigneur* or something of the sort. What do you say, Miss Edgerton?''

"Are you sure you wish my company, sir?'' Sophy couldn't resist asking. "Aren't you afraid I'll tread on your toes, or faint in your arms, or do something equally shocking?''

Dennis chortled but said nothing. Marcus, although a little red about the ears, was not discomposed. "I'm feeling quite daring this evening, ma'am,'' he said banteringly, "and am quite willing to take my chances.''

"Well, then, how can I refuse?'' she said a bit breathlessly, rising and taking his arm.

"*I'm* the one who's going to do something shocking,'' Dennis threatened as they began to walk away. "I'm going to fetch a pair of dueling pistols, that's what I'm going to do!'' But Sophy and Marcus merely laughed and went on to the dance floor.

The music had scarcely begun, however, and Marcus had just whispered, "You may step on my toes as much as you wish, my dear, but you won't faint, will you?'' into her ear, when there was a commotion at the far end of the room. The far wall was lined with three pairs of French doors leading to a balustraded terrace, all of which were closed against the driving rain. But Mrs. Maynard had seen a face staring in at them from one of those doors and had fallen down in a swoon.

The music stopped, a crowd of ladies circled Mrs. Maynard and endeavored to bring her round with salts, burnt feathers and cold cloths. Marcus, with several of the other men at his heels, ran out into the rain to catch the miscreant. But the darkness and the downpour soon drove them to retreat, and they again returned empty-handed. By that time, Mrs. Maynard had come to her senses and was enjoying the sensation of being the center of an attentive audience. She was able to repeat her story three or four times before the crowd began to wander away. As far as she was concerned, the evening was an unqualified success.

The doughty searchers shook the raindrops from their hair and shoulders and returned to their activities. Card games and conversations were resumed, the musicians picked up their instruments, and the dancers took their places on the floor. "Well, Miss Edgerton," Marcus said teasingly, circling her waist with his arm and leading her into the Grand March, "you are a source of constant amazement. I know you threatened me with something shocking, but how did you manage to arrange *that* little mischance?"

Sophia, completely taken aback, stared up at him in horror. How *could* he think that she would have had anything to do with such a frightful incident? If he had struck her a blow on the face, she couldn't have felt more assaulted.

Marcus needed only one glimpse of her stricken eyes to realize that he'd been completely misunderstood. "Good God, Sophy, I was only joking!" he explained hastily. "You can't think that I—! I would never believe that you could have had anything to do with a Peeping Tom. Don't look at me so, girl! Don't you believe me?"

Sophy could hardly trust herself to speak. Her insides were quivering in affronted outrage. His explanations meant nothing to her; she couldn't even hear them. That he could imagine her to be so malevolent, so troublesome, so offensive was beyond anything she had anticipated. She was hurt to the bottom of her soul.

But her calm had to be maintained, the dance had to be danced, the amenities of civilized behavior had to be upheld. Somehow she managed to remain in step, to go through the motions without stumbling, to keep herself in time to the music. Marcus kept trying to tell her she'd misunderstood him, but she merely nodded. She couldn't trust herself to say a word. She knew she couldn't have kept her voice steady. At the end of the dance, she walked quickly from the floor, bid her grandmother a brusque good-night and left the room.

Marcus did not attempt to follow her. He was both ashamed of himself and furious with her. He'd known from the first that she was the sort to take offense at nothing. He'd only made a foolish little joke. Perhaps he shouldn't have said it, but he'd meant no harm. Blast the girl! Over-sensitive, overwrought and impassioned, she had an uncanny and provoking way of turning the most commonplace of circumstances into an emotional melodrama. This was just exactly the sort of contretemps he had anticipated all along. She was a tiresome, galling, irksome, infuriating troublemaker, and he would be damned if he would spoil his evening by chasing after her and trying to calm her down!

He threw himself into the activities of the ballroom with a vengeance. He danced twice with Iris, once each with his mother, little Fanny, Mrs. Carrington, and the spectacular Mrs. Ashley-Davies. He played a game of silver-loo with Dennis and Bertie, he told a number of funny stories at the late supper that was served buffet-style after midnight, and he behaved very much like the merriest of bridegrooms.

But the memory of a pair of horror-stricken eyes haunted him. Like an ulcer, it ate at his spirit without pause. Even after he'd gone to bed, he couldn't shut his eyes. That vexatious girl, whether she was aware of it or not, had managed, as usual, to destroy his peace of mind.

As for the vexatious girl in question, she too couldn't fall asleep. She didn't love him at all, she told herself. She hated him more than she would have thought possible. He had made up his mind about her the first moment he'd looked at her, and so great was his conceit that his opinions could not be changed no matter what she did. He thought of her as a zany, histrionic disaster from the first, and that was how she would remain in his eyes. Very well. If that was what she expected, that was what he would get. If he had found her behavior disturbing before, it would be *nothing* to what he would find in the week to come. "There are some possibilities for mischief you wouldn't *dream* of, my lord," she whispered into the darkness. "Just wait!"

Chapter Fourteen

SOPHY KNOCKED OVER the coffee pot the next morning. Marcus had come down to breakfast late, having been unable to fall asleep until well after dawn. His eyes were heavy-lidded and darkly circled, and an unpleasant pain was hammering away behind his left temple. His mood exactly matched his physical condition; sluggish and dyspeptic, he nevertheless had to face a houseful of guests to whom the daily routine was becoming boringly familiar and for whom he would have to concoct some entertaining diversions. To make matters more difficult, the rain was continuing to fall in a depressingly purposeful way, as if it intended to take permanent hold of the landscape.

He found the breakfast room occupied only by Sophy and Bertie, who were engaged in a low-voiced dispute which ceased the moment he appeared. He bid them a brusque good-morning, helped himself to a piece of dry toast, an egg and a cup of tea from the sideboard, and sat down at the table. Taking a quick look at their non-communicative expressions and lowered eyes, he decided that non-interference was the better part of valor, and he picked up his *Times* and buried himself in it. "Would you care for a cup of coffee, your lordship?" Sophy asked with over-bright friendliness.

Marcus regarded her suspiciously from over the top of the *Times*. "No, thank you," he said, "I've already taken some tea."

But she seemed not to be listening. She had already picked up a cup and saucer and was reaching for the coffee-pot which was standing on a tray in the center of the table. Belatedly, she looked up at the tea cup he had indicated. "Oh, you have *tea*—" she began, retracting her hand hastily. It clumsily struck the handle of the coffee-pot which she had just too-precipitously set down. The pot toppled over, the spout aimed right at him. The steaming brown liquid flooded the cloth and dripped over the side of the table while they all stared, frozen.

"*Sophy*!" Bertie cried in ill-concealed disgust.

"*Aaaah*!" shouted his lordship as the hot coffee reached his lap. He jumped to his feet muttering a curse and wincing in pain.

"Oh, I'm so *sorry*!" Sophy murmured, staring in apparent confusion at Marcus who, with arms spread wide, the newspaper still clutched in his right hand and soggy with brown wetness, was looking down at the awkward stain which was still spreading on his pale-yellow breeches. For a moment, while the pain still stung, he shut his eyes, bit his lips and remained immobile. But after a moment, Bertie came round to his side and attempted to dab at him with a serviette. Sophy asked, "Are you all right?" in a frightened little voice, and he opened his eyes.

He stared at her furiously but didn't utter a word. She tried to apologize again. "I'm most dreadfully—" she began.

"Spare me, please," he said abruptly. He threw the newspaper to the floor and strode rapidly from the room. But he cast a sharp glance at the girl as he passed her. Her expression was quite a familiar one. She looked completely contrite, but he'd seen that unfathomable glimmer at the back of her eyes before. The infuriating wench was laughing at him again.

In the afternoon, Mr. Carrington's eyeglasses disappeared. After half the servants in the household assisted Marcus in searching for them for well over two hours, the pince-nez turned up safe and snug behind a cushion on an easy chair which Sophy had occupied all afternoon while she had been engrossed in a novel. She had been, she said, completely unaware of the search.

In the evening, she lost a number of pennies in an easygoing game of copper-loo, and when the reckoning was made, she was so appalled at her losses (a sum of less than half a guinea) that she made a scene and ran out of the room in a huff.

By this time Marcus had had enough. He knew now that Sophy was shamming it, and he didn't like the game a bit. He followed her out of the room and stopped her at the foot of the stairway. "Just a minute, my dear," he said, catching her by the arm. "I'd like to have a word with you."

She raised her eyebrows coolly. "Yes, my lord?"

"How many more of these incidents shall we have to put up with before you will have punished me enough?" he asked, giving her a level look.

"Punished you? I don't understand."

"Oh, yes, you do, my girl. You understand me perfectly. It is *I* who don't understand. What have I done to so mortally offend you? I'm perfectly willing to make amends, you know."

Sophy tried to wrench herself from his hold. "I don't know what you're talking about," she said coldly and pulled herself free.

She managed to get up the first step. "Damn you, Sophy," he said between clenched teeth. He grasped both her shoulders and pulled her down with such violence that she fell against him. "I'd like to give you another shaking!"

She glared up at him furiously. "Go ahead," she challenged nastily, "if that sort of histrionic, impassioned behavior suits you."

Though the irony of her tone was not lost on him, it had little effect. He had lost control. He wanted to shake her senseless. He wanted to wring her neck. His pulse pounded in his ears, and he felt as furious as he had the other night when she'd returned from her ride over the downs and had slipped off her horse into his arms. His grasp on her tightened, and he saw her wince. Her lips trembled, and some unaffected part of his brain noted that she had a very pretty mouth. It was full-lipped, soft and very vulnerable. He leaned closer, not quite knowing why. She stared up at him, unmoving, her breath suspended.

The sound of his mother's voice behind him struck him like a pistol shot, even though it was calm, modulated and somewhat amused. "Really, Marcus," she said, walking past him in her usual, floating way, "you are much too severe with that child. Stop bullying her." And she continued down the hall without a pause and disappeared into the library.

Shaken, he loosened his hold on Sophy, who made a little sound (was it a laugh? a sob?) deep in her throat, tossed him a completely enigmatic look, and ran up the stairs. But he didn't move, except to look at his hands which were shaking. What had come over him? He had lost his head and had almost wanted to kill her, but he'd *actually* been of the verge of . . . ! He could scarcely believe it of himself. He didn't understand himself at all. He sat down on the bottom step and put his hand to his forehead. What troubled him was that, despite her tricks, despite her taunts, despite his distaste for her character and his own lack of control, he had actually been about to *kiss* her! And what bothered him most of all was that he hadn't done it.

The rain stopped during the night, and the morning brought another perfect June day. Many of the guests rose early, for the rain-washed air was inviting, and the out-of-doors beckoned. Marcus spent a good part of the morning in the stables, seeing that those who wanted to ride were properly mounted. By ten, they had all been dispatched except Iris, who, mounted and ready, was waiting for Marcus to saddle his own horse and ride with her. Just as Marcus was about to jump up into the saddle, Sophy appeared in the stable-yard. She was dressed in her becoming riding costume with its rakish, plumed hat, so her intent was obvious.

Marcus had been dreading the moment when he would have to face her, and the fact that the moment would now take place in front of his betrothed did nothing to make him less uneasy. But Sophy smiled at him with perfect complacency, bid Iris a cheerful good morning and nonchalantly asked if he could mount her.

Marcus rubbed his chin thoughtfully. "I have only the mare—which I would not *dare* to suggest—and my Spanish stallion, who might be a bit too skittish—"

Sophy looked at him from the corner of her eye, her brows raised haughtily. Marcus shrugged. "Oh, very well, *take* him!" he said, throwing his arms out in a gesture of hopelessness, "but don't expect a moment's sympathy if you break your neck."

The groom saddled the stallion, Marcus helped her up, and Sophy rode off with a merry wave. Iris looked at Marcus thoughtfully as he mounted. They rode out sedately and were well along the bridle path before she spoke. "You were almost *rude* to Miss Edgerton, I think," she suggested quietly. "It is not at all like you, Marcus."

"It's no more than the wench deserves," Marcus answered grumpily. "Come down this way. I want to show you the view from the hill."

Iris recognized that he'd purposely turned the subject, and she said no more about it.

Sophy meanwhile rode her stallion across the fields with real pleasure. He was remarkably fleet-footed and seemed to enjoy as much as she the freedom to run free through the open fields. She gave him his head, and they flew over the ground like the wind. It was not until she saw Bertie at the edge of the field that she drew the stallion to a stop. "I say," her cousin said admiringly, "that mount is *something like*!"

"Isn't he a beauty?" she agreed with a broad smile, leaning forward to stroke the animal's neck. "It makes one feel amost forgiving toward a certain gentleman."

Bertie glanced at her with a quick look of relief. "Do you mean it, Sophy? You won't carry on any more—?"

She grimaced and shook her head. "I said *almost*."

Bertie, annoyed, spurred his horse and galloped off. But after a few minutes he relented and turned back. Drawing alongside her, he asked teasingly, "Where's your new swain?"

"What new swain?" Sophy asked, startled. She felt the tingle of a blush as the memory of her scene with Marcus at the foot of the stairs flooded her mind. Had Bertie seen them? Was this his way of suggesting to her the impropriety of intimate encounters with a man who was betrothed to another?

But Bertie had not seen them at all. "How many swains have you? I mean Stanford, of course."

"Oh," Sophy said in well-concealed relief. "He's not a swain, you gudgeon. I saw him on the lawn playing his *gowf*. It seems to be a passion with him."

"I thought *you* were his passion."

"Stanford? You *are* a gudgeon."

Bertie shrugged. "Perhaps I am. I don't pretend to know anything about petticoat fever. But he does buzz about you like a fly."

"Only flirting, Bertie. It doesn't mean anything."

They turned their horses to the bridle path that edged the field and ambled along side by side. But Bertie's brow was puckered as if he were wrestling with a knotty problem. "I don't understand," he muttered at last. "What's the difference between flirting with a girl and . . . er . . . something more . . . more . . . ?"

"More significant?" Sophy suggested helpfully, trying to hide a grin. "Why, Bertie? Are you in the petticoat way, all of a sudden?"

Bertie reddened and looked sheepish. "Don't be a goose. I only thought it was time to . . . er . . . practice a bit. One has to learn *sometime*."

"I see. Well, as to your question, Bertie, I'd say that the difference between flirting and actual courtship is the feeling behind it. Flirting is just for fun—for practice, I suppose, to use your word—and the other is more serious."

"Have you ever had one of those . . . er . . . more serious affairs?"

Sophy laughed. "Several," she answered promptly.

"*Several*? But you've never even been betrothed!" Bertie, much shocked, stared at her in confusion.

Sophy tried to clarify the matter. "Well, you see, the feeling didn't last long enough to lead to a betrothal."

"Then I still don't understand. Why wouldn't you call that flirting?"

"Because while it lasted, it *felt* serious."

"I see," Bertie said thoughtfully. "What you're saying is that Stanford doesn't feel anything serious toward you, while on the other hand, someone like Dilly does."

"Dilly?" Sophy asked curiously. "Are you speaking of Lawrence Dillingham? I'd forgotten all about him. Are you suggesting that the idiot fancies himself in *love* with me?"

Bertie shrugged. "So he says. And from what little I know of the matter, it seemed so to me. Of course, the clunch hasn't written a word to me since we left, so he may have gotten over it by this time."

"I sincerely hope so," Sophy said fervently, "or we shall not have the least pleasure in his company when we get back."

Bertie was not interested in matters so far into the future. It was the present that concerned him. "Does one always *know* if one is flirting or involved in something more serious?" he asked, carefully casual.

"No, not always," Sophy answered, looking at him curiously. "Bertie, are *you* thinking seriously of—?"

"Of falling in love? No, of course not. Besides, she doesn't even *look* at me, especially if Stanford's anywhere in the vicinity."

Sophy's mouth dropped open. "Fanny? You've taken a fancy to little *Fanny*?"

"Confound it, that's what I don't know!" he burst out. "Until yesterday, I'd have laughed at the mere suggestion. But last night, Mama made me dance with her while Stanford was busy flirting with you, and—"

Sophy's lips twitched. "And—?"

Bertie shook his head in bewilderment and self-disgust. "Dashed if I know. She kept looking over her shoulder at Stanford. I might have been a piece of furniture for all the notice she took of me. Made me so blasted angry, I wanted to wring the chit's little neck!"

Sophy was about to laugh, but something in his tale struck a chord, and the laugh caught in her throat. She stared at her cousin in sudden fascination. "You wanted to wring her neck, and you think it might be . . . *love*?"

"Sounds idiotic, I know. But it *felt* like love. Something like. And today, I can't seem to get her out of my mind. . ."

This engrossing subject so absorbed them that they didn't hear hoofbeats until Marcus and Iris were almost upon them. It was with real reluctance that they dropped their conversation and turned to greet the other riders.

The bridle path was not wide enough for four abreast, so Iris rode ahead with Bertie as Marcus drew up alongside Sophy. "How do you like Picaro, Miss Edgerton? He's one of my favorites, you know."

"Is that his name? Picaro? Is it Spanish?"

"Yes. It means rascal. Has my rascal been behaving himself?"

"Oh, yes, just beautifully," Sophy assured him, patting the horse affectionately.

"It was wise of you to start off your acquaintance with him with this easy canter. When you get to know each other, after a couple of days, you'll be able to gallop with him quite easily. You'd be quite amazed at the speed he can reach."

Sophy stiffened and turned a pair of glinting eyes at him. "*Would* I?" she asked coldly. The wretched man had done it to her again. He'd assumed she needed days to know her mount, when she'd had his measure in minutes! *Why, you overstuffed pomposity*, she wanted to say, *I've already raced him*! But she held her tongue. "Why don't we go out in the field," she suggested brightly, "and try a slightly brisker pace right now?"

Marcus looked a bit dubious, but he suspected that a show of caution would offend her. "Very well, if you like," he agreed. "Iris? Bertie? Do you want to have a little run across the field?"

The four turned off the path into the field and began to canter. The pace was mildly brisk, far slower than Sophy had earlier raced Picaro, but Marcus made the mistake of cautioning Miss Edgerton "not to overdo it." She responded by flashing Bertie a speaking look and surreptitiously giving her horse a sharp jab with her spur. The horse broke into a flying gallop. Sophy threw out her arms dramatically and screamed.

Bertie, who knew perfectly well that she was shamming, swore viciously under his breath, but Iris cried out in alarm, "He's *bolting*!" Marcus immediately spurred his horse into action, shouting back over his shoulder at Bertie, "Go and fetch the groom!"

Bertie, with a snort of disgust, turned his horse and started for the stables. But Iris remained immobile as she watched the riders rapidly disappearing from view. Her eyes were distended in alarm. "Oh, my God!" she breathed, gripping her reins with white-knuckled tightness.

Bertie drew up beside her. "Don't worry, Miss Bethune," he said, a slight edge of sarcasm coloring his tone, "you can take my word that Sophy will be quite all right."

Iris turned her head slowly in his direction. Her eyes had taken on a blind look, and it was a long moment before she seemed to bring him into focus. "I wasn't thinking about her," she said.

Sophy's hat had blown off, and she laughed in sheer pleasure as the wind whipped her face and hair. She heard the thunder of a second horse behind hers, and she knew Marcus was following. She leaned forward, putting her arms about the horse's neck, pretending to be hanging on for dear life. Feigning an expression of terror, she cast a look behind her. It was Marcus, all right, pushing his mount to the limit. But she had no intention of letting him catch up with her just yet. Let him suffer, she said to herself viciously.

They thundered across the fields like the wind. They sailed over stone walls and hedges as if they were winged. Sophy had not enjoyed such a wild ride since her devil-may-care childhood. With Marcus close behind to add to the tension, her blood raced with excitement. She would have liked to ride on forever. But looming up before her was a wide creek—too wide to jump. There was no time now to let Marcus catch her. She wouldn't be able to continue with the pretense that the horse had ridden away with her. She would have to rein in her horse and end the game. Stopping now would reveal to Marcus that she'd had control of the animal all along, but she had no other choice. She had to end the game.

Marcus, intent on closing the small gap between them and plucking her to safety, was completely unprepared for Picaro's abrupt halt. As he thundered up alongside the horse, he saw clearly that the girl was reining in. "*Sophy, you—!*" he burst out furiously, taking no notice of the stream just ahead. But his horse noticed. The surprised animal instinctively reared up in rebellion, sending his rider flying through the air. Then the disconcerted beast charged ahead, splashing through the creek and galloping off to parts unknown.

Marcus landed heavily on the bank of the creek. He felt a sharp crack of pain and knew no more. When a series of strange sensations began to creep into his consciousness, he had no idea how long he'd been senseless. His first awareness was of a blinding pain in his head and another in his leg. Something cool and wet had been laid across his forehead. And an urgent, tearful voice was murmuring brokenly, "Please don't be dead! Please, *please* don't be dead!"

"Sophy, shut up," he muttered grumpily, not attempting the tremendous effort of opening his eyes. "I'm not dead!"

"*Marcus!*" she gasped joyfully, and he felt his shoulders being lifted. It took him a moment to realize that he was being pressed against her in a tremulous embrace. He had evidently been lying with his head on her lap before she'd hugged him. The movement caused his head to throb more violently, and even his leg seemed to respond adversely to the shift of his position, but he made no complaint. Despite the pain, there was something eminently satisfying in being clutched against her breast. Her softness was a luxurious pillow, and he could smell the fragrance of her skin. She was gently rocking him, making small, crooning noises of relief. He sighed and snuggled against her, not aware that his arms had tightened around her at the same time. He refused to think. He wanted only to stay just where he was, snuggly ensconced in her embrace. There would be plenty of time to think later.

"Marcus, you haven't gone off again, have you?" she asked hesitantly after a while.

"No," he murmured, not moving.

"Do you think you might try to stand? To see if you're all right?"

She was certainly an irritating female. Couldn't she leave well-enough alone? He stirred and tried to sit up, but his head swam alarmingly.

"Oh, Marcus, you *are* hurt!" she said in horror.

He opened his eyes and frowned in pain. "What did you expect, you little wretch?" he muttered, feeling the back of his head to determine the source of his pain.

"Oh, dear," Sophy moaned, "you've a dreadful lump—"

"I'm quite aware of that, ma'am." A wave of resentment washed over him. The girl had not only caused this painful injury; she'd made a complete fool of him, tricking him into believing the horse had bolted with her. They might both have been *killed*! "I suppose I ought to be grateful to you," he added sullenly, rubbing the throbbing lump on his head, "for the fact that my skull is still intact."

"I . . . I'm so *sorry*!" she said in abject misery. "I never *dreamed* that such a thing would happen."

"Are you trying to pretend that you set off on this mad chase without intending to do me *some* sort of injury?"

"Marcus! You can't believe—! Please don't look at me so. I *never* intended to do you harm!" But here her eyes wavered under the glare of his anger. "Not *this* sort of harm."

"No? Then *what* sort of harm had you in mind?" The pain in his head and ankle was becoming more intolerable, he was becoming aware of a soreness in his shoulder and arm, and the only source of comfort seemed to come from venting his spleen on the person who had brought him to this fix. "You'd *already* abused me, insulted me, embarrassed me, scalded me, set my house afire, endangered my guests, terrified me nearly out of my wits, and driven me to the brink of madness. What is there *left*, short of outright murder?"

Sophy lowered her head, her eyes overflowing with tears which rolled down her cheeks unheeded. Marcus made a shaky attempt to get to his feet. She rushed to his side to assist him. "Don't touch me!" he growled, having worked himself up to a real fury. "*Just don't touch me!*"

He dragged himself to a nearby tree and pulled himself up by clinging to its trunk. Sophy followed behind him, arms pathetically outstretched to assist him if he fell. But he managed without her help, the effort so exhausting him that he leaned against the tree, panting.

"Do you think you could climb up on P-Picaro?" she asked timidly, indicating the horse who was munching placidly on the grass nearby.

He shook his head. "If you want to help me," he said to her curtly, "find me a branch or a stick that I can use as a cane."

"You can't mean to *walk* home! That ankle may be broken! You'll do yourself terrible harm."

"Oh, will I?" he asked with a twisted, ironic smile. "How convenient that would be for you. You could then say, with impunity, that all this is *my* fault!"

One look at the girl's white, anguished face told him he'd gone too far. "I shan't have to walk home," he said in quick explanation. "My groom must be on the lookout for us by this time. I only mean to get out in the open where he can find me."

"B-But your ankle—!"

"Isn't broken. Only a sprain."

She found a branch, stripped it of leaves and gave it to him. He took it wordlessly and, without a glance in her direction, started to limp homeward. Sophy hurried alongside, pleading with him tremulously to lean on her. He waved her aside. "Get on the horse and ride ahead," he ordered. "There's no earthly use in your hanging about."

But Sophy wouldn't leave him. As Marcus limped out of the shelter of the trees and started across the field, Sophy ran to pick up the horse's reins. She led the animal into the clearing and fell into step a few paces behind her crippled victim. They made a bedraggled, pathetic procession: Marcus, hobbling and wincing with each painful step, led the way; Sophy, dishevelled and tear-stained, the embodiment of mortified anguish, followed meekly a few paces behind; and, bringing up the rear, the horse, Picaro, plodded along peacefully, completely indifferent to the human distress in front of him.

Chapter Fifteen

AT LEAST HER grandmother had agreed that it would be advisable for them to leave. That decision had been made at the conclusion of a very long, very difficult discussion between them. It had been painful enough, earlier that day, to have to sit, humiliated and miserable, in the corner of the drawing room, shunned by everyone in the household while they'd waited for news of Marcus's condition. But when everyone else was relieved by the doctor's report (he'd suffered only a mild concussion, a sprained ankle and various minor bruises and would be up and about in a day or two), Sophy still had ahead of her the ordeal of facing her grandmother.

Exhausted, red-eyed, and wracked with sobs, she had confessed the entire story to the tight-lipped Lady Alicia. She had spared no detail, from the circumstances leading to the eavesdropping at the theater to the events of the wild race to the creek. When she began, she'd hoped that her grandmother would grant that she had some justification for her behavior—that Marcus's consistent disparagement of her character would be a sort of vindication. But even to her own ears, her motivation sounded flimsy, and as the story unfolded, she became more and more ashamed.

But her grandmother hadn't scolded. In fact, she'd said very little beyond asking a few questions to clarify the

tale. Her face rigidly composed, the old lady had listened
patiently to every detail, had nodded in agreement when
Sophy suggested that they leave at first light the following
morning, and had rung for Miss Leale. She'd ordered the
worried-looking abigail to bathe the girl immediately, feed
her some broth and put her to bed. Sophy was curiously
upset by the lack of a scolding. If her conduct was beyond
censure, the enormity of her crimes must be terrible indeed.
She had burst into a fresh flood of tears and had to be led,
weeping, from her grandmother's room.

But Lady Alicia was not unaffected by Sophy's story. It
was quite obvious to her that her granddaughter had fallen
in love with Marcus. The young Earl was the complete
antithesis of the sort of man Sophy might hope to attract.
He was repelled by the very qualities which made the girl
what she was. That knowledge had wounded Sophy, and
the wound cut deep. Alicia had no doubt that it would heal
in time, but the scar would always be with her. Her heart
twisted in pain for her granddaughter—the goddess Venus
was ever a spiteful bitch!

Sophy refused to go to bed until her things were packed.
She wanted nothing to delay their departure the following
morning. But when she tapped at her grandmother's door
the next day at the stroke of seven, bonnetted and cloaked
for the journey, she found Lady Alicia still in her bed.
"Grandmama, why aren't you ready?" she demanded impatiently.

"I shall be ready in due course," Alicia responded
calmly. "We shan't be able to go much before noon."

"Why not?"

"Because, my dear, you cannot run off in secret, like a
thief with the family silver in his sack. We must say
proper goodbyes to Charlotte and her guests. And *you*, my
dear, must pay a call on Lord Wynwood, ask after his
health and make a sincere and proper apology."

"Grandmama, *no*!"

"Granddaughter, *yes*! And since we must permit him to
sleep for at least another few hours, our departure must be

postponed until you've had a talk with him. I think you should explain everything to him, just as you did to me. It's the only course I consider seemly.''

Her grandmother was adamant and would brook no argument. Sophy had no choice but to acquiesce. Two hours later, when she'd learned from his man that Lord Wynwood was awake and willing to see her, she tapped at his door. In the hopeful expectation that the interview would be brief and that she could quit this place—the scene of so much humiliation—immediately thereafter, she had not removed her cloak, and she carried her bonnet clutched in her hand. A female voice bid her to come in. Timidly, she pushed open the door.

Marcus, wearing a green, frogged dressing gown, was lying on a chaise in a large, sunny alcove of his bedroom. His head was cushioned by a huge pillow, and his left foot, thickly bandaged at the ankle, was resting on a tufted bolster. Iris Bethune sat at his side, an open newspaper in her lap. "Oh, I didn't mean to interrupt . . ." Sophy said awkwardly.

"You're not interrupting," Marcus said with a leer. "We've been expecting you."

Iris looked quickly from one to the other. "We've quite finished with the important news," she said, folding the paper and rising. "Marcus doesn't like being read to, in any case." She patted him gently on the shoulder. "See you later, my dear."

Sophy felt very much the intruder. "Please don't go on my account," she urged. "I shall stay only a moment."

Marcus hooted. "If you think you'll escape me as easily as that, Miss Edgerton, you're out in your reckoning. It will take more than a moment to hear what I have to say to you."

"Don't tease her, Marcus," Iris said kindly, crossing to the door. "And remember that the doctor said to refrain from any exertion until the headache is gone."

The warning was aimed more at Sophy than at Marcus. Sophy colored, and Iris, having made her point, quickly left the room. There was a moment of awkward silence. "I . . . I hope, your lordship, that you are . . . er . . . feeling more the thing . . ." Sophy ventured unhappily.

" 'Your lordship,' is it? How is it that I was 'Marcus' when I lay in your lap yesterday, and I've been reduced to 'your lordship' today?"

Sophy crimsoned. "I *never* called you Marcus!" she protested vehemently.

"Yes, you did. Several times. But I don't intend to be thrown off the track by irrelevant discussions. Sit down, please. There are a few matters I'm determined to clarify before this interview is over."

"I'm afraid, sir, that . . . er . . . I haven't much time . . ." She tried surreptitiously to edge toward the door. If matters became insupportable, she could merely dash out of the room.

"Haven't much time?" he asked impatiently. "What flapdoodle is this?"

"Well, you see, we'll be leaving as soon as . . . I mean, the carriage has already been ordered—"

"Carriage? You're thinking of *leaving*?"

"Yes, sir. My grandmother and I thought—"

"Well, you can both think again. I won't have it." He eyed her askance. "Is this one of your tricks to avoid answering my questions? It won't wash, my girl. Sit down, I say, or I shall have to get up and use force."

Sophy made a restraining gesture and scurried to the chair vacated by Miss Bethune. "The doctor said you're not to exert yourself."

"Then see that you do nothing to *force* me to exertion. Now, Miss, if you'll take off that cloak, we may be comfortable."

She obediently untied the cord at her neck, let the cloak slip back from her shoulders, and turned nervously to face him. "What . . . what is it you wish to ask me, sir?"

"What do you *think* I wish to ask? Why did you *do* it?"

"Ride off that way, you mean? I . . . haven't a very good reason, I'm afraid." She turned the bonnet round and round in her fingers. "I suppose I wanted to show you that I could ride Picaro as well as you."

"Well, you certainly showed me," he said drily.

"I'm truly sorry that you were injured because of my foolishness," she said, the bonnet trembling in her unsteady grasp. "I never meant it to be more than a little . . . joke. . ."

She braced herself to receive his cutting retort. But Marcus said simply, "I know that." She looked at him in surprise. He was looking a bit shamefaced himself. "I didn't mean all those malevolent things I said to you yesterday. I realized as soon as I came to my senses that you didn't mean to injure me. It was only the pain that made me so rancorous—the pain and the humiliation . . ."

"Humiliation?"

"Yes . . . of being thrown." He glanced up at her with a sheepish grin. "I'd never been thrown by a horse in my life before."

"You are being very kind to me, my lord," Sophy said, her eyes on the bonnet in her lap, "but you didn't say anything to me yesterday that I haven't said to myself. I've been very foolish and headstrong . . . I've tried to ruin your lovely houseparty, and . . . I've caused you . . . bodily injury. I can only h-hope you'll forgive m-me . . . and that you'll be able to . . . to forget all this after I've gone." With that humble and penitent apology, she rose from her chair and started hurriedly for the door.

But he sat up and caught her arm as she brushed by the chaise. "Sophy, *don't*! There's no need for this . . . self-castigation. Do you think I don't know that I'm somehow at fault in all this? From the day of your arrival, I've felt your disapproval. I know I've somehow offended you. Can't you tell me what it is I've done? I want, more than *anything*, to find a way to . . . end these hostilities between us."

Sophy was dumbstruck by his sincerity. She turned her head away so that he wouldn't see how shaken she was. "There *was* something," she admitted reluctantly, "but it seems so . . . so *insignificant* now."

"I won't find it insignificant."

"Yes, you will. You *must* find it so. It all seems so *silly* now."

He said nothing, but merely watched her while she gathered the courage to tell him. After a momentary struggle, she faced him. "It was . . . you see, I was utterly *affronted* . . . when you said I was a . . . shatterbrained hysteric—"

"Sophy! I *never* said a thing like that to you!" he objected, horrified.

"Not to me. To Stanford. I . . . overheard you at the theater."

"The theater? I don't—" He wrinkled his brow in his attempt to recall the incident. "Oh, good God! I seem to *remember* . . . ! It was at Drury Lane . . . Coriolanus! But how could you have heard—?"

Sophy blushed painfully. "I saw you coming down the corridor together. It was shortly after I'd made that . . . scene at the bookstore, do you remember? I didn't want to face you, so I . . .hid behind a door. You and Stanford stopped just outside my hiding place to talk. There was nothing I could do but remain where I was and listen."

"You overheard our entire conversation? Good Lord! It must have been hideously vulgar. Dennis and I can be quite . . . ungentlemanly in our private talks. Sophy, I . . . I don't know what to say!"

"There's nothing you *ought* to say. It was a private conversation, and I had no right—! Besides . . ."

"Besides?"

She turned away again. "Besides, I'm beginning to agree with your assessment of my character," she said with a little catch in her voice. "I *am* a sh-shatterbrained hysteric. And a . . . a zany little d-disaster, too."

He winced. "I was *afraid* you might have overheard that bit of malignity."

"I don't b-blame you for it," she said with a tiny sob. "Not any more. It's all quite t-true!"

Deeply shamed, Marcus clumsily lowered his bandaged foot to the floor and stood up. Sophy jumped up and ran to him. "Marcus, what are you *doing*? The doctor *told* you—!"

"The devil with the doctor!" Ignoring the pain which his implusive action brought on, he pulled her roughly into his arms. "Sophy," he implored, "you can't believe that I *still* think of you that way! You must *know* that my feelings have passed far beyond . . ." He paused helplessly, not knowing how to prove to her that those cruel words, uttered in an ignorant past, had no longer any meaning or reality for him. Pinioning her to him with one arm, he

tilted her face up to his with his other hand. She was
staring at him in wide-eyed breathlessness. Her lips, still
swollen from a night of weeping, looked so achingly
desirable that his innards clenched in a hungry spasm. As
had happened once before, he felt himself irresistably
drawn to kiss her. This time there was no interruption. His
mouth found hers, and he pressed her to him with a
pleading urgency.

The fervor of this unexpected and illicit embrace left
them both shaken and amazed. They stared at each other
for a long moment. Then he dropped down on the chaise
and buried his head in his hands. When she managed to
regain control of her breathing, Sophy approached him and
put a hand on his shoulder. "It's all right, Marcus," she
said softly. "It . . . was only an . . . accident. I don't . . .
refine on it too much."

He lifted his eyes to hers. "No. You . . . we . . .
mustn't. I hope you can forgive me. I don't know what's
happening to me." He grinned at her with wry self-mockery.
"It's *I* who has become the shatterbrained hysteric."

"Don't be so silly. Please lie down again, Mar—Lord
Wynwood. I would not like your mother or Miss Bethune
to think I had upset you."

"You needn't be afraid to call me Marcus," he said
with a touch of bitterness. "There's nothing improper in
that, at least." Paying no attention to her request that he
lie down, he grasped the hand she'd placed on his shoulder.
"You won't leave, will you, Sophy? Promise me you'll
stay til the end of the week. I won't believe myself forgiven
if you go."

She hesitated. Her feelings were so confused that she
didn't know what she wanted, or what was the proper
course of action. "But . . . there's nothing to forgive—"
she vacillated.

"Please, Sophy, you *must* stay. It's only for a few days.
We *need* those days, if only to prove to ourselves—and
each other—that we can be sensible and . . . normal. And
that we can . . . part as friends."

Sophy nodded. She couldn't resist his appeal. She helped
him to lie back on the chaise and went swiftly to the door.

Her feelings were in a turmoil and would require several hours of calm reflection to be adequately soothed. In the meantime, the only thing she knew was that she'd never been happier in her life . . . nor more miserable.

Chapter Sixteen

LADY ALICIA HADN'T PACKED. Her friend Charlotte, having learned of her intention to leave, simply refused to permit it. "I shan't have you running off like this," she'd declared, adamantly seating herself on the edge of Alicia's bed. "Yes, I'm quite well aware that my son has sustained a few injuries as a result of a riding accident, but I will not hear of anyone's taking the blame for it. No, don't argue with me, my dear. I have no time to bandy words. Mrs. Cresley wishes to consult me about tomorrow's menus, so I must be off. Put away those trunks immediately and come downstairs. My yellow tea roses have bloomed in the night, and I'd like to show them to you."

She had moved gracefully but inexorably to the door in her customary cloud of sheer silk. But before she drifted out, she reminded Alicia to refrain from berating Sophy for an occurrence which was not the girl's fault. "It would be presumptious of mere mortals to credit or blame ourselves for the things which should properly be laid at the door of Fortune herself," she said poetically.

Therefore, when Sophy returned from her talk with Marcus, she found her grandmother already reconciled to remaining for the duration of the allotted fortnight. Each was quite surprised at the other's sudden change of mind, but they each decided to refrain from asking questions which might disturb the equilibrium. It was best to let sleeping dogs lie.

Their unspoken accord was the beginning of a new phase of this unpredictable adventure. It presaged two days of unalloyed pleasure. The weather and everyone's disposition turned uncommonly sunny. When the other guests realized that Lady Wynwood and Marcus did not hold Sophy responsible for his accident, the atmosphere cleared. The air rang with laughter and good will. Even the children frolicked on the lawn without dispute as their elders strolled the grounds, flirted and sported with renewed zest, and smiled in satisfaction at everything around them.

There were only two clouds darkening the bright horizon, and even they did not appear to be threatening. One dark cloud was Marcus's infirmity. But even though his sprained ankle prevented him from partaking in sport, his headaches had all but disappeared and his spirits seemed to be as high as always. The other cloud was the mystery of the reappearing face in the window. Like a ghoulish apparition, the pallid face would be discovered at the onset of darkness in the window of whatever room had been selected as the evening's gathering place. But even this cloud did not seem to betoken a storm, for the apparition caused no harm and would promptly disappear as soon as it was noticed. It soon ceased to be a cause for hysteria. It became, instead, a puzzling but minor nuisance.

Of course, since even Wynwood in June was not quite heaven, not everyone could be expected to be happy at all times. Little Fanny Carrington was not always happy. She was not faring very well in her efforts to attach Dennis Stanford. It was inexplicable to her, and to her sympathetic sister, that the otherwise-knowing dandy could prefer Miss Edgerton to Fanny. The sisters spent hours studying Fanny's face in the mirror with critical objectivity and were agreed that Fanny had by far the better face; Miss Edgerton's nose (being too small and inclined to turn up ever so slightly at the tip) was markedly inferior to the straight purity of

Fanny's. Miss Edgerton's hair, too, was unremarkable, being not really red but quite brown in most light, while Fanny's glinted with golden highlights at all times. And Fanny's hair had the added advantage of being quite long and straight, which permitted her to dress it in an infinite variety of styles, while Miss Edgerton's short curls could merely be brushed into a single, simple, unstylish mode. Cissy pointed out in fairness that Miss Edgerton's eyes were "speaking," but she was quick to add that her mouth was much too full to give her any pretensions to real beauty.

Thus the girls were at a loss to account for Mr. Stanford's preference. The only possibility that presented itself to them was that Miss Edgerton was old enough to wear her gowns cut enticingly low at the bosom. Therefore, in order to enter into a more equable competition with her rival in matters of bosom-display, Fanny proceeded to pull her dress down as far as she could, tucking the neckline into the top of her stays. But her mother would invariably yank the dress up almost to the neck, a height that Fanny and Cissy considered childishly prudish.

The tug-of-war between mother and daughter grew more violent with each passing day, until one of the dresses tore under the strain. Mrs. Carrington (who had at first found the battle somewhat amusing) lost her temper, slapped her daughter soundly and warned her that the next time Fanny lowered her neckline, she would be banished from all adult society for the remainder of their stay.

This ended Fanny's attempt to compete with her rival in matters of décolletage. Sophy was acknowledged to have the bosom-advantage, but the sisters declined to accept as inevitable Sophy's untimate victory in the battle for Mr. Stanford.

Bertie, whose mild attempts at flirtation were remarkable only in the lack of notice that was taken of them, nevertheless managed to maintain his natural amiability. Mooning about after a "petticoat" was not his style, and further discussion with Sophy on the nature of "serious attachments" convinced him that what he felt for Fanny could not be very serious. So he continued to admire her

golden skin, perfect nose and coltish movements from a
safe distance, gave her an occasional, extravagant compliment, and accepted her arrogant disdain with a complacent
disregard. For his cool-headed acceptance of the situation
and his praiseworthy lack of self-pity, he was complimented
highly by his observant host. Marcus had regarded the boy
with affection and interest since the night at West Hoathly,
and often sought out his company. Bertie was highly
flattered by the attention he received from Marcus. He had
achieved a highly-valued place in the select circle of
Marcus's intimates. He might be considered a failure as a
beau, but that failure was more than mitigated by his
having gained a friend.

For Sophy, the peaceful hours had the quality of
convalescence. Her sensibilities had long been rubbed raw
by the awareness of his lordship's scornful disapproval.
But now she felt so comforted by that last talk with him
that her spirit was suffused with a healing, if melancholy,
serenity. She moved through the hours in a haze of
bittersweet contentment, at the center of which was the
delicious secret that he cared for her a little—a secret
edged on the outer fringes of her consciousness by a
wistful acceptance of the knowledge that he never could be
hers.

Even the moment in which he'd discovered her playing
with the dogs did not shake her euphoric composure. He
and Iris had come strolling through the field behind the
stables and had discovered Sophy romping with two of the
hunting dogs. "I see your pathological fear of dogs does
not apply to hunters," Marcus had remarked drily, the
twinkle in his eyes the only sign that he remembered their
last intimacy.

"I am embarked on a program of self-improvement, my
lord," she'd responded, grinning guiltily. "I'm slowly
building up my courage to face Mrs. Carrington's Shooshi."

Since the hunting dogs were twice the size of Mrs.
Carrington's spaniel, Marcus emitted a hearty guffaw. Iris,
who didn't know that Sophy's scene with the Carrington
dog had been a pretense, didn't understand this exchange
at all. But she chose not to ask for enlightenment; she

merely smiled politely and passed by on Marcus's arm.
Neither Sophy nor Marcus noticed the strained quality of
that smile.

After dinner on the evening of the second day of the
new, harmonious *entente*, while the usual card games were
being organized in the drawing room, Mrs. Carrington sat
down at the piano in the adjoining music room and played
a few light airs for her own amusement. She played quietly,
not wishing to distract the card-players from their concentration or the young folk from their flirtations. But the
music carried her away, and before she knew it she was
playing a little French dance tune with lively gusto. Dennis,
who was holding a very unpromising hand in a game of
Hearts with Cissy Carrington, perked up his ears. "I say,
Mrs. Carrington," he called to her, "is that a waltz you're
playing?"

"Yes, it is, Mr. Stanford. It's called *Valse Gracieux*.
It's only recently been published. Do you like it?"

To Cissy's annoyance, he dropped his cards and went to
the music room doorway. "It's charming. Would you play
it again? Perhaps I can find a partner and dance to it."

"Oh, do you know the steps?" asked Iris with interest.
"They say that the waltz is the rage in Paris."

Lady Alicia looked up from her cards long enough to
comment acidly that Paris had ever been the center of
vulgarity and debauchery, and that the popularity of the
waltz in that city only proved its unacceptability.

"Oh, pooh, Grandmama," Sophy put in. "Even the
patronesses at Almack's have given their approval to an
occasional waltz. Don't be so old-fashioned."

Lady Alicia shook her head in disapproval. "At Almack's
too? Shocking! What *is* the world coming to? Such gyrations
would never have been permitted in my day." With a
grunt, she turned back to her cards.

Dennis came up to her chair and put an arm around her
shoulders. "But, Lady Alicia," he pleaded with his most
polished smile, "surely you'd have no objection to our
indulging in a little waltz here in the privacy of Wynwood?"

She pushed his arm away playfully. "Coxcomb, don't

think to cut a wheedle with *me*! I'm not a simpering miss. But go ahead and dance, if you want to. What does it matter what *I* think? If the patronesses at Almack's have given the dance their sanction, there's precious little difference *my* opinion will make. So go away and leave me to my cards.''

There was a burst of approval from the younger set at Lady Alicia's "permission," and an area in the center of the drawing room floor was cleared. Mrs. Carrington agreed to play for them. "Now," Dennis asked, standing in the middle of the room with arms outstretched, "who will waltz with me?"

"Oh, let me!" Fanny volunteered, running up to him.

"Have you ever danced the waltz?" Dennis asked suspiciously.

"Well, no, but . . . I can learn it quickly, I'm sure."

"I'm sure you can, my dear, but I think you should sit and watch it for a while before you try. Isn't there anyone here who has tried it before?"

There followed a moment of silence. Fanny returned to her chair and Iris looked at Sophy questioningly. "Didn't you say you had danced it at Almack's, Miss Edgerton? *Do* show us how to perform it—I would *so* much like to learn."

Sophy edged back into her chair. "I . . . I *have* performed it once or twice, but I'd rather not . . .''

"Why not, Sophy?" Dennis demanded.

Sophy cast a quick look at Marcus who was sitting on the sofa next to his betrothed. "I'm not very expert," she said lamely.

Marcus smiled at her encouragingly. "Don't be shy, Sophy. We will not be a critical audience."

Sophy made a face at him. "No, I'm sure you won't. You'll all be sitting here waiting for me to take a tumble, or to charge into a lamp table. Well, I won't do it! I've turned over a new leaf, and I shan't do *anything* that can even *remotely* lead to disaster."

This new outspokenness on Sophy's part was a refreshing change, and they all laughed. But Marcus didn't let her excuse go unchallenged. "I'm perfectly sure that no catastrophe will result from a bit of waltzing,'' he said with a grin.

''And as soon as you've demonstrated the steps, you may stop if you wish,'' Iris suggested. ''Would that be agreeable?''

Other voices joined to urge her to agree. Sophy couldn't refuse without appearing curmudgeonly. So she nodded to Dennis, who promptly crowed with success. With pomp and ceremony, he offered Sophy his arm. Mrs. Carrington played an amusing little fanfare, and Sophy was led to the floor.

For several minutes, she and Dennis demonstrated the movements of the waltz to a very slow piano accompaniment. They kept at arm's length while Dennis explained exactly what they were doing: step, together, back, step, together, turn . . . It all looked quite simple and very decorous.

''Now show us what it looks like when you're really doing it full tilt on the dance floor,'' Bertie suggested.

''Oh, yes, *do*!'' Iris urged. ''Now that we've learned the nature of the movements, we shall truly appreciate a look at the finished performance.''

''Of course,'' Dennis agreed with alacrity, ignoring Sophy's hesitation. ''Music, please, Mrs. Carrington—loud and lively!''

The music started briskly, and Dennis swept the reluctant Sophy into his arms. They swirled into the dance with graceful elegance. Dennis was a polished dancer, holding his partner with a strong guiding hand at her back and tilting her so that she leaned back on his arm at just the right angle. They whirled into their first turn to the sound of an admiring gasp from the onlookers.

But their pleasure in the waltz was to be short-lived. The dancers had barely executed the second turn when there was a loud rattle at the windows. Two of casements burst open—they had been pushed in from outside. There was a frightening crash of breaking glass, and a male figure tumbled in through the flying debris. While the women screamed in fright, the intruder scrambled to his feet and made directly for Dennis. ''*Unhand* that girl, you cad!'' he cried, swinging his fist at Dennis's jaw and sending him sprawling to the ground.

The women shrieked even louder. Sophy, paying no attention to the wild intruder, dropped to her knees beside her fallen partner. Sir Walter and Julian jumped up from their cards, overturning the card table with a crash. Mr. Carrington rose so hastily from the chair in which he'd been reading that it, too, fell over, bringing down with it a nearby end-table and triple-branched candelabrum. While he stamped out the flames, Sir Walter and Julian rushed toward the miscreant, followed closely by Bertie and the limping Marcus.

Sir Walter and Julian reached him first and, without much trouble, wrestled the fellow to the ground. There he lay on his stomach, with Sir Walter twisting the fellow's hands behind his back in an iron grip, while Julian perched astride his rump. ''It's the Peeping Tom!'' Mr. Carrington chortled, his pince-nez falling off his nose in his excitement. ''We've caught the Peeping Tom!''

''Turn him over,'' Marcus said, ''and let's have a look at him.''

Julian obligingly got to his feet. The men formed a defensive circle around the intruder, while Sir Walter released the fellow's hands and turned him over. It was a tall, lanky dark-haired youth who stared up at them, his eyes blinking in terror from a pallid face. ''Good God!'' Bertie exclaimed aghast. ''It's *Dilly*!''

Sophy, who was attempting to revive Dennis without success, froze. Dilly? Lawrence Dillingham? What on earth was he doing *here*? But Dennis groaned and stirred, and she turned her attention back to her patient. Fanny had, by this time, come to her aid and knelt on Dennis's other side, moaning and wringing her hands.

Meanwhile, the others were staring at Bertie in astonishment. ''Do you *know* this fellow?'' Marcus asked.

''Yes, of course I do. It's Lawrence Dillingham. Known him for years. Didn't know he was a Peeping Tom, of course,'' Bertie explained.

''I ain't a Peeping Tom,'' Dilly muttered.

''No, you're a blackguard and a *murderer*!'' cried Fanny,

bursting into the circle and staring down at the hang-dog villain.

"Ain't no murderer, either," Dilly said, sitting up and staring at the overwrought girl.

"Oh, yes, you are!" Fanny insisted. "Just *look* at what you've done!" she pointed a trembling finger in Dennis's direction, then rounded on Dilly angrily. "See? You're a *monster!*" And she slapped him hard across the face. Dilly fell back, gaping at the girl in injured innocence.

Dennis, however, was far from dead. He sat up dazedly and felt his aching jaw. "Wha' happened?" he muttered in bewilderment.

Mr. Carrington, meanwhile, grasped his daughter's arm and pulled her away. "Stay out of this, you silly child," he said in an angry whisper. "You're making a spectacle of yourself."

Sir Walter looked down at his quarry. "Well, if you're not a Peeping Tom, what *were* you doing out there?"

"Ask your son," Dilly answered brusquely, rubbing his cheek.

"Me? I don't know anything about this," Bertie said in vehement denial.

Dillingham lifted himself on one elbow and looked lugubriously at Bertie. "Fine friend *you* are."

"I'm no friend at *all,*" Bertie told him flatly. "Not yours, anyway. Not now. Not when you go peering into windows and breaking into people's homes like a common thief. What on earth *are* you doing here?"

"*You* know," Dilly mumbled, his frightened eyes roving over the faces looking down at him.

"I *don't* know!" Bertie declared impatiently. "How would *I* know what lame-brained rig you're involved in?"

"That's the very question I'd like to ask, Mr. . . . er . . . Dillingham," Marcus cut in. "Just what *is* your rig?"

"Bertie can tell you," Dilly insisted. "I told *him* to do it, but he didn't want to."

"You told *Bertie* to break into my house?" Marcus asked, confused.

"He's gone off his hinges!" Bertie declared.

"Are you denying, *Mr.* Edgerton," Dilly said with

sudden spirit, "that I asked you to keep an eye on her?"

Bertie's mouth dropped open. "Oh, my Lord! Is *that* . . . ? I don't believe it! Is *that* what you've been doing?"

"What? What's the fellow talking about?" Sir Walter asked.

"I think m' jaw's broken," Dennis said, feeling the side of his head gingerly.

"You *are* off your hinges!" Bertie was muttering to the miscreant on the floor. "You ought to be locked away!"

"That's what I think," Dennis muttered. "Damned mushroom broke my jaw!"

Bertie shook his head incredulously. "Have you been skulking about *all this time* just to . . . just to . . . ?"

Dilly shrugged glumly. "What else?"

Sir Walter was rapidly losing his patience. "I don't see how you've managed—even with those monosyllabic words you use—to make yourself clear to my son, Mr. Dillingham, but do you mind trying to explain yourself to the rest of us?"

Dilly sat up, looked around again at all the faces watching him, scratched his head and said cautiously, "I only wanted to . . . keep an eye on her, you see. To make sure she wouldn't go and get herself betrothed. They're bound to do it, these females, when they go away from home. My own sister—"

Julian broke into a loud guffaw. "Do you mean to say that you've done all this to keep a guard on your *sweetheart*?"

Dilly nodded embarrassedly.

"Who is she?" Mr. Carrington asked curiously. "One of the housemaids?"

"No, no," Julian offered, suddenly recollecting the fellow's words when he first burst in. "He must mean—"

"That's right, sir," Dilly said proudly, getting to his feet and pointing out past the circle of people surrounding him. "It's *she*!"

The circle broke as all heads turned in the direction he'd indicated. Sophy looked up to find every eye on her. She raised herself slowly, like a girl in a dream. "*M-Me*?" she stammered, her bewildered eyes travelling over the shocked faces gaping at her like a circle of accusers in a nightmare. Bertie's face, beet-red and unhappy . . . Lady Charlotte, too surprised to smile . . . Grandmama, white as a handkerchief . . . Marcus . . . Marcus with his eyebrows raised in enigmatic aloofness . . .

The floor tilted beneath her feet, and the faces and the walls behind them began to spin slowly around until all she could see clearly was Dilly's pointing finger. And their eyes . . . Marcus's eyes . . . all watching . . . waiting for her to speak . . .

"All this s-spying . . ." she heard herself say, ". . . all this con-confusion . . . the b-broken windows . . . D-Dennis's jaw . . . all this because of . . . because of . . . *m-me*?" And for the first time in her life, she dropped to the floor in a dead faint.

Chapter Seventeen

AFTER THE DEBRIS had been swept away, the broken windows mended, the tables righted and the bric-a-brac replaced; after the racing pulses had been slowed and the excitement calmed; after Fanny had been chastised, Dilly sent off to a back bedroom, Dennis's jaw found to be merely bruised and Sophy merely humiliated; after the mystery had been solved and the whole story told; after several brandies had been imbibed and a midnight supper eaten—after all that, a good number of the household were able to find the whole affair to have been very funny.

And of course, in a way it was. If one ignored the pathetic aspects, one had to see the amusing side. An innocent, impressionable, heartsick young man, so addled by infatuation that he couldn't bear to permit his lady-love out of his sight—such a character had often been the subject of farce. And the details of Dilly's tale *were* quite farcical. He had followed Sophy to Sussex, rented a room at the nearest inn (a full seven miles distant), and had ridden across the downs every night to spy on her. He had done it every evening for almost two weeks, rain, wind and darkness notwithstanding. He had endured much suffering (ludicrous though it was): he'd lost his way when there was no moon, he'd been soaked to the skin in a drenching downpour, he'd lost his hat, fallen off his horse and been scratched by brambles when he'd had to hide in a thicket. Yet he had not failed on a single evening to keep his self-imposed tryst.

The climax had occurred, of course, in true farcical style, when he'd looked into the drawing room window and seen Sophy struggling in the arms of a would-be seducer. The fact that the struggle was being placidly observed by a roomful of people did not penetrate his love-crazed mind. He'd burst into the room in a rage and a shower of broken glass to save her, but in reality the "seduction" had only been a waltz. ("If that was a dance," he was heard to say later, "it is the most lascivious exercise ever invented!") All the heroics had been for nothing—that alone was worthy of a hearty laugh.

But perhaps the most humorous part of the comedy was the ending—when Sophy was roused from her swoon. She had not a word to say to the *chevalier galant* who'd endured dangerous combat for her sake. Not only did she deny him a word of thanks, but she cast him a look of such disdain and loathing that he cringed. From then on, she did not turn her eyes in his direction, and she left the room as soon as she could politely make her exit.

So the comedy ended, with the "heroine" completely out of reach and the "hero" sitting glumly in the corner of the drawing room wondering why on earth he'd gotten himself into this coil. Lady Charlotte kindly insisted that he join the guests for a late supper, and Bertie tried to cheer him by assuring him that, besides making a great cake of himself, no real harm had been done. But nothing erased the hang-dog look from his face until Fanny, also feeling quite put-upon and humiliated, sat down beside him. "I'm very sorry I slapped you, Mr. Dillingham," she whispered apologetically. "I didn't understand . . ."

"Oh, that's all right, ma'am. I deserved it," he said with a quick glance at her face.

"No, you didn't. You were . . . very brave and honorable, even though you were mistaken about the necessity for your action. Cissy says so, too."

"Cissy?"

"My sister."

"Oh." Dilly gave her an affecting smile of gratitude.

"You are both very kind." With a sudden surge of courage (brought about by the conviction that, having made such a complete ass of himself, he could fall no lower and had therefore nothing to lose) he added brazenly, "Your sister is as kind as you are. Is she as pretty, too?"

Fanny, taken by surprise, blushed and giggled. "Oh, Mr. Dillingham, you *are* a bold one!"

"Am I?" he asked in pleased surprise. "*Thank* you! Oh, I mean . . . that is, that doesn't mean that you think me rude, does it?"

"Oh, no, not at all. To call a girl pretty cannot be considered rude. At least, I don't *think* so . . ." She considered the matter carefully. "A bit *forward*, perhaps . . ."

"I've never thought of myself as forward, Miss . . . Miss . . . I don't believe I know your name."

"I'm Fanny Carrington. Oh, dear, I see my mother looking for me. I suppose I ought to . . ."

Her disappointment in having to end their *tête-à-tête* was so obvious that Dilly was flattered. And when they rose, and she offered him her hand, his depressed spirits lifted hopefully. "Will I see you tomorrow?" he asked eagerly, grasping her hand awkwardly.

"Won't you be gone by then?"

"Lady Wynwood has offered me a room for the night."

Her face brightened. "Oh, how lovely! I mean, then I suppose I shall see you . . . at breakfast?"

"At breakfast," he promised. He watched after her as she ran off to join her mother. There was an open-mouthed expression of awe on his face and renewed hope in his eyes. Thus is the ease with which farce can sometimes transpose itself into romance!

The one person who could find nothing at all funny in the events of the evening was Sophia Edgerton. For her, the world had collapsed in tragic calamity. "*We need these days*," Marcus had said, "*to prove to ourselves and each other that we can be sensible and normal.*" And she had tried so hard to do just that. Even when she'd seen him sitting hand-in-hand with Miss Bethune, and her heart had ached with jealousy and longing, she'd smiled brightly and behaved like the perfect guest. She had felt, with a deep, instinctive awareness, that he was proud of her. It had really seemed possible that, when the fortnight came to an end, they *would* be able to part as friends. If friendship was not the relationship she dreamed of in her secret thoughts, it was at least something salutary. But now, even *that* small comfort was denied her.

The events of the evening replayed in her memory with the distortions of a nightmare. To her mind, the room had been a shambles, Dilly had seemed a vulgar, clownish baboon, the faces of the guests had looked at her with obvious revulsion, Dennis had been irreparably mauled, and Marcus's eyes had filled with disgust. And she had fainted. *Fainted*! The very thing that Marcus (when he'd considered her a hysteric) had predicted she would be likely to do. Just two days after he'd told her that he no longer believed it (she could still hear his voice saying those beautiful words: "*My feelings have passed far beyond . . .*"), she had proved the worst to be true. Only a shatterbrained hysteric would have climaxed the cataclysmic evening with a swoon.

For many hours she paced her bedroom, trying to find a hint, a speck, a *crumb* of evidence to sustain her disintegrating self-esteem. But there was nothing in the debris but disgrace and shame. Marcus had suspected, during her earlier debacles, that she was shamming. This time, however, it must have been evident to him that the lurid melodrama was no counterfeit. It was real, and she, he would have to believe, had inspired it. All the witnesses would have to believe that she'd encouraged Dilly's affection. They would have to believe that only an overwrought and demented girl could encourage the affections of so overwrought and demented a beau. (Imagine anyone believing that she would ever consider a fool like Dilly as a suitor!) But she had no doubt at all that after this wretched night's work, Marcus would be convinced that she and Dilly would make a perfect match!

When these agonizing reflections had been repeated in her mind so often that she became numb to the pain of them, she began to think of the morrow. Unfortunately, humiliation was not fatal. She would not die in the night. She would have to go on with her life somehow. But not here. No matter what other confusions beset her brain, this fact was brilliantly clear—when morning came, *she could not be here*.

At first light, Sophy scratched at Bertie's bedroom door. There was not a soul stirring, not even the servants. But she was already fully dressed, wearing her travelling cloak and bonnet, and carrying an over-stuffed bandbox. She had packed only the most necessary clothing and a book in which was pressed a single pink rose.

When there was no answer to her repeated tapping, she turned the knob stealthily and crept inside. Bertie was sprawled on his bed, deeply asleep. His bedcovers were rumpled, his hair matted and his face appealingly flushed and innocent. She hated to disturb his peaceful slumber, but time was pressing. In a half-hour's time, the servants would begin to bustle about. She must be gone by then. She shook his shoulder firmly. He shuddered, puffed out his breath and turned over. "Not yet, Mincher," he muttered.

"It's not Mincher. *Do* wake up, Bertie."

One eye opened suspiciously. "Sophy?"

"Yes, it's me. Please, Bertie, get up."

The eye closed as if to ward off an unpleasant sight. "No. *Go 'way*," he said bluntly. "You're up to some scheme. Don't want to know about it. Don't want anything to do with it. Jus' go 'way."

"Bertie, you *must* help me. I don't know how I shall manage if you don't."

He opened both his eyes with exaggerated caution. "Manage what?" he asked, prompted by a momentary curiosity. But his common sense took over, and he thought better of it. "No, don't tell me," he said quickly, putting his hands over his ears. "I've had enough of your childish tricks. One would think, after last night, that you'd had enough."

"*Bertie*!" Sophy exclaimed in offense. "I'd expect that sort of chastisement from the others, but surely *you*, at least, shouldn't blame me for last night."

At this he sat up. "Don't be a wet-goose. *No one* blames you. I say, why are you wearing a bonnet? Where are you going?"

"That's just it, Bertie. I want to go home."

"Home? To London?"

She shook her head and bit her underlip before replying. "To . . . to Wiltshire."

"Wiltshire? Do you mean you want to go to *Edgerton*? Why?"

"It's the only place I have left," she said mournfully. "They don't know anything about . . . about all this. About the riding accident, and Dilly, and all the rest. If I rusticate there long enough, perhaps people will forget, and I'll be able to go back to Grandmama's one day."

"Sophy, you're overdoing it again. No one blames you for Dilly's lunacy. There's no need to—"

"No, you're out there. They're *bound* to blame me. *You* know that I never encouraged Dilly, but the others will never believe that. How could they? Why would any man with a grain of sense in his head behave the way Dilly did if he didn't feel possessive of me?"

"But Dilly *has* no sense. Anyone can see that."

"No, they can't. How could they? He has a perfectly respectable reputation. He's never done anything so ridiculous before, has he? His behavior before last night had been quite unexceptional."

"I suppose so," Bertie admitted. "Except about you."

"Yes, you told me the other day that he'd spoken to you about me."

"All the time. He was loony on the subject from the first. I don't know why you didn't notice it yourself."

"No, I never noticed anything out-of-the-way." She blinked as she was struck by a sudden memory. "Except the day we left for Wynwood. He *did* come round and babble some nonsense at me about not becoming betrothed! I didn't know what he was talking about."

"Yes, he said the same to me. Perhaps we both should have set him straight *then*." Bertie shook his head in sympathy for his friend. "Poor Dilly. He was quite a good fellow until love struck."

Sophy sat on the edge of the bed and sighed in doleful agreement. "Yes, love can make perfectly sane people behave very strangely."

Bertie peered at her shrewdly. "Are you speaking of Dilly? Or of yourself?"

"I'm just . . . speaking generally," she said hastily, but her face was suffused with color.

"Good Lord!" Bertie gasped as he was struck with an idea so staggering that he fell back against the pillows. "You're not . . . ! You haven't . . . ! Sophy, don't tell me it's . . . *Marcus*!"

"I won't tell you anything of the sort!" she answered crisply, turning her face away from him.

But Bertie was not convinced by her denial. "Of *course*! I should have guessed. It all adds up. *That's* why you've been behaving so . . . so . . ."

"Go ahead and say it! So *insanely*."

"But, Sophy," he said in sympathetic concern, "he's *betrothed*. And he don't even *like* you!"

Sophy leaned her head against the bedpost. "I . . . kn-know . . ."

Bertie's slight experience with the tender passion had enlarged his understanding and had given him some inkling of the pain of unrequited love. He swung his legs over the side of his bed and sat beside her. "Don't cry, Sophy," he pleaded softly. "Please don't cry."

"Oh, B-Bertie," she sobbed, turning and casting herself into his sympathetic embrace, "what am I to d-do?"

"I don't know," the harassed young man muttered unhappily, "but I wish you'd stop crying. You're soaking my nightshirt. It ain't even proper for me to be sitting next to you in my nightshirt at all—even if you *are* my cousin."

"I'm s-sorry," she sniffed, sitting up and mopping her eyes with the ends of the ribbons of her bonnet, "b-but at least you can understand now why I m-must g-go home."

"No, I can't understand. What good will it do to run away?"

"I've already t-told you. I can't f-face him . . . !"

"But have you forgotten your stepmother? I can't see

what good it will do you to deliver yourself into *her*
clutches.''

Sophy got up and faced him purposefully. "I have no
other choice. Will you take me, Bertie? I can't ask Miss
Leale to go with me, for she would only carry the tale to
Grandmama. And I can't very well go all that distance
unescorted.''

Bertie felt himself much put upon. Fond as he was of
her, he didn't relish the prospect of stealing away from
Wynwood in this underhanded style. But the girl obviously
needed his help. "Very well, I'll take you, though I don't
like the idea one bit!''

"Oh, Bertie, *thank* you!'' She threw her arms around his
neck in an appreciative hug. "Now hurry and dress. I'll
run down to the stables and have the groom . . . Oh,
dear!''

"*Now* what?''

"We'll need a curricle and pair. I can't very well steal
them from Marcus, can I?'' She frowned worriedly. "And
Grandmama's carriage is too large and decrepit to make
good time.''

"Besides, if you take *hers*, how will she be able to get
home?'' Bertie pointed out.

"Well, you'll be coming back here, won't you? The trip
will only take you a couple of days—you'd have it back
here in plenty of time for her departure.''

"In that case, take my father's laudalet. It's much lighter
and needs only a pair.'' To make off with his father's
carriage was not admirable behavior, but Bertie salved his
conscience by telling himself that borrowing was not as
bad as stealing.

The details settled, Sophy picked up her bandbox and
headed for the door. "Do hurry, dear,'' she urged. "The
servants will be up and about at any moment.''

"I'll hurry,'' he muttered grumpily. But before she left,
he raised an admonitory finger and wagged it at her. "I
have just one thing more to say to you, my girl,'' he told
her firmly. "This is the last time—the *very* last time—
I become involved in your escapades. Whatever happens in
future, whatever harebrained notions you take into your

head, you are *not* to include me. The next time you have need of an ally in your plots, you are to forget that you know me. Is that *clear*, Miss Edgerton? You are to forget I'm your cousin, you are to forget I'm the partner-in-crime from your childhood, you are to forget that I even *exist*!''

Chapter Eighteen

FOR SEVERAL HOURS after their stealthy departure, the runaway pair were not missed. Since many in the household were sleeping off the effects of the night before, it was assumed by those who were up and about that Sophy and Bertie, too, were safely in their beds. The only inhabitants of the breakfast room by the hour of ten were Alicia, Charlotte and Isabel (who were readying themselves for a shopping trip to Cuckfield), and Dilly, Marcus and Fanny. If Dilly had hoped for an invitation to remain at Wynwood, he was doomed to disappointment, for Charlotte bid him a blithe *bon voyage* before herding her companions out to the waiting carriage, and Marcus merely asked him quietly if he had sufficient funds with which to pay his shot at the inn and make his way back to London. Dilly replied with pride that he was quite plump in the pocket and thanked his host for his generous hospitality.

Dilly hoped that Marcus would then take himself off on his own concerns and leave the breakfast room to him and the young lady, but Marcus, having no idea that Dilly's amorous leanings had taken so aburpt a turn, felt obliged to remain to see the boy off. Fanny and Dilly were forced to speak in the most distant and formal way. "May I ask you to pass the biscuits?" was the most daring of their exchanges. At last, having no further excuse to hang about, Dilly offered his hand to his host to say goodbye.

"I'll see you to your horse," Marcus insisted, reaching for his cane. Marcus didn't expect Fanny to follow them out, but she did. He was puzzled by it until Dilly, about to climb into the saddle, turned to the girl. "May I come to call on you in London, Miss Carrington?" he asked, awkward at being forced to say it in front of his host, but carrying on anyway.

"I should be . . . delighted," Fanny said with a becoming blush.

Marcus, suddenly comprehending the situation, wanted to laugh out loud. That they *both* could have switched their affections so readily, especially after their attachments to two others had been so blatantly displayed only the night before, struck him as ludicrous in the extreme. He made a hasty retreat to permit them a private parting, bursting into unrestrained laughter as soon as he was out of earshot. He wondered if it would be a breach of taste or of some moral code to tell Sophy about the little scene. He would have liked to share his amusement with her.

The shopping expedition was an unqualified success, the ladies returning with a number of boxes and parcels to show for their exertions. But Lady Alicia noticed an agitated Miss Leale hanging about near the stairway. "What is it, Leale? You look as if you've lost your best friend. Have you mislaid the curling iron again?"

"No, ma'am," Miss Leale said agitatedly, ignorning the slur. "If you'll step into the sittin' room fer a bit, I've a little somethin' to show ye."

The "little somethin' " turned out to be a note from her granddaughter, telling her where she'd gone. Lady Alicia's lips tightened on reading it. When she recovered from her initial shock, she stalked out of the sitting room and handed the note to Charlotte. "Read *that*," she demanded bitterly, "and then let me hear you tell me again what a sweet and charming creature my granddaughter is." Without waiting for a reply, she marched up the stairs and did not reappear for the rest of the day.

Charlotte, the note still in her hand, went searching for her son. She found him in his study. Placing the note on the desk before him, she asked mildly. "Do you think, my love, that we should do anything about this?'' And she slipped into a chair while he glanced over it.

Dear Grandmama, Sophy had written, *You needn't say it—I'm a silly chit. You've told me often enough. But I'm sure you will understand that I can no longer remain under this roof. I have brought havoc on this peaceful, orderly household too often. Last night was the last straw. I cannot bring myself to face anyone this morning. I'm sure you can make my excuses. Say everything that I should have said myself. I do not want you to be worried about my safety. Bertie is taking me to Papa. I know you will say that I won't enjoy having to deal with my stepmother, but perhaps the discipline will be good for me. You've always said that I lack discipline, and I see now that you are right. After a while, when the gossip has died down, if you should want me, I will gladly come back to you. In the meantime, please don't think too badly of me. I have been remiss in many things but never in my love for you. Your devoted Sophy.*

Marcus closed his eyes for a moment. Then, with a sudden, sharp explosion, he slammed the letter down on his desk and jumped up. Turning to stare out the window, he said tightly, ''What do *you* think we should do about it? I, for one, find the whole matter highly distasteful. The girl has given us not a moment's peace since she arrived. My duty as her host can scarcely apply now that she's gone away.''

''Yes, you're quite right,'' his mother said gently.

''Confound it, Mama,'' he said, rounding on her impatiently, ''I know you too well to be taken in by 'you're quite right.' You had a plan when you came in here. Well, *out* with it! What is it you think I should *do*? Ride out after her and bring her back by force?''

She smiled at her son as benignly as if he'd merely said good afternoon. ''I made no suggestion at all. But if you think you *should* ride out after her, I would have no objection. I'm sure I could manage the evening here without you.''

''Thank you very much, but I have no intention of performing so ridiculous an act. Why should I?''

Charlotte directed her attention to the Norwich shawl around her shoulders which didn't seem to be arranged to her satisfaction. "There's no reason in the *world* for you to do so, my dear. *I'm* not the one who suggested it. I only thought that, if you *wished* to do it, it would be such a boon for poor Sophy. I am sorry that she left here thinking that we blame her for last night's little incident. If you went after her, you could tell her—"

"Save your breath, Mama. I shall do no such thing. Last night's 'little incident' may not have been her fault, directly, but it would never had occurred if she hadn't been here, now would it? When you first told me you'd invited her, I *warned* you that she was the sort to generate crises. Little did I dream how right I was!"

"Yes, you were. Nevertheless, I found her to be such a taking little thing, didn't you?"

Marcus opened his mouth to respond and suddenly found himself at a loss. A sharp pain seemed to constrict his throat. He hastily turned back to the window and stared out at the lawn. He had a clear, almost hallucinatory recollection of the way she'd looked that morning when he'd watched her from this very spot, racing about with the children, her skirts raised to reveal a tantalizing bit of ankle. "Yes . . . I suppose one could say she was . . . taking," he said at last, "although that detail has nothing whatever to do with the matter at hand. I'm sorry, Mama, if I disappoint you, but . . . I have no *right* to go after her . . . to tell her what to do or where to go. No right at all."

"Yes, I see that, of course," his mother said agreeably, seeming to take no note of his dejected air as he stared out at the lawn. She gathered up her skirts and rose. "I'll see you at dinner, then," she said and left him to his musings.

He returned to his place at the desk and picked up her letter. A rereading left him with a stronger feeling of disgust than the first reading had given him. The maddening creature had been unable to maintain her equilibrium for more than two days. Running away like this for no good reason—the girl was a ninny! And she'd left behind nothing but this foolish, uncommunicative little note—in which there was not a *word* for *him*. As far as this farewell message was concerned, he might never had existed! Well, her machinations, dramatizings and explosions were no longer his problems. He was glad to see the last of her. He crumpled her note into a little ball and threw it in the wastebasket. Now he could forget her. As far as he was concerned, the disturbing little nuisance could go hang!

Marcus was not at his best that evening. His manner was curt and his smile, on the rare occasions when it appeared, was forced. He found the evening unspeakably dull and was glad when he finally was able to make his way to bed.

The next day, Lady Alicia took her leave. Her granddaughter's departure had hurt her. She no longer felt pleasure in socializing, even with her beloved Charlotte. Home and solitude were what she now craved. Though both she and Charlotte looked a little misty-eyed when they parted, Charlotte bravely maintained her smile, and Lady Alicia remained crisp and acerbic to the last.

Sir Walter and Isabel remained to wait for Bertie—he had their carriage. But they both felt that they, too, should be taking their leave. They sensed a slight, unspoken air of desolation about the place—as if the houseparty had gone on just a bit too long.

When Bertie finally returned, he seemed reluctant to talk about Sophy or the trip he'd made. Sophy had been deposited safely with her father and had sent them all her sincere regards and her regrets that she had not bid them goodbye in person. Marcus asked, with elaborate disinterest, if she had seemed happy. Bertie answered that he supposed so—although Lady Edgerton, Sophy's stepmother, was a veritable dragon, and he didn't see how *anyone* could be happy in her company for very long. That was all the news Bertie offered, and it did nothing to brighten Marcus's mood.

Sir Walter did not delay his family's departure after Bertie returned. He gave the boy barely enough time to pack, and then he and Isabel said their goodbyes. Bertie and Marcus shook hands affectionately, and Bertie earnestly requested that Marcus get in touch with him on his return to London. They departed in a dull drizzle. The houseparty seemed to be dwindling down to a rather depressing finale.

It was still drizzling later that evening when Iris requested an opportunity to talk to Marcus privately. He took her to the library and shut the door. "Is anything wrong, Iris?" he asked, pouring two glasses of Madeira.

"I wish you will sit down, Marcus, please," she said in a rather sepulchral tone. "I don't care for any spirits at the moment."

Marcus obediently sat down beside her on the sofa. "I hope you don't mind if *I* take a drink. This drizzle seems to have settled in my bones."

"Yes, I've noticed that," Iris said.

Marcus, about to raise the wineglass to his lips, stayed his hand. "Why? What do you mean?" he asked, puzzled.

"Only that your attitude has not been cheerful. I had not been aware, before, that you were so unsteady in your moods."

"Unsteady? That word is a bit strong, isn't it?"

"Perhaps. But I think you'll agree that you had not previously been the sort of man who pokered up or fell into the dismals with no apparent provocation."

"Do you find me that sort now?" Marcus felt a wave of irritation. Her remarks sounded very much like a scolding. But he was not a schoolboy and didn't enjoy being treated like one. A sarcastic retort leaped to his tongue, but he bit it back. Better to laugh this off, he told himself, than to launch into a quarrel. A quarrel was the last thing in the world he wanted at this point. So he smiled his most charming smile. "Poor Iris," he said, patting her hand. "You see me at close range for the first time, and, in less than two weeks, the truth about me is revealed. The bloom is off the rose."

"You think this is a subject for levity, my dear, but I'm afraid I find it a bit more serious than that," she said, frowning.

"I cannot find it so. Perhaps the strain of entertaining house guests for so long is taking its toll on me—being on display has always put me in the dismals—but I don't think you need fear that I shall be a brittle-tempered spouse.''

Iris shook her head and said carefully, ''I don't think you will be my spouse at all, Marcus. Please forgive me, but I think we should reconsider our troth. I think, after all, that we don't suit.''

''Don't *suit*? Iris, you must be joking! Or have I done something to offend you? Surely I've not been so moody that I've frightened you off! You cannot be so delicate that an occasional frown disconcerts you.''

Iris turned away in irritation. ''You must not try to put *me* on the defensive, Marcus, for I am not the guilty party.''

''Then *I* must be the guilty one—but I scarcely think that a bit of moodiness is sufficient grounds for—''

''It's not the moodiness alone that brings me to this pass, I assure you. If you will look into your heart with your usual honesty, my dear, I'm sure you'll find sufficient cause for guilt.''

He dropped his eyes and drank his Madeira in a gulp. ''I don't know what you mean,'' he said stiffly. Then he smiled at her again. ''I've often heard husbands complain that their wives accuse them of misdemeanors they won't name, but I didn't think you were the sort who—''

''I am not your wife. Therefore it is not my place to name what I think is your 'misdemeanor'. I can only say that I've felt for many days that I am not . . . in the center of your . . . preoccupations . . .''

Marcus was struck with a pang of contrition. ''Yes, you're right,'' he said shamefacedly.''I *am* guilty of neglect of you. I never should have suggested that our betrothal be celebrated here. If I had permitted your mother to hold the ball she so dearly desired, I would not have had to play host and could have spent my time at your side as an affianced . . . er . . . lover should.''

''Perhaps, in those circumstances,'' Iris said softly, her eyes lowered to her folded hands, ''I would not have had the opportunity to notice that you've never been a lover at all.''

There was a protracted silence. Marcus stared at her in admiring dismay. She had a large measure of integrity and honesty that set her above the ordinary. How could he have permitted himself to hurt her so? Yet her intelligence made it difficult for him to reassure her or to ease her pain. She had evidently seen through his scrupulous politeness to the emptiness of his feelings. He had no idea what to do about the problem now. "I've told you that I'm not at ease in displaying my feelings," he explained lamely.

"Yet I've seen you on *several* occasions show flashes of genuine warmth."

"Have you?" he asked, grasping at the straw with relief. "Then you *know* how deeply I feel for you."

"That warmth was not directed toward me."

The simple directness of her statement left him powerless to speak. His mind whirled with protestations of innocence, with excuses and explanations, with pleadings of forgiveness, with all the things that a woman would expect on such an occasion. But her soft-spoken sincerity had disarmed him. He couldn't cheapen her forthrightness by defending himself with shoddy, wheedling lies. "I'm sorry," he said miserably. "You deserve better . . ."

"Yes, I do."

He turned to her earnestly and took her hand in his. "Will you give me the chance to make it up to you? I promise to try my utmost. Nothing will stand in the way—"

"No, Marcus," she said gently, removing her fingers from his grasp. "I never wanted a *mariage de covenance*. That is all our marriage would be to you. I prefer to wait for a love-match. It is not too late for me to find one."

There was not much that Marcus could find to say after this. No matter how sound his reasons for wishing to marry Iris had been, love had not been among them. And his Uncle Julian had been right about love—when one was possessed by it, all other reasons for marriage became pointless. He accepted, with a feeling of crushing guilt, the finality of her declaration that their betrothal was at an end. When she went to the door, he remained standing at the window, his head lowered in dejection.

"I won't tell Mama anything of this until we've returned

to London," Iris said before leaving, "so I hope you'll say nothing to anyone yet. Mama is sure to make a dreadful scene, and I would rather face it at home than here. I'll make the announcement to the newspapers as soon as Mama is told."

He looked at her helplessly. "I wish you every happiness, my dear. You're a—"

She smiled at him wistfully. "Yes, I know. A great gun."

So the calamitous houseparty came to an end. Lady Bethune, her sister, her sister's children and Iris piled into the Bethune coach the next day and left for home. Lady Bethune was effusive in her goodbyes to her hostess, repeatedly asking Charlotte to come to London as soon as possible so that the two mamas could discuss the wedding plans. Lady Wynwood smiled and nodded pleasantly to all suggestions, but when Lady Bethune reviewed the conversation later, she could remember no definite date or arrangement. "Lady Wynwood is certainly a vague sort of creature," she remarked to her family disgustedly.

Dennis, who'd been enjoying the respite from Fanny's attention, now found himself being pursued again. With the house so thin of company, the girl had little else with which to amuse herself. But Dennis had no patience left to deal with the little minx. He packed his bags hurriedly, thanked his friend for a memorable rustication, jumped into his curricle and left for London, urging Marcus to follow as soon as possible. "Too much country life is bad for the brain," he warned as his curricle disappeared around the bend of the drive, "so don't dally too long."

The Carringtons were the next to take their departure. At the end of a fortnight precisely, their carriage appeared at the front door. When the baggage had been loaded and the children herded aboard, Fanny delivered herself of an emotional thank-you for a stay which she would "remember all the days of my life." Then Mrs. Carrington kissed her hostess tearfully and followed her daughter into the coach. Mr. Carrington took off his spectacles, shook Marcus's hand firmly and said, "It was a most entertaining visit, my boy. Most entertaining. Can't remember a time when I've been so diverted." With that, he climbed aboard and signaled for the coachman to start. But the carriage had no sooner begun to roll when the butler came hurrying down the steps with their forgotten dog in his arms. "*Wait!*" he shouted, chasing the lumbering equipage down the driveway. "You've forgotten your little *Shooshi!*"

Mrs. Carrington screamed in horror, leaned dangerously out of the carriage window and grasped the almost-forgotten Shooshi in her arms. "Goodbye again!" she clarioned, waving the animal's paw in farewell as they disappeared from sight.

That left only Uncle Julian, but Marcus refused to permit him to leave. Now that he could relax, he wanted the company of the old fellow whom he was only now getting to know. Julian readily agreed to stay on. The two men spent the next few days in riding, playing chess and walking companionably through the woods. In the evenings, they sat with Charlotte on the terrace enjoying the balmy breezes and reminiscing about the family's past. Then, after Charlotte had gone to bed, they talked on late into the night, about everything from Napoleon's misguided strategy in Russia to Julian's youthful misadventures. It was the sort of quiet companionship that Marcus most enjoyed, and the two came to an affectionate intimacy they had never had before.

Although the old gentleman learned a great deal about his nephew during those times, Marcus did not talk about his betrothal at all. If the omission struck Julian as peculiar, the matter was explained by an item he found in the *Times* one morning at the end of June. "What's *this?*" he asked his nephew in surprise. "Can they have made a mistake?" He pointed to the place on the page and passed the paper to Marcus.

Marcus didn't really need to read it. "Yes, it's true. I've only been waiting for this to appear before I told you. She's jilted me, I'm afraid."

"I see," Julian said knowingly. "Have you told your mother?"

"Not yet." He sighed. "I suppose I'd better do so now, before she hears about it from some gossipy neighbor."

"Do you think the news will disappoint her?"

"I don't know. With Mama, it's hard to tell. I never knew whether or not she really *liked* Iris. Kept calling her Miss Bethany or some such misnomer."

"I wouldn't worry about your mother. Always takes things in her stride, Charlotte does. Never known a woman so unflappable."

Without ado, Marcus went in search of her. He found her in the greenhouse, repotting some seedlings, her full sleeves rolled up and her silk gown covered by a large, soiled apron. She smiled at him absently. "Off for a bit of riding?" she asked.

"No, not now. I've come to show you this item in the *Times*." He offered it to her.

"Hold it for me," she said, wiping her hands on the apron. "My hands are too dirty." He held it before her face, and she scanned it quickly. Then she looked up at him with eyebrows raised and read it again. "Did you know about this?" she asked.

"Yes," he said, leaning back against a worktable. "Iris told me about her feelings before she left."

"I see. Then it was something that happened *here* that caused her to change her mind?"

"So it seems. My abstracted behavior and the lack of attention to her made her realize that I was not sufficiently . . . how can I put it? . . . enamored of her."

His mother nodded. "She is a wise girl. I noticed the same thing."

Marcus frowned in irritation. "Oh, you *did*, did you? Well, if you had not saddled me with a collection of mismatched and troublesome guests to supervise, neither one of you would ever have noticed anything!"

Charlotte casually turned to her flowerpots. "I knew you didn't love Miss Bethany even—"

"Miss Beth*une*, Mama, Beth*une*!"

"Bethune, then. I knew you didn't love her even before she set foot in the door."

"How astute of you! Next I suppose you'll tell me that you arranged to ask your little Sophy to visit in the full expectation that her antics would so distract me that Iris would be driven off.''

Charlotte's lips curved in a half-smile. "I make no claim to such god-like prescience. Do you think me a witch?''

He eyed her askance. "I sometimes wonder.'' He walked around the worktable so that he could see her face. "Then am I right in assuming that you are not too disappointed at this turn of events?''

"No, not at all. Are you?''

"Not disappointed. Only ashamed that I may have caused pain where it was not deserved. But I'm curious, Mama. Did you not *like* Iris?''

"I liked her very much. She's a fine, respectable, and well-bred young woman. But I felt from the first that she was not the sort of girl you need.''

"You may be right.'' He picked up a seedling and played with it absently. "I wish I knew what sort of girl I *do* need,'' he said glumly.

His mother regarded him with her enigmatic half-smile. "You know *exactly* the sort you need.''

"Nonsense. I don't know what you mean,'' he said in disgust. "I wish you would not always speak in riddles.''

"I mean Sophy,'' she said promptly, not looking up from her potting.

"*Sophy*! What are you *saying*, Mama?''

She took the seedling from his hand and placed it carefully in its new pot before she answered. "I'm saying,'' she declared when the seedling was properly set, "that you should ride to Wiltshire without delay, rescue the girl and marry her.''

He stared at his mother aghast. "Marry *Sophy*? *Marry* her? Have you gone *mad*? Can you imagine the sort of life we'd have together? Can you picture the horror of it? I would never know a moment's *peace*. Just *think* what my days would be like. There would be tears at breakfast because I didn't compliment her hair, and diatribes over dinner because I'd skipped luncheon. If we were going out for the evening, she would want to stay cozily at home, but should I suggest the cozy evening, she would rail at my selfishness in keeping her locked away from society. When I'd leave to attend to matters of business, she'd weep at the prospect of terrible loneliness, and when I'd return she'd greet me at the door in wild distraction over some trumpery household crisis. If I smiled at one of her friends, I'd be jealously denounced for flirting, but if I didn't smile, I'd be accused of snobbery. I should live on the razor's edge of suspense, wondering what crisis she'd next have me face. Not a day would pass without some calamity or misadventure of her making. Cataclysm and catastrophe would become part of my ordinary existence. I'd become intimately acquainted with apprehension, consternation, perturbation and foreboding. As the days would pass, I'd find my bride more and more melodramatic, overwrought and maddening. And as the years would pass, instead of finding her more mellow and serene with maturity, I would find that she'd presented me with half-a-dozen children—all girls!—who would be every bit as impetuous, disquieting, skittish, impassioned and histrionic as their mother. *Marry* her? Why don't you rather send me off to fight Cossacks in winter? Or to sail down a waterfall in a cockleshell? Or to explore the heart of darkest Africa? Or to push a rock up a mountain like Sisyphus. *Marry* her?" He paused, cocked a sheepish eye at his mother who was smiling at him tolerantly and asked, "Do you think she'll *have* me?"

Chapter Nineteen

SOPHY HAD HOPED THAT, by maintaining a quiet, guarded tongue and an agreeable, modest demeanor, she would manage to live with her Evangelical stepmother in a modicum of peace. But Lady Edgerton, her suspicions aroused by the unconventionality of Sophy's return, was belligerent and hostile from the first moment of her arrival. Sophy had been sent home in disgrace, Lady Edgerton was convinced, because of some heinous, immoral transgression, and she would not rest until she had ferreted out from the girl all the details and had meted out the proper punishment.

Lady Edgerton, born Oriana Scarpe, was a formidable woman. A product of the union of an outspoken, loose-living father and a prudish mother, she early embraced the philosophy of John Wesley in its most extreme form. Her life was the very model of virtuous, Christian womanhood. Her time was spent in reading sermons, attending services, quoting from scriptures and doing good works. Her beliefs held strongly to the narrowest interpretation of the Evangelical moral standards.

Her late-in-life marriage to Lord Edgerton had come as a great shock to the families of both sides. Lord Edgerton had been a widower for several years and had shown no inclination to remarry. Nor had he ever exhibited the slightest religious propensities. He had no interest in life comparable to his love of his horses. He rode them and bred them and talked of them. Oriana Scarpe, on the other hand, had never ridden in her life. Of course, one could understand that a woman in her forties, who had never been married, might succumb to an offer from a gentleman of rank and property. But Lord Edgerton's reasons for *making* the offer were never understood. Miss Scarpe had neither wealth nor beauty, being a large, red-faced woman with narrow eyes and closely-crimped dark curls which hung over her ears, making her look like an angry jurist with a black wig. But they *had* married, much to the amazement of their families and acquaintances, and they lived together in apparent harmony, each one changing not a whit to suit the other.

Lady Oriana had immediately ordered daily family prayers which were attended by all the servants, but not by the master; and Lord Edgerton went about his daily exercises on horseback, a practice in which his wife never joined. Thus the two went their separate ways, as if to prove that marriage need have little or no effect on people of strong character.

The victim of this strange union was Lord Edgerton's sixteen-year-old daughter. The new Lady Edgerton looked upon young Sophia as an unruly hedonist; the child, completely unschooled in the devout and holy life, rode her horses as wildly as a boy, took too great a pride in her appearance, wore dresses that were as vulgar as a courtesan's and spoke with the free tongue of a doxie. Her stepmother set about converting the girl to moral virtue in the only way that seemed effective—by breaking her spirit. The resulting struggle only made Sophy miserable and roused an unalterable resentment in her bosom against the monster who had become her stepmother. Sophy's flight to her grandmother in London had been the result.

Lady Edgerton regarded her return as a sign from above that she had been given a second chance to convert her stepdaughter to the ways of the righteous. Sophy was not only expected to attend "family" prayers with the servants, but she was forced to endure long sessions of private devotions with her stepmother three times a day. In addition, she was subjected to an endless series of questions regarding her activities in the years of her life with her grandmother (whom Lady Edgerton denounced repeatedly as an irreverent, godless incorrigible who would burn in Hell) with particular emphasis on the circumstances which had caused Sophy to return to the fold. Sophy explained repeatedly, and as calmly as she could, that she'd come home because she'd been embarrassed by the persistence of an unwanted suitor. But her stepmother suspected a much more lurid motive and would not be content with that simple explanation.

Sophy, inwardly burning with fury at the insults to her grandmother and to her own moral conduct, nevertheless tried to maintain her outward equanimity. If matters became unbearable, she told herself, she could always go to her father for help. Her father had always indulged her, calling her his little poppet and pinching her cheek with hearty affection. But one day, at luncheon, when her stepmother was berating her with unusual venom, Lord Edgerton had merely said, "Oriana, stop badgering the girl," and had taken himself off to the stable. At that moment, it became clear to his daughter that Lord Edgerton managed to maintain a peaceful relationship with his wife by staying as far away from her as possible.

So Sophy was forced to bear the endless scoldings and sermonizings without hope of assistance or sympathy. Lady Edgerton was convinced that Sophia had sinned—although the exact nature of the crime was withheld from her—and Sophia must be punished. The girl was kept indoors, even on the warmest summer days, to sew a heaping pile of shirts for the poor and to listen to her stepmother's renderings of the sermons of Whitefield and Wesley.

After a few weeks of this grim life, Sophy noticed a change in her stepmother. She became, suddenly, more cheerful and less critical. She told Sophia to dress her hair and put on a more cheerful gown than the dark blue bombazine she had been heretofore required to wear. The reason for the softening became clear in short order: Lady Oriana had arranged for a suitor for her stepdaughter!

Lady Edgerton was not so blind that she didn't realize that Sophia disliked her. The presence of a stubborn, willful girl in her well-run, exemplary household was a

constant source of irritation. If she could marry Sophia off
to a respectable and virtuous gentleman, would not her
obligations to the girl be fulfilled? The husband could then
take over the reformation of her character. And, happily,
she knew the very man. She had a cousin, not a day above
forty, who was the vicar of a small parish near by, and
who had a growing reputation for the awesome effects of
his hell-fire sermons.

When her stepmother's object became clear, Sophy
attempted to resist. She explained patiently that she'd just
endured a difficult time with an unwanted suitor, and that
she couldn't face the ordeal of entertaining another. She
intended never to marry, she declared fervently, and she
hoped Lady Edgerton would not require her to subject the
gentleman in question to useless embarrassment.

"Nonsense, my dear, of *course* you'll marry. It is the
duty of good Christian women to do so. The Reverend Mr.
Scarpe, a cousin of mine on my father's side, will be
calling this afternoon. I want you to welcome him with
cordiality—showing proper restraint, of course—and to
say nothing . . . I repeat, Miss, *nothing*! . . . which might
discourage him from making an offer."

"But, ma'am, you don't understand. There is nothing I
can say to encourage him. I cannot *think* of matrimony, at
least not at this time."

"And why not, Miss? In what debauchery have you
indulged to make you feel thus unworthy?"

The rudeness of the question left Sophy speechless.
Realizing that arguments would be useless, she bit her lip
and took herself off to change her dress as ordered. She
reappeared later in a puce-colored jaconet gown completely
unsuited to the hot weather but quite decorous in its high
neckline and long sleeves, which Sophy felt was the most
unflattering item in her wardrobe. Characteristically, her
stepmother was quite pleased with it.

Unfortunately, the Reverend Mr. Scarpe was pleased
with it, too. The moment he laid his protruding black eyes
on Sophy, they shone with a lascivious light. Mr. Scarpe,
a round-shouldered, balding gentleman, whose barrel-like

body was set on a pair of long, spindly legs, had not often come upon a young woman of Sophy's undisguisable charms. He could barely conceal his leering eagerness to acquire this toothsome creature for his own. He sat down beside her on the sofa in the shaded drawing room and, disregarding the fact that Lady Edgerton was observing the proceedings from across the room, allowed his knee to bump into hers. Sophy inched away and tried to distract him with a polite question about the composition of his parish. "A most loyal and God-fearing flock," he said complacently. "I doubt if a finer group could be found in all England. Although, of course, I, like John Wesley, look upon the *world* as my parish. But tell me, Miss Edgerton, about yourself. How is it I've not seen you here before?"

"I've been residing with my grandmother in London," she explained, feeling his knee again and inching away.

"Living amidst all 'the pomp and vanity of this wicked world,' I have no doubt," her stepmother interjected coldly.

" 'Judge not according to the appearance,' *John*, 7:24," the vicar quoted solemnly. "I'm sure this little flower remained pure in the midst of the sinning around her. 'Unto the pure all things are pure,' *Titus*, 1:15." He beamed at her benignly.

"Hummph!" her stepmother grunted, but, not wishing to endanger the success of her objective, she held her peace.

Sophy, who had reached the end of the sofa and found herself trapped, jumped up. "Perhaps Mr. Scarpe would like a lemonade. Shall I get some, ma'am?"

"No, thank you," Lady Edgerton answered quickly. "I'll see to it myself." And with a meaningful look at her cousin, she left them to themselves.

Sophy took an armchair halfway across the room. But the vicar would not be outmaneuvered. He rose, took hold of a straight-backed chair and dragged it as close to the girl as he dared. Perching upon it and leaning so close to her she could feel his breath, he smiled at her broadly. "You need not be shy with me, my dear. I can see that your life with Lady Edgerton has not been easy, but in me you have found a friend.''

''Lady Edgerton has been very kind,'' she said mendaciously.

The vicar raised his eyebrows. ''I have eyes and ears, Miss Edgerton. 'He that hath ears to hear, let him hear,' *Mark*, 4:9. I believe I have it in my power to ease your lot, you know.''

The afternoon was very hot, and a fine beading of perspiration appeared on Mr. Scarpe's upper lip. He reached into his pocket to take out his handkerchief and mop his face. The action dislodged the edge of his neckcloth, which stood up like a tiny cat's tail against his neck. Thinking it a fly, he brushed at it, intent on the girl's face.

Sophy restrained the urge to laugh. ''Indeed, sir, you need have no concern for me. My lot is not so very difficult.''

''Perhaps not yet,'' he said urgently, attempting to brush away the ''fly'' and lean toward her at the same time, ''but you should not delay too long in setting up an establishment of your own, with a husband to protect you and children to bring you joy. 'Walk while ye have the light, lest darkness come upon you,' *John*, 12:35.'' He shifted in his chair as he attempted to catch at the annoying ''fly.''

''I have no intentions of marrying,'' Sophy said bluntly, hoping to quash his pretensions as soon as possible.

He dabbed at his face with one hand while he swished away at the ''fly'' with the other. ''You cannot be serious, Miss Edgerton! A young lady of your—if I may say so—spectacular charms must not be permitted to keep them to herself. You must stop thinking like a child.'' He reached out and patted her arm. ''It is time to 'put away childish things.' ''

''Are you not going to give the source?'' Sophy asked acidly, thrusting his hand from her arm. It fell to her lap where the infuriating lecher kept it, turning his palm to feel her thigh. ''Sir, I must ask you to—'' She moved her leg aside.

Her lack of encouragement of both his words and his

attempts at physical intimacy left him completely undaunted. "*Very* spectacular charms," he repeated, snatching both her hands. Still bothered by the "fly," but with his hands more interestingly occupied, he resorted to a twitch of the shoulder and head to shake the "fly" away. If Sophy were not so angry, she would not have been able to restrain her laughter.

"Please, sir," she said irritably, "I wish you will release my hands. I'm certain my stepmother would not approve—"

"Lady Edgerton knows that my object is matrimony. She wishes me to make my case as strongly as possible . . ."

"I assure you that this is pointless," Sophy said desperately, trying to get away from his clutch and the smell of his breath. "My way of life is not what a man of the cloth would wish. I am quite shatterbrained and flighty—not given to holy thought or good deeds . . ."

"Don't trouble about that, my dear. I will teach you. In time, you will be a model wife for a clergyman. 'For the fashion of this world passeth away,' *First Corinthians*, 7:31. And think of the happiness we would find while I instructed you . . ."

A beatific vision filled his mind of this succulent morsel ensconced in the sitting room of his cottage, bending over a book of his sermons while he perched on the arm of her chair stroking her white neck. Quite overwhelmed with the idyllic possibilities of the scene, he released her hands with the object of sweeping her into his arms, but he was momentarily distracted by the "fly," and stopped to twitch and swat. Sophy, quite aware that he was about to reach for her, took advantage of her temporary release and jumped up from her chair. The precipitous movement caused him to rock back. His chair tipped over backwards, and he fell to the floor with a crash.

Sophy first reacted with concern. "Are you hurt?" she asked, looking down at him. He had raised himself on one elbow and was blinking up at her in bemused anger. "You . . . you did that on *purpose*!" he cried in wounded dignity.

"No, truly, I—" But the sight he presented gave her an uncontrollable urge to giggle. His face was flushed, his purpled lips clenched in anger, his neckcloth now completely askew, and his thin legs sprawled wide apart. She had a flash of memory of a picture of Humpty-Dumpty in her old *Mother Goose*, and she almost expected Mr. Scarpe to crack like an egg. A giggle bubbled from her throat, which caused Mr. Scarpe's cheeks to grow purple. This made the giggle grow to a chortle, and Sophy found herself laughing unrestrainedly.

That was the scene on which Lady Edgerton re-entered. Mr. Scarpe lay on the floor, raised on one elbow, glaring with distended eyes at the hilarious Sophy, his scraggly hair dishevelled, his neckcloth askew, and his legs spread indecently wide. And Sophy, heedless of the look of horror on her stepmother's face and the murderous look in her erstwhile suitor's eyes, pressed her hands against her aching sides and continued to roar with laughter.

After the vicar had taken his leave (for the first time in his life bereft of a fitting line of scripture with which to embellish his exit), Lady Edgerton, trembling in agitation, ordered the girl to her room. "And there you will remain locked," she intoned darkly, "until you write a note of apology to Mr. Scarpe and beg him to renew his suit."

"I shall *never* write such a note," Sophy declared vehemently. "Your Mr. Scarpe is a lecherous, sanctimonious *weasel*, the sort who pinches a girl surreptitiously under the very noses of her parents. You may lock me in my room and feed me bread-and-water for a *month*, but I won't write a *word* to that . . . that . . . *humbug!*"

"That you can speak so of a man of the cloth is proof of the depravity of your soul," Lady Edgerton declared. "But a few days of complete isolation will change your mind. We'll see how much spirit you'll show when I'm done with you."

Sophy put her chin in the air and marched to the stairs. "Wait 'til Papa hears about this. He won't permit you to lock me up for long."

But Lord Edgerton, uncomfortable as he was to learn that Sophy was being kept prisoner in her room, nevertheless could not face a quarrel with his wife. After a mild attempt to plead his daughter's cause, he succumbed to the logic of his wife's claim that his softness had brought his daughter to this pass, and that if he wished for the girl's character to be strengthened, he must permit his wife to exercise firm control.

After a couple of days, Sophy's hope of rescue by her father was gone. She spent a few hours weeping bitterly at her fate, and then she began to plot her escape.

It was at this point that Marcus arrived at Edgerton to see Sophy. Once he'd realized that he wanted to marry her, despite the dire predictions he'd made to his mother, his impatience was unbounded. The match would probably be a disastrous one, but disaster or not, he couldn't wait to see her and take her in his arms again. If it meant a lifetime of calamity, he would face it. For he knew now that without her he was only half alive.

As his curricle neared the Edgerton estate, he grew unbearably restive. It was completely unlike him. He'd always been the most contained of men. He had never been hasty or impatient. He had always taken the circumstances of life in easy stride, each thing as it came. This fretful, tense anxiety was both painful and exciting, a strange and disquieting sort of happiness. The serene and peaceful life he'd envisioned with Iris Bethune had paled into oblivion. With an eager tightening of the throat and a racing pulse, he banged the knocker of the Edgerton's door.

And aged and doddering butler led him to the drawing room with the pace of a snail. Then he waited interminably for someone to come. While he waited, he permitted himself to dream of an eager, shining-eyed Sophy bursting into the room with arms outstretched. Instead, he was greeted with icy politeness by a florid Lady Edgerton who said something about Sophia's being unable to see visitors. "What?" he asked stupidly, unable to control the devastating disappointment that swept over him. "Is she ill?"

"No, my lord," Lady Edgerton explained. "She is quite well. She is, however, being held *incommunicado* at the moment."

"*Incommunicado*? I'm afraid I don't understand. Why?"

"It is a private matter. Suffice it to say that she will be receiving no visitors in the near future."

Marcus blinked at the implacable woman as if she were a creature from a nightmare. "I don't think you quite understand," he said after a pause. "I've come all the way from Sussex without stopping. My business with her is quite urgent. If you send up my name, I'm certain she'll agree to see me."

Lady Edgerton snorted unkindly. "Yes, I'm certain she *would*! It is *I* who am keeping her from social intercourse at this time."

Marcus had heard from Bertie that Lady Edgerton was a veritable dragon, but this was more than he bargained for. All his persuasive powers were useless against her implacable resolve. What had Sophy done, he wondered miserably, to deserve such drastic punishment?

The only inroads he was able to achieve in the impregnable fortress of Lady Edgerton's will were her invitation to take dinner with them and her promise to permit him to speak to her husband alone. But the brief meeting with Sophy's father did little good. Although Marcus admitted the purpose of his visit and asked Lord Edgerton for his permission to make his addresses to his daughter, Lord Edgerton could promise him nothing. "My wife is determined that Sophy shall marry her cousin. You've met my wife, so I needn't tell you that her mind, once made up, is absolutely unmoveable."

Marcus clenched his fists in irritation. "But obviously, Sophy doesn't wish for the match. You cannot mean to *force* her—"

"Oriana has determined on it. I'm afraid, my boy, that there's nothing any of us can do about it."

Dinner time passed with interminable sluggishness, the aged butler serving with his usual snail's gait. Lord Edgerton kept up a flow of hearty talk about a new-born foal he had hopes of training for racing. Marcus answered in monosyllables. Lady Edgerton's conversation consisted entirely of polite inquiries as to the quality of the various dishes which were served. His answers were equally polite, but since he couldn't taste a thing, his mind being preoccupied with other matters, his hostess could not consider his absent-minded responses as an enthusiastic endorsement of the condition of her kitchen.

When the covers had been removed and the port placed at Lord Edgerton's elbow, Lady Edgerton asked her guest if he would care to join her for evening prayers. "No, no, my dear," Edgerton demurred quickly, "you must leave him to me. I want to take him to the stables and show him the foal."

Marcus hoped that Edgerton's excuse to his wife was a ruse to deliver to Marcus some secret message of hope, or to help Marcus concoct a plan by which his wife's purpose might be circumvented. But he was doomed again to disappointment as Edgerton took him to the stable without even mentioning Sophy's name and paraded the foal before him proudly. Marcus could barely maintain an appearance of civility as Edgerton enumerated the little foal's many virtues. He said a few words in praise of the animal and, utterly depressed, put out his hand to bid his host good-night.

"No, no, you mustn't dream of leaving now," Edgerton insisted. "It's growing quite dark already, and the nearest inn is several miles off. You *must* stay the night. We might even get in a bit of riding in the morning, if you've a mind."

Marcus hesitated. The Edgerton household was not one which would normally attract him, but Sophy was under this roof. If he remained, perhaps he might find a way, somehow, to find her room. He thanked his host profusely and accepted the invitation. Then he excused himself for the purpose of fetching his horses and seeing to their disposal for the night.

As he strolled around the side of the building, heading for the front drive, he looked up at the windows. A few of them showed lights, for the twilight was rapidly deepening. He wondered if one of the lights came from Sophy's bedroom. The building was three stories high. If her room was on the second floor, he might reach it by climbing one of the trees. But the third floor looked completely inaccessible.

Good Lord!, he thought, *the girl has driven me to plotting a break-in*! He should have known it would be like this. He couldn't visit her politely in her drawing room as he would any ordinary girl, oh no! Not Sophy! With *that* girl, it would have to be a scene, a drama, a spectacle. If he were to see her this time, it would have to be by stealth, by climbing up to her window like a damned Don Juan!

Immersed in these ruminations, he was startled by the sound of a falling object—something bulky and heavy which landed a few feet from where he stood. It was a bandbox, hastily packed (with bits of delicate clothing sticking out around the edges) and tied by means of a number of colored ribbons which had been knotted together. Something about the box suggested Sophy. Who else would solve her baggage problems with such draggletailed ingenuity? He looked up, his pulse beginning to race again. To his amazement, he saw a rope-ladder, made from a few twisted bedsheets which had been knotted together, being tossed from a third-story window. He stepped back into the shadows of the shrubbery and waited.

As he expected, a figure climbed out onto the sill and lowered itself awkwardly onto the rope. It was surely Sophy; he could make out a head of dark curls. She had pinned up her skirts, revealing a pair of stockinged legs which curled around the twisted sheets with endearing lack of skill. Trembling, and clutching at the sheet with taut fingers, she lowered herself little by little until, to her obvious horror, she found herself at the end of her rope, from which she dangled more than one story above the ground. He could hear her gasp as she looked down at the ground which was too frighteningly far below her to permit a safe jump.

He gave a choked laugh. It was just exactly like the girl to use a rope which was too short. It seemed just exactly right that his first glimpse of her should be this one. But the sight of the girl dangling there in midair, unable either to pull herself up or to jump down, was too much for his equilibrium. He sat down on the grass, lowered his head in his arms and gave way to uncontrollable hilarity.

Chapter Twenty

"WHO *IS* IT?" she whispered into the darkness. "Who's *there*?"

But the choking laughter continued unabated.

"Will you stop laughing, whoever you are, and come over here to *help* me? Who is it?"

"A white knight, of course, to rescue you," he whispered back when he'd regained his breath. "And not a moment too soon, from the look of things."

"*M-Marcus*?" she asked in a choked voice, in which the only emotion he could recognize was astonishment.

"At your service," he said with a slight, ironic bow as he came to stand beneath where she dangled.

"But . . . what are you *d-doing* here?" She tried to look down at him from her precarious perch. "Why did you . . . c-come?"

"Don't you think you'd better come down before we make the necessary explanations? Unless you'd rather stay where you are. I, of course, have not the slightest objection to conversing with you like this—the view of your legs is unspeakably delightful, and—"

She uttered a horrified gasp. "And you, sir, are unspeakably rude to refer to them," she managed to exclaim. "You must know that I didn't expect to be *observed* during my climb."

"I beg your pardon. Well, shall you jump? Or shall I ask your father for a ladder."

"Oh, *no*, don't ask *anybody* for *anything*, or I shall be discovered! Do you think you can catch me?" she asked dubiously. "I'm not a lightweight, you know."

"Have no fear. I shall manage."

With a brief intake of breath, Sophy let go her grasp on the rope and fell into his hold. The impact made him stagger backward, but he kept his balance and managed to hold her against his chest for a moment or two longer than was absolutely necessary. When he set her on her feet, they both were breathless. "Are you all right?" he whispered.

"Yes. Are you?"

"Never better. Now what?"

"Now I think we'd better run for our lives. Have you a carriage?"

"Right around the bend."

Without another word, he took her hand and pulled her behind him to the waiting carriage. With a flick of the reins, he started the horses bowling down the drive. "Oh, good heavens, I've left my bandbox!" she cried, clapping her hands to her mouth.

He pulled the horses to. "I'll run back for it," he said, putting a leg over the side.

"No, no!" she said in terror. "We'll be caught! Let's just go on." But he had already gone. The moments seemed interminable before he returned. He tossed the bandbox into the curricle behind their seats and jumped up beside her again. He started the horses and soon they had left Edgerton far behind. Her tension eased as the distance between them and her stepmother increased. "I don't know how to thank you," she said after a while, "although I cannot *imagine* how you came to be waiting under my window at just the right time."

"It's the talent of white knights to arrive in the nick," he said cheekily. "Otherwise, how would you ladies-in-distress manage your lives?"

Sophy did not like the arrogance of his tone. It seemed to her that he always managed to see her at her worst. "I was not *really* in distress," she said defensively. "I was just momentarily nonplussed."

He chuckled. "Indeed? I'm sorry then that I came out of hiding. I should have remained where I was and watched you get yourself out of that fix."

"You are straying from the point, sir," she said primly. "I had asked how you came to be at Edgerton."

"I came to be there, ma'am," he said, mimicking her tone, "to pay a call on you. But I was told you were not receiving visitors."

Sophy made a face. "The old dragon had locked me up, just because I'd sent the vicar sprawling."

He bit his lip. "Oh, is *that* all? How *can* she have been so narrow-minded? Although I dare say if it had been the *curate* she might have been persuaded to forgive you."

"You needn't be sarcastic. I know you think I dote on these disasters, but—"

"Why, Sophy, how *can* you believe I think any such thing! Dote on disaster? *You*? Nonsense. Just because you inspired a daft young man to break into my home for love of you, just because you ran away from my home in the dead of night without a word to me, just because I find you locked away like the princess in a fairy tale and then discover you hanging from a rope more than a story above the ground, you think I believe you dote on *disaster*? My dear girl, you misjudge me!"

Sophy felt the sting of tears behind her eyelids. There it was, that tone of disparagement. Why was it that every time he came into her life she was involved in some mishap or calamity? Why had he come along at just the wrong moment and found her dangling in the air? Just a moment ago she'd been grateful beyond words for his rescue, but now it seemed a most unfortunate coincidence. How could she ever win his respect if he kept discovering her in the act of blundering into some chaotic misadventure? Her throat tightened painfully, but she swore she would not let herself cry. "You needn't say anything more, sir. I suppose it would be useless for me to expect you to believe that none of those things you've just enumerated was my fault. They might have happened to *anyone*."

"Is that so?" Marcus asked drily. "I wonder why they don't happen to me."

"Oh, *you*! You are too perfectly precise and orderly to fall into scrapes," she said promptly.

He threw a quick glance at her. "Is that a set-down, Miss Edgerton? By that you mean, I suppose, that I'm a pompous prig."

Sophy didn't answer. She had once described him in just those words, but it was a long time since she'd felt that way about him. To her he *had* become the white knight, but there was no point in revealing her feelings—she would only be more humiliated.

But to Marcus, her silence meant agreement. Something in his chest seemed to grow numb. He fixed his eyes on the road, and the lines around his mouth hardened. "Where am I taking you, ma'am?" he asked coldly.

"To London, if you please. I've no place to go except to my grandmother's. My return will be a shock to her, I'm afraid. She's bound to give me a dreadful scold, but it will be like music when compared with my stepmother's sermons."

Marcus nodded, and they drove on in silence. It was only when the twinkling lights of London began to appear that he spoke again. "At the risk of sounding more like a prig than ever, I'd like to suggest that this might be the proper time to unpin your skirts. We shall be coming into populated areas soon, and, unbelievable as it may seem, we might encounter some types who are even more priggish than I."

Sophy choked and reddened to the ears. "You might have said something *before*!" she accused, looking down in hideous embarrassment at her exposed legs.

"I suppose I should have," Marcus said with a trace of the amusement that had marked his tone earlier that evening, "but that was expecting too much pomposity, even from me. The view was too attractive."

Sophy hastily undid her skirts and arranged them decorously over her limbs. She eyed him covertly as they plodded along through the increasing traffic. Truth to tell, it was comforting to have him at her side. Now that the pain of her humiliation was subsiding, she had to admit that she'd had no real plan to take her back to London when she'd climbed out of that window. She had taken a foolhardy risk. The act may have ruined forever his respect for her, but from a practical point of view she'd been fortunate that he'd been waiting there. "You never told me, sir, why you came all the way to Wiltshire to see me," she reminded him softly.

Even in the darkness she could see him stiffen. "It was nothing. Only an impulse . . ."

"An impulse? You?"

He gave a rather bitter laugh. "Yes, I. It's not like me to behave impulsively, is it? I've always held that impulsive behavior is foolish behavior. I shall try not to behave so foolishly again."

Sophy didn't understand why he sounded so angry, or what he was talking about. But he didn't respond to her questions, and eventually she stopped asking. The rest of the ride was passed in strained silence, during which Sophy remembered with a pang the joyful gleam in Marcus's eyes when he'd helped her down from the rope . . . a gleam which, somehow in their subsequent conversation, she had caused him to lose.

Lady Alicia didn't learn until the following morning that her granddaughter had been restored to her, for Sophy had refused to permit the overjoyed Miss Leale to waken her during the night. As soon as Alicia was told the news, she hopped out of bed and scurried to Sophy's bedside. Sophy awoke with a start, took one look at the old lady's brimming eyes, and the two fell into each other's arms. They laughed and wept and kissed each other until Lady Alicia regained her self-control. She sat down on the side of the bed and demanded to be told all. Sophy faithfully recounted the story of the vicar's ludicrous courtship, her stepmother's punishment and the fateful rescue at the hands of Lord Wynwood.

Lady Alicia looked at her granddaughter quizzically. "How strange. Did Lord Wynwood tell you why he'd come?"

"He merely said it was an impulse. I must admit,

Grandmama, that it's been puzzling me. What can he have wanted?''

Lady Alicia had a theory, but she thought it best to keep it to herself. ''If it was something of importance, we'll discover the answer before long. In the meantime, my love, I hope this marks an end to the excitement you've been generating.''

''Oh, yes,'' Sophy sighed pathetically, ''I hope so too. I've had quite enough tremors and palpitations to last a lifetime.''

For the next few days, Sophy remained quietly at home. Her grandmother often noticed that she seemed to watch out of the window as if waiting for a visitor, but none came. Soon, however, the news of the girl's return began to spread, and callers began to knock at the door. One of the first was Sir Tristram Caitlin, whose pursuit of Sophy had been quite marked before she'd gone to Wynwood and who showed every sign of intending to continue. Dennis Stanford called, indicating his continuing interest in fixing her affection. And shortly thereafter, Bertie sauntered in.

He was greeted with such an affectionate hug that he blushed. ''You'd think you hadn't seen me for years,'' he laughed, wriggling out of her embrace.

''It *feels* like years! Where's Dilly? Afraid to show his face here, I expect,'' Sophy remarked.

''No, I don't think that's it,'' Bertie told her with a grin. ''You'll never credit it, but the gudgeon's gone and tumbled for *another* female!''

''Really? *Already*? I must say, Bertie, that's quite the most lowering news I've heard since my return. One would think the fellow would wear the willow for at least a month.''

''He didn't wear it for a *day*!'' Bertie said in disgust. ''He fixed on the new girl the day after he broke in to the Wynwood drawing room.''

''The next *day*? You don't mean it! Are you saying it was someone at Wynwood? But who—?''

''Fanny Carrington, who else? If *you* think his abrupt turn-about is lowering, how do you imagine *I* feel? Losing out to that scarecrow is hardly likely to lift *my* self-esteem."

Sophy laughed. "Poor Bertie. It must have been a shock to learn that Dilly managed to lure her away from Dennis Stanford."

Bertie grinned sheepishly. "Right! That bobbing block must have depths we haven't discovered." He took an awkward turn about the room, pausing and glancing at his cousin in some concern. Then he said, with calculatedly casual nonchalance, "Speaking of affairs of the heart, has anyone told you about the item about Marcus in the newspapers?"

She looked up quickly. "About Marcus? No. What item?"

"It seems that Miss Bethune jilted him. My father showed me the item in the *Times*."

"*Jilted* him? *No!*" Sophy paled, reddened, and paled again. "She *couldn't* have! Bertie, are you sure?"

He shrugged. "Ain't likely to find mistakes in the *Times*."

Sophy, speechless, dropped down on the sofa and stared ahead of her with unseeing eyes. Marcus, *free!* For the first time since she'd met him, he was unentangled. Could this mean something to *her?* Her heart began to pound alarmingly. Had this news anything to do with his visit to Edgerton? "When *was* this, Bertie?" she asked, trying to make sense of the events. "Yesterday?"

"No. A couple of weeks ago, I'd say. Why?"

Her pulse thumped in her ears. A couple of weeks ago! Before he'd come to Edgerton. Good Lord, had he come to tell her . . . to ask her . . . ? She didn't dare pursue the thought. Her knees were turning to water. What had he intended, that night in Wiltshire? Whatever it was, he'd discovered her dangling at the end of a twisted sheet. Oh, God! She had frightened him off with another *calamity!* On an impulse, he'd come to see her . . . perhaps even to . . . make an offer! But she'd confronted him with another disaster, and it had been one too many.

Bertie was looking at her uncomfortably. "What's the matter, Sophy? You're shaking!"

"Bertie, you're my dearest c-cousin in the w-world, but . . . g-go home."

"Go home? Why?"

"Because, fond as I am of you, I d-don't want an audience right n-now. You see, I th-think I'm g-going to c-cry!"

Two long days passed. In those two days, she learned that Marcus had indeed been jilted, and that he was in residence in his London townhouse. But he did not come to call. The reason for his absence was plain—he'd found her incorrigible. He'd been able to forgive the debacle over Dilly's break-in, but the incident at Edgerton had undoubtedly ruined her last chance.

Those were her thoughts in moments of rational calm. During other moments—times of real misery and self-loathing—she told herself that there had been nothing at all significant in his visit to Edgerton. Perhaps his mother had sent him there to make certain she was safe. Lady Charlotte was like that. Sophy had blown up the importance of the entire matter. She'd refined on it too much. Just because Marcus had forgotten himself one day and kissed her was not reason enough to suppose . . . to suppose . . .

Sophy didn't cry or take to her bed or make any sort of scene. She didn't even speak about the weight she carried in her chest. Only late at night, alone in her bedroom, she would take out from under her pillow a little book in which she'd pressed a pink rose.

Her grandmother watched for three days while her granddaughter moved through the house in a fog of pain. It hurt her to watch the girl valiantly trying to behave in a rational and orderly way while her dreams fell completely apart. This, then, was the disaster Alicia had predicted. Sophy was paying the price for her flaws, and the only place where the wreckage showed was in the girl's eyes.

Alicia could not bear those haunted eyes. She had to do something, and quickly. Before another day had passed, she took her pen in hand and poured out her heart in a letter to her friend Charlotte.

*   *   *

Marcus did not go back to Wynwood after he took Sophy to her grandmother. He returned to his London residence and tried to resume his normal life. The impulse that had led him to seek out Sophy in Wiltshire he now recognized for the foolish whim it was. He must have been deranged to have believed that a match between a wildly impulsive creature like Sophy and a staid, precise prig like himself was possible. It was best to put the entire matter out of his mind.

But returning to his former way of life was not easy. He found himself brooding, losing his concentration when he worked at his desk, and losing his temper with the servants. He forgot appointments, found his mind wandering in the middle of serious conversations with his friends, and, one evening when at his club with Dennis, he even became so cast away on brandy that he'd made a *scene*! Dennis had told him later that *he*, Marcus Harvey, had stood up in front of everyone at the club and recited something from Shakespeare at the top of his lungs. Marcus didn't need to be told what he'd said:

> *"Love is a spirit all compact of fire,*
> *Not gross to sink, but light, and will aspire!"*

Those lines had been running through his head for weeks.

Somehow, these signs of the disintegration of his character didn't even trouble him. Compared to the pain that had manifested itself in his chest when he'd given up the idea of declaring himself to Sophy and was always with him, the rest was nothing. And if he was changing, what was wrong with that? If Sophy could get wind of the story of his making an ass of himself at the club, she couldn't very well call him a prig any more, now could she?

One day, two letters arrived for him addressed in female hands. One was a typically cheerful letter from his mother, who, after rambling on for two pages about insignificant nonsense, mentioned some news about Sophy. The name seemed to leap out at him from the page. *You will be glad to learn*, she wrote, *that Alicia has noticed a profound change in her Sophy. Since her return from Edgerton, the girl has been behaving in a remarkably sensible, orderly and well-controlled manner. Since you seemed to find her so disquietingly impetuous, I'm sure you'll be glad to learn that her character has so improved.*

His reaction to those casual sentences was a wave of extreme irritation. Her character improved? What rubbish! He wasn't glad at all! Didn't his mother realize that he liked her just the way she was?

The other letter, by some strange coincidence, was from Lady Alicia. *Please forgive me,* she wrote, *for the long delay in writing to you, but it has been much on my mind that I have not properly thanked you for your service to my dear granddaughter on her departure from Edgerton. I would like to thank you in person. Is it possible for you to call tomorrow morning at eleven? It would give great pleasure to your affectionate friend, Alicia Edgerton.*

Marcus paced the floor with the letter in hand. It was not an invitation he could easily refuse without being considered uncommonly rude. But what if Sophy were present? Could he bear to see her again? Just the thought of it set his fingers trembling. What was happening to him? Had he so far fallen into the sickness of love that his character was completely destroyed? Certainly not, he assured himself. He could surely pay a simple call without disintegrating into mush. He would pay his respects to Alicia, offer a polite greeting to Sophy, and take his leave, thus proving to himself that he was still the self-controlled, sensible man he had always been.

The following morning, when Alicia and Sophy lingered over their morning coffees in the breakfast room, Alicia remarked casually that she'd sent a note round to Lord Wynwood requesting that he drop by this morning.

Sophy froze. "Grandmama! *Why?*"

"I have not yet had the opportunity to thank him for his kindness in rescuing you. I don't think it right to procrastinate any longer, do you? After all, it's been almost a month since he restored you to me—"

"No . . . only three weeks . . ."

"Three weeks is quite long enough. At any rate, he should be calling at any moment," Alicia said composedly.

Sophy jumped up frantically. "Then, Grandmama, I hope you will excuse me. I must leave at once. I can't—"

She ran to the door as she spoke, but she was too late. Escape was cut off by the appearance of the butler at the door. "Lord Wynwood, my lady," he announced. And Marcus walked in.

Chapter Twenty-One

SOPHY STOOD ROOTED to the spot, her face drained of color. Neither she nor Marcus looked at one another. But Alicia rose from the table and crossed the room with a warmly welcoming smile and arms outstretched. "Marcus, my dear boy," she exclaimed, "so good of you to come at the request of an old lady."

She embraced him and kissed his cheek. "I'm always delighted to be at your disposal, Lady Alicia," Marcus said, "although I assure you it is not at all necessary for you to . . . er . . . thank me . . ."

"Perhaps not for you, but it is for me. You know, you rescued my dear girl from virtual imprisonment, and it is not something I will take lightly or easily forget." She smiled at him benignly, and then, to Sophy's extreme dismay, she headed for the door, adding blandly, "No doubt Sophy will wish to add her thanks to mine. I'll leave you two in private so she may do so properly."

They were alone. Sophy could hardly breathe. She had been able to behave naturally with him in the past because she'd believed him safely rivetted to another. Now, however, her discomfort was overwhelming. And Marcus was doing nothing to ease her mortification. He merely stood there in the middle of the room, turning his hat in his hand and looking irresolute. "I . . . er . . . do most sincerely thank you, my lord," she said hesitantly. "I don't know . . .

what would have become of me if . . . if you hadn't come along.''

He made an impatient movement of his hand. What was the sense of these polite, meaningless exchanges between them? ''That was most politely expressed,'' he said curtly, ''but quite unnecessary, since you thanked me quite adequately when we said goodbye at your door.''

Stung by his tone, she turned away, moving blindly to the window and leaning on the sill. ''It would have been more gracious of you merely to have accepted my thanks without criticism,'' she said quietly.

There was a pause. ''Yes, you're quite right. I . . . I'm sorry. I don't seem to know how to speak to you lately.''

She turned and looked at him curiously. ''No? Why not?''

''I'm not sure. I seem to have lost my . . . courage.''

''I shouldn't think you'd need courage to talk to *me*,'' she remarked in surprise.

''No, I don't suppose you see yourself as . . . er . . . formidable.''

''Formidable? *Me?*'' She couldn't help smiling. ''How silly! You didn't seem to find me so at Wynwood.''

''No, not at Wynwood. You became formidable at Edgerton.''

''Really? To be called formidable cannot be a compliment, can it? *Is* it a compliment? I cannot imagine what I did at Edgerton to make it difficult for you to speak to me. What did you want to say to me there?''

''The same thing I want to say to you now. It's something I never said before to . . . to anyone. I'm finding it deucedly difficult to tell you that . . . that I love you.''

Sophy felt the floor lurch beneath her feet. There was a sharp constriction in her stomach, and she swayed slightly and closed her eyes. ''*Sophy!*'' he said sharply, tossing his hat on a chair, crossing the room in two strides and grasping her shoulders. ''Sophy, if you faint now, I'll wring your *neck*!''

She had opened her eyes and was gazing up at him with the most dazzling, breathtaking look of wide-eyed wonder. ''I have no intention of faint—'' she murmured dazedly.

But he gave her no chance to finish. The joy in her face had given him all the courage he needed. He crushed her to him and kissed her with the ruthless ardor of a passion long delayed. Sophy, who wanted to hear more of these delightful revelations, felt for a moment that she didn't want to be kissed. She waved her arms about in feeble rebellion, but soon the rebellion ceased. This outrageous behavior, she realized, was exactly what she'd dreamed of for so long, so she closed her eyes, let her arms find their way around his neck, and surrendered.

After he'd released her, and the floor had steadied beneath her feet, she opened her eyes. He was smiling down at her, the most disconcerting warmth shining from his eyes. "*Marcus*," she asked breathlessly, "are you sure you know what you're *doing?*"

"No, my love, not at all. I'm quite besotted. Love, you know, has a way of making even the most orderly people behave like zanies."

"But . . . but you *can't* love me! Bertie says you don't even *l-like* me!"

He grinned and kissed the tip of her nose. "He's quite right. I dislike you excessively. But not nearly as much as I love you, it seems."

She shook her head. "I don't think one can love someone one dislikes, can one?"

"Yes, quite easily. You see, my sweet, I've learned to my surprise that liking and loving are two very different and unrelated emotions."

"I don't believe that at all," she said dubiously.

"Why not? I think you feel the same way yourself. Didn't you tell me that you disliked me, too?"

"*I?* Never!"

"I remember it distinctly. You called me a pompous prig."

She was about to argue the point, but even if she'd never said it, she'd certainly thought it. She lowered her eyes to the uppermost button on his coat and began to twist it nervously. "Well, I didn't mean it. Not a word. The truth is that I like you very much. I only said it for . . . for . . ."

"I know," Marcus cut in drily. "For dramatic effect."

She flicked her eyes up at him and lowered them again. "Yes, I'm afraid so."

In the silence that followed, she continued to twist the button until it was in danger of coming loose. "I know you don't . . . like me. And I'm not at all likely, no matter how hard I try, to make myself as . . . self-possessed and . . . even-tempered and well-behaved as . . . as Miss Bethune," she admitted painfully.

Marcus lifted her chin and forced her to look at him. "If I'd been able to love Miss Bethune even a fraction as much as I love you, we would still be betrothed. She sensed, however, that I had completely lost my heart to a hysterical little madcap, and she gave me my freedom. It took me some time to understand myself, Sophy, but I now realize that you—just exactly as you are—are the very girl I want."

"Marcus, really?" His words were so delicious to hear that she almost couldn't believe them. "Do you mean that you won't *mind* my getting into scrapes and causing calamities and falling into all sorts of terrible disasters?"

He threw back his head and gave a shout of laughter. "You are asking a bit much of me, aren't you, Sophy? Of course I shall mind. I fully expect to give you daily scoldings and weekly thrashings. But if you always have the assurance that I love you whatever you do, and that I shall be there to pull you out of your difficulties, perhaps you won't get into them quite so frequently."

Sophy responded with a shivery sigh and a blissful smile, and she slipped her arms around his waist and snuggled into his embrace. "Does this mean," she asked shyly, "that you are going to ask me to . . . to marry you?"

He rubbed his cheek against her hair. "In due time," he teased, now quite obnoxiously sure of himself.

"In due time! What do you mean?" she demanded, pulling herself away from him. "When?"

"This afternoon at three," he responded promptly, pulling her back again.

"I'm otherwise engaged this afternoon at three," she

said saucily. "I've promised to ride in the park with Tris Caitlin. And Dennis Stanford has arranged to meet me there, too."

"Has he, indeed?" Marcus asked, raising one eyebrow threateningly. "As I told my mother before I left for Edgerton," he added with a half-regretful sigh, "I shall certainly end by strangling you." But he softened his dire threat by kissing her again.

When she'd regained her equilibrium, Sophy's fingers returned to his coat button. "Perhaps I might send them each a note," she suggested demurely, "saying that a sudden emergency in the family prevents me from keeping our riding engagement."

"That would be very kind," Marcus murmured and bent his head to show his appreciation.

But she held him off. "Do you think," she asked, her voice hesitant but quite serious, "that there *can* be a happy marriage when one of the partners holds the other in dislike?"

His eyes glinted down at her with malicious amusement. "Well, we shall learn the answer to that for ourselves one day, shan't we?"

That was not the response she'd wanted. She glared up at him, ready to do battle. But he laughed and pulled her into his arms again. "Well, you maddening, provoking, irritating chit, aren't you going to tell me that you love me and will be delighted to become my wife?" His tone was challenging and smug, although his lips were distractingly pressed to her forehead.

"Certainly not," she answered promptly.

His head came up with a jerk. "What?" he demanded with very satisfactory dismay.

She looked up at him, demurely innocent. "Not until three o'clock, when you've asked me properly," she said. Then, twisting her arms tightly around his neck, she raised her lips for another kiss.

At Wynwood, where Julian was lingering out the summer, Charlotte handed him the letter she'd just received from Marcus. Julian read the first paragraph and gave a whoop of joy. "He's *done* it!" he chortled. "Gotten himself shackled to the right female at last."

"Not shackled yet. He says we're to give a party first to announce it. He wants at least two hundred guests."

Julian couldn't believe it, but there it was in the letter in his nephew's precise, firm hand: *at least two hundred in attendance*. He shook his head in wonder. "Two hundred!" he laughed. "What's come over the boy? I know love changes a fellow, but this—!" He looked across the table at his sister, sitting there calmly adjusting her shawl about her shoulders. "Aren't you astounded?"

"Not at all," Charlotte said placidly.

Julian cocked a suspicious eye at her. "Don't play that serene-and-all-knowing game with me. I'd wager a monkey to a groat that you were sick with worry the night of his betrothal. And a good many days before and after, as well."

Charlotte smiled at him complacently, rose gracefully and threw the shawl about her neck with an insouciant toss. "I never had a moment's concern," she said serenely, gliding to the door. "Not a single moment's concern." And she floated from the room in her cloud of gauzy silk.

ritalu